W9-AFI-491

Also by Roxana Robinson

A Perfect Stranger

A Perfect Stranger

and Other Stories

ROXANA ROBINSON

Random House
New York

Copyright © 2005 by Roxana Robinson

Published in the United States by Random House, an
imprint of The Random House Publishing Group, a
division of Random House, Inc., New York.

RANDOM HOUSE and colophon are registered
trademarks of Random House, Inc.

"The Face-lift," "Treatment," "Family Christmas," and
"Assistance" first appeared in *The Atlantic Monthly,*
"Intersection" in *Ms.* magazine, "At the Beach" in
Good Housekeeping, "Blind Man" in *Dædalus.*

LIBRARY OF CONGRESS CATALOGING-IN-
PUBLICATION DATA
Robinson, Roxana.
A perfect stranger: and other stories / Roxana Robinson.
p. cm.
Contents: Family Christmas—The face-lift—
Assistance—Choosing sides—At the beach—Blind
man—The treatment—Assez—Intersection—Shame—
The football game—Pilgrimage—A perfect stranger.
ISBN 0-375-50918-6
1. United States—Social life and customs—Fiction.
I. Title.
PS3568.O3152P47 2005
813'.54—dc22   2004059537

Printed in the United States of America
on acid-free paper

Random House website address: www.atrandom.com

2 4 6 8 9 7 5 3

Book design by Dana Leigh Blanchette

This book is for dearest Lucy
with much love

ACKNOWLEDGMENTS

I would like to give grateful thanks to C. Michael Curtis, at *The Atlantic,* for his impeccable editorial eye; to J. Seward Johnson, for hospitality in Key West; to Anne Greene, of Wesleyan University, for her warmth and encouragement; to the John Simon Guggenheim Foundation, for its generous support; and to my family, as always, for theirs.

CONTENTS

A Perfect Stranger

Family Christmas

At Christmas, we went to my grandparents'.

My grandparents lived outside New York in a private park, a strange nineteenth-century hybrid between a club and a housing development. The Park was enclosed by a thick stone wall, and at the entrance was a pair of stone gateposts, and a gatehouse. As we approached the gate, a man appeared in the doorway of the gatehouse, sternly watching our car. Our father, who knew the gatekeeper, would roll down his window and say hello, or sometimes he would just smile and wave, cocking his hand casually backward and forward. The gatekeeper would recognize my father then and nod, dropping his chin slowly, deeply, in confirmation of an unspoken agreement, and we would drive through the gates into the Park.

One year there was a gatekeeper who did not know my father. The new man stepped out of the gatehouse as we approached and waved heavily at the ground, motioning for us to stop. He was frowning in an official way.

"He's new," said my father, slowing down. "Never seen him before."

My mother laughed. "He probably won't let us in," she said.

My father pulled up to the gatehouse and rolled down his window. "We're here to see my family, the Weldons," he said politely. "I'm Robert Weldon." My father looked like his father: he had the same blue eyes, the long straight nose, and the high domed forehead. The gatekeeper glanced noncommittally at the car, and then he nodded. He was still frowning, but now in a private, interior way that no longer seemed to have anything to do with us. He gave us a slow wave through the gates, then he went ponderously back into the little house.

The four of us children sat motionless in the back. After our mother spoke we had fallen silent. Our faces had turned solemn, and we had aligned our legs neatly on the seats. Our knees matched. Our docile hands lay in our laps. We were alarmed.

We did not know why some cars might be turned away from the Park gates. We had never seen it happen, but we knew that it must happen: Why else would the gatekeeper appear, with his narrowed eyes and official frown? We knew that our car did not look like our grandparents' car, nor any of the other cars that slid easily in between the big stone gateposts without even slowing up. Those cars were dark and sleek. They looked fluid, liquid, full of curves, as though they had been shaped by speed, though they always seemed to move slowly. Those cars were polished, the chrome gleamed, the smooth swelling fenders shone, and the windows were lucid and unsmudged. Those cars were driven sedately by men in flat black hats and black jackets. It was the driver who nodded to the gatekeeper. The passenger, who was in the back seat, never next to the driver in the front, did not even look up as they drove through the gates.

Our car, on the other hand, was a rackety wooden-sided station wagon, angular, high-axled, flat-topped. The black roof was patched, and the varnished wooden sides were dull and battered.

Our car was driven by our father, who did not wear a black jacket, and next to him in the front seat was our mother. The two slippery brown back seats were chaotic with suitcases, bags of presents, the four of us children, and our collie, Huge. We felt as though we were another species when we arrived at this gate, and it seemed entirely possible that we would be turned away. The rules of entry and exclusion from the Park were mysterious to us; they were part of the larger unknowable world which our parents moved through but which we did not understand. It was like the struggle to learn a language, listening hard for words and idioms and phrases, being constantly mystified and uncomprehending, knowing that all around us, in smooth and fluent use by the rest of the world, was a vast and intricate system we could not yet grasp.

After we were through the gates, my mother turned to us.

"Well, we made it," she said humorously. "They let us in this time." She smiled and raised her eyebrows, waiting for us to answer. My mother was small and lively, with thick light brown hair parted on one side and held with a barrette. She wore her clothes casually; sweaters, and long full skirts.

We said nothing to her. We disapproved of my mother's levity, all of us: Sam and Jonathan, my two older brothers; Abby, my older sister; and me, Joanna. I was the youngest, and the most disapproving.

Inside the gates, the road meandered sedately through the Park, which was on the slopes of a small steep mountain. Up on the top, along the ridge, the land was still wild and untouched. Deer moved delicately through the thickets, and we had heard there were bobcats, though we had never seen one. Down along the narrow paved roads all was mannerly, a landscape of wide lawns, great towering shade trees and luxuriant shrubberies. Unmarked driveways slid discreetly into the road's docile curves. Set far back, even from this narrow private interior road, were the houses. Tall, ornate, gabled and turreted, half-hidden by brick walls, stonework, and the giant old trees that surrounded them, they stood comfortable and secure within their grounds.

Our grandparents' house was called Weldonmere, and it stood below the road, at the bottom of a wide sloping oval of lawn. The driveway traced a long semicircle, starting from one corner of the front lawn, swooping down to the house at mid-point, then back up to the road again. Along the road stood a screen of trees: dogwoods, cherries, and an exotic Japanese maple, with small fine-toothed leaves, astonishingly purple in season. Down the hill, protecting the house with its benevolent presence, stood a great copper beech, dark and radiant. Its dense branches, like a vast layered skirt, swept down to the lawn, and beneath them were deep roomy eaves, where we played in the summer. Now all these trees were bare, and mantled with snow.

Weldonmere was white, with pointed Victorian gables and round neoclassical columns. At the front door was a big porte cochere, and above it the house rose up three stories to the scalloped blue-black slates of the roof.

My father stopped the car under the porte cochere, and we cascaded out. Huge darted alertly into the bushes, his long nose alive to a new universe. We children, following our parents through the brief shock of cold air, lurched stiffly into the big square front hall. We stood among the suitcases on the Turkey carpet, blinking in the light of the chandelier. Our parents called out to the household in a general and celebratory way.

"Well, hello! You're here!" Grandpère appeared in the doorway to the living room. Grandpère was tall and dignified, with a neat thick silver mustache. He held himself very straight, like an officer, which he had been, or a rider, which he still was. There was about him an air of order, he was always in charge. Grandpère carried his gold watch on a chain in his pocket, and he wore a waistcoat, which was pronounced "weskit." He was a formal man, courtly, but kind. Underneath the mustache was always the beginning of a smile.

"Hello, Robert! Sarah, children." His voice was deep, his manner ceremonial. He included us all in his smile, and he opened his arms in a broad welcoming gesture.

Grandmère appeared behind him. Grandmère was narrow and elegant. She wore a long dark dress, and her white hair was parted on the side. It was straight at first, then turned to dense mannerly curls, pressed flat against her head. Her mouth was eternally pursed in a gentle smile. Grandmère was from Charleston, South Carolina, but her mother's family had been from Baton Rouge, where they spoke French. She had been brought up to think English was common, which was why we called our grandparents "Grandpère" and "Grandmère."

"Here you all are," Grandmère said faintly. She sounded pleased but exhausted, as though we were already too much for her. She stood gracefully in the corner of the arched doorway, leaning her hand against it and smiling at us. We milled around, taking off our coats and being kissed.

Huge had come inside, and now held his plumy tail tensely up in the air, his head high and wary. Tweenie, Grandmère's horrible black-and-white mongrel, snake-snouted, sleek-sided, plump and disagreeable, appeared in the doorway behind her. The two dogs approached each other, stiff-legged, slit-eyed, flat-eared. They began to rumble, deep in their throats.

"Now, Tweenie," Grandmère said, not moving.

"Oh, gosh," said my father from the other side of the room. "Get Huge, will you, Sam?"

Sam was the closest, but we all took responsibility for our beloved Huge. We all began shouting, and pummeling his solid lovely back, sliding our hands proprietarily into his deep feathery coat. "Huge!" we cried, sternly reminding him of the rules, and demonstrating to the grown-ups our own commitment to

them. Of course this was hypocritical. We believed that Huge
could do no wrong and was above all rules, and that Tweenie
was to blame for any animosity, in fact for anything at all. We
thought that Huge was entirely justified in entering her house
and attacking her, if he chose to do so, in her own front hall, like
some pre-Christian raider. Huge ignored our calls to order,
shaking his broad brown head, his eyes never leaving Tweenie's
cold stare. I laid my head against Huge's velvet ear.

"Huge," I said, holding him tightly around the neck, "no
growling."

We did not touch Tweenie: she bit us without hesitation.

"Now," Grandpère said firmly, "Tweenie, come here."

The authority in his voice quieted us all. Tweenie paid no
attention, but Grandpère strode across the rug and took her
powerfully by her wide leather collar. Tweenie's growls rose suddenly in her constricted throat, and she twisted her head to keep
Huge in sight as she was dragged away.

"Oh, dear," said Grandmère gently. "Tweenie gets so upset
by other dogs."

Huge, unfettered and unrepentant, trotted triumphantly in
small swift circles on the rug, his thick plumy tail high.

"Huge," I said sternly and banged on his back. I looked at
my father for praise, but he was making his way toward us
through the luggage. When he reached us, he grabbed Huge's
collar.

"Now, *hush*," my father said sharply to Huge. Huge, who
had never been trained in any way, ignored my father completely. My father pulled him in the other direction from Tweenie, and Huge whined, twisting his great shaggy body to get a
last view of Tweenie's smooth repellent rump. Tweenie was being
slid unwillingly, her feet braced, past the front stairs and past the
little closet where the telephone was, through the small door behind the staircase that led into the kitchen quarters.

Grandpère opened the door. "Molly," he called, "take the

dog, will you?" Without waiting for a reply, he closed the door behind Tweenie's reluctant rump and returned to us, brisk and unruffled.

"She gets upset," Grandmère murmured again, smiling at us in a general way.

"We'll take Huge up with us," my father said and turned to us. "Let's get settled now, let's get our things upstairs."

We set off. The staircase was wide and curving, with heavy mahogany banisters and a carved newel post. The steps were broad and shallow, and the red-patterned carpeting was held in place by brass rods. Lugging our suitcases behind us, we went up in slow motion, step by step. On the second-floor landing there was a door which was always closed.

One afternoon I had climbed the stairs by myself. When I reached that landing, instead of going on to the upstairs hall, I stopped at the small closed door on the right and opened it, though I knew I should not. I looked in: a narrow hallway, with closed doors on either side. I stepped inside. It was hushed and dim; everything seemed different there. The ceiling was lower and the floor was uncarpeted linoleum. I walked silently, on my toes, down the hall. I pushed open one of the doors and peered into a small bedroom. It held a narrow wooden bed, a small bureau, and a chair. Everything was perfectly neat. The window looked out the back of the house to the garage. The curtains at the window were limp, and the air seemed muted and dark. A clock ticked in the stillness. I stood without moving, looking at everything, staring into a world I didn't know. My heart began to pound, and when I heard someone coming up the back stairs from the kitchen, I fled back to the front hall.

Later I asked my mother what was behind that closed door on the landing. She said it was the servants' wing, and that we must never go in there, as it would disturb them. That was where they lived, she said. I didn't understand this, for how could you live in a place like that? How could you compress a whole life into that one small room with nothing in it, in someone else's house?

There were no servants in our own house. My father had been a lawyer in New York, like Grandpère, but he had given that up. He had left the law and the city, and moved to Ithaca in upstate New York, where we now lived. My father worked for the university, helping poor people in the community. I'd heard him tell people about making this change, and from the way he said it I knew it was something unusual, and that we were proud of it.

We lived outside town, in an old white clapboard farmhouse. There was only one bathroom, and the house was heated by a big wood-burning stove in the middle of the living room. In the winter, after supper, we sat around the stove and my mother read out loud, and my father peeled oranges for us. While we listened, my father pulled the oranges apart, separating the succulent crescents and passing them to us: fragile and treasured. Then he unlatched the heavy iron hatch on the stove and threw inside the thin bruised-looking orange peels. We heard the faint hiss as they gave themselves up to the red heart of the stove. We closed our eyes for a moment, listening, and feasting on the sweet fragrance the peels gave up.

At Weldonmere we slept on the third floor. Abby and I were in one room, the boys in another. Our room overlooked the porte cochere, and it had been our father's when he was little. It had low twin beds, foot to foot, and a velvety engraving of a Raphael Madonna and Child. The boys' room overlooked the back lawn, and beyond it the small pond that gave the house its name. Our parents slept on the second floor, with Grandmère and Grandpère. We children were alone on the third floor, and we liked this. On Christmas Eve we felt boisterous and wild, and we didn't want the presence of our parents to constrict us. In the morning, we were not allowed to go down the front stairs for our stockings until it was light, and on some Christmases the four of us had sat, lined silently up on the landing, shivering, waiting for the first gray pallor of day to lighten the darkened rooms below.

This Christmas we had arrived late. The drive was a long one, and by the time we got there, it was dark, and Grandmère and Grandpère had already had dinner. Our parents were to have trays in front of the fire in the living room, and we children were sent into the kitchen, where Molly would give us our supper.

Molly was Irish and fierce, with pale blue eyes and a cloud of fine white hair. She had slim arms and slim legs and a thick middle. Her hands and feet were small, and she moved fast. She wore a white uniform, a white apron, and brown lace-up shoes with thick low heels. She ruled the kitchen absolutely. We never did anything to make Molly mad. She would have our heads. That's what she told us, shaking her own wild white head fiercely, and we believed her.

Molly had a husband named Bud, but he was a mysterious figure, like the bobcats; we had never seen him. We did know Molly's son, Richard, who was my grandparents' chauffeur. He was fat, and moved slowly. We children had a poor opinion of him. We called him Ree-ard, which we thought was funny. When he wasn't driving my grandparents' long black car, Ree-ard sat on a chair in the kitchen, near the back stairs. He took off his black coat and sat in his shirtsleeves, his white shirt vast and billowy. He looked like a lump, and sometimes Molly told him that, whirling suddenly from the big stove and rounding on him, laying into him without mercy. Molly might do that to anyone, at any moment—erupt into a high foamy rage, and say things with her fierce, thin Irish lips that you never wanted to hear.

But Molly was nice to us, and we liked her. That evening we pushed through the swinging door into the pantry and filed into the kitchen. Molly turned at once from the stove.

"Ah, here they all are, then," she said, her Irish accent thick. Molly's mouth didn't smile easily, but her eyes did. "Come over here and let me have a look at you." We presented ourselves expectantly, waiting to see what she would find. "You're growing," she said warningly to Sam, as though this was something he should look out for, and to me she said accusingly, "Where's that tooth gone?" I had no answer, but I knew she was not angry. She put her hands on our heads approvingly, as though we belonged to her, then she moved briskly back to the stove. "I'm going to take this out to your parents first, so you all sit down at the table and don't make any trouble." We didn't need to be told that. Making trouble in Molly's kitchen was the last thing in the world we would consider doing.

We sat and waited for her to come back. Tweenie lay on a towel next to her bowl, which had milk in it. She eyed us disagreeably.

"I hate Tweenie," I said and made a face at her.

Jonathan always disagreed with me. "She's just a *dog*," he said scornfully. "Why would you hate a *dog*?"

"She looks like a snake," Abby said. "Look at her."

We looked at her. Tweenie looked back at us, ready to bite.

"Where's Huge?" Jonathan asked.

"In with the grown-ups," Sam said. "We can't bring him in here because he'll upset Tweenie."

"Oh, *Tweenie*," I said with loathing, rolling my eyes.

Molly pushed through from the pantry, her low bosom and portly middle preceding her. Her neat lace-up shoes pointed outward when she walked. "Now, then," she said energetically, "come get your plates and I'll put some food on them." We lined up, and Molly loaded our plates. We sat down again at the table. Molly was at the stove, her back to us.

"Where's Richard?" Sam asked her politely, his mouth full.

Sam was the oldest, and could ask these questions of grown-ups. I would never have dared: Ree-ard was a comical figure to us, and I could not have discussed him with a grown-up. There were things that we talked about only among ourselves, and that was our true world—where we said the things we meant, and where we spoke freely and directly. Then there were the things we said to adults, and those were often false, or constrained and mannered. You had to be careful in talking to grown-ups, it was like talking to foreigners. They expected to hear certain things; they didn't always understand you.

I myself had little practice in talking to grown-ups. I was the youngest, and was seldom asked my opinion. I did not understand how to blend the two ways of talking, or how to bridge the gap that lay between them. I knew that if I asked about Reeard I would be scolded for being fresh. But Sam could do it with impunity, his face and voice ingenuous. He asked as though it were a serious question, as though we thought Richard were a serious person.

"Oh, *Richard,*" Molly said, hissing the word, sounding bad-tempered at once. "Where is Richard," she repeated rhetorically, and shook her head. She set the lid on a pot and wiped her hands on her apron, and we said no more about Richard.

Besides Richard, Molly had a daughter named Margaret. We seldom saw Margaret, she didn't live at Weldonmere. She didn't even live in the Park. She lived somewhere else, in an apartment, and she worked in an office, for a married man. My father worked in an office, and he was a married man, but somehow these things set Margaret in a mysterious region, exotic and sinister.

In the car, my father had spoken to my mother in a voice slightly lower, more private, than the one he used for the whole car. It made me alert at once, and I leaned forward, listening. My father said to my mother, "Margaret's going to be there."

My mother looked at him and said, "And—?"

My father, not looking at her, said, "I suppose so."

My mother turned away and said, "Poor thing."

I was listening to them as I always listened to my parents, in order to understand the world, though what they said often made things more confusing. The tone of voice my parents used about Margaret meant, I knew, that they would not answer my questions about her. If I asked my mother what she had meant by "Poor thing," or why it was so serious and important that the man Margaret worked for was married, she would smile at me and make her voice louder and more public and say, "Oh, it's just a conversation I'm having with your father, that's all." She would tell me nothing. I knew that this language I was trying to learn could not be learned directly, that it was something that had to be absorbed blindly and obliquely. I knew that we were to have no help with it. We would have to learn it through signs, inflections, looks and sighs and tones of voice.

Sitting at the kitchen table, I watched Abby eating. If I didn't eat fast enough, or if I didn't eat the vegetables, she might tell on me, if she were in a spiteful mood. Now she was pretending to ignore me, but I watched her anyway, as I ate. I ate the soft pillowy lima beans one by one, watching Abby's fork across the table. I looked at her face when I was halfway through and saw that she was watching something behind me. She picked up her milk glass and drank, still watching, her eyes intent. I turned around.

At the far end of the kitchen was the back staircase that led up to the servants' wing. I had never been up it. Now, sitting on the upper steps and looking at us, was a little girl, my age. She was pretty, with dark blue eyes and brown hair thick around her face. She was wearing a long pale blue nightgown, tucked down over her feet. Her hands were hidden in her lap, and she was watching us. I had never seen her before, this girl my age. She was with us here in the house, sitting on the back stairs, looking at us.

The four of us watched her as we ate, not speaking. The girl did not move. She was watching us through the wooden banisters. Once she raised her hand to tuck back her hair, which had fallen across her face. Her skin was very pale. She put her hand back into her lap and then leaned her face against the banisters, looking through them as though they were bars.

She was living here in the house. I wondered if she would be there in the morning, opening presents under the tree. Would she have a stocking? I felt a kind of private outrage rise up in me: how could there be a girl like me here, my age, my size, in our family's house?

Molly, hearing our silence, turned from the stove and saw our stares. She looked at the staircase and erupted.

"You get out of here," she said to the little girl, and started over toward her. "Get back up those stairs. You're not to come down here, and you know that. I told you that, go on, get up there."

Before Molly could reach her, the little girl stood and ran back upstairs. She didn't look at us; she fled. We saw her feet, which were bare, and the bottom of her pale blue nightgown, and then she was gone. Molly turned without looking at us and went back to the stove in a temper, banging the pots. We looked at each other in silence and went on eating.

When we were finished, we were sent through the pantry into the dining room and then the living room beyond, where the grown-ups were. They were sitting in front of the fireplace, on big sofas and chairs covered in blurry flowers. Huge lay on the rug, and he raised his head when we appeared, his tail thumping.

Coming into the living room, we passed the Christmas tree, tall and glittering. We stopped, staring at the packages beneath it, eyeing them for size, trying to decipher names on the tags.

"I have more than you do," Jonathan said to me under his breath.

"You don't," I said, tilting my head sideways to look for my name.

"Come over and say hello," my father said. Sam was nudging a package with his toe, trying to shift it so the tag was visible. "And leave the presents alone. Don't start pushing them around."

"*I* wasn't," Abby said virtuously and went over to sit on the sofa between Grandmère and Grandpère.

"Sam," my father said, and Sam left the packages and went over, giving an athletic kick in the air on the way, to show that he had really been practicing soccer, not nudging presents. I went over by the fire, and I felt the heat on my face. Outside there was snow on the long lawn that sloped down to the pond and the creek beyond. I could see the Christmas tree in the corner, rising in shimmering tiers, fragrant, brilliant, intricate. This was the reason we were here—stockings, presents, the boundless glitter of anticipation—but it was all before us still. There was nothing to do now but wait. The night ahead was endless, and I felt myself tingling with impatience and excitement, but our parents and grandparents seemed content here, sitting by the fire and talking, indifferent to the time moving so slowly.

I climbed onto the flowered sofa next to Grandmère. I loved the way she smelled, powdery and soft, and I loved her silvery curled hair. She smiled at me and patted my hand. "Sit here with me, Joanna," she said, though I already was. Grown-ups were like this, awkward in their speech, saying things you already knew, or things you couldn't understand. I smiled back at her and put my hands in my lap. She put her arm around me, and I leaned against her and gazed into the fire, and waited for it to be Christmas morning.

My father was talking about his work. I don't know when exactly I began to hear the noise from the kitchen. I looked across at Sam, who was leaning against my father's chair. He looked back at me, and we both listened. No one else seemed to hear it, they were all listening to my father's story.

"It's hard to get people from below the poverty level involved with community projects," he was saying. "We try to encourage anyone who's willing. We try to make it easy for them, and whatever they want to do, we try to help. Well, there's a single mother, with two children, pretty far below the poverty level. She had volunteered once or twice at school, and then she told the counselors she wanted to set up a kids' summer program."

In the kitchen, something was happening. I could hear muffled noises, bumps and crashing sounds, and then voices, but they were indistinct. It was hard to imagine anything boisterous going on in Molly's kitchen. Unless—it was too much to hope for—Tweenie had attacked someone?

"We told her we'd advise her, and we helped her set it up, but she was a dynamo, and she really did it all herself. And she paid for everything, supplies, and refreshments, whatever her costs were. She took eight children, five days a week for two months, and she charged nothing." My father paused and took a sip from his coffee cup. He was sitting in an armchair across from Grandpère. "Well, I knew she couldn't afford it, and I heard afterward she'd done a very good job. In the fall I wrote a report on the program and applied to the state for a small grant. Just a few hundred dollars, to cover her costs for the season and start her off for the next, if she wanted to go on."

I heard a real crash, now, in the kitchen. Sam and I looked at each other.

"Tell about going to see her," my mother said. She was holding her cup and saucer in her lap and watching my father.

"She lives way outside town, and doesn't have a telephone, so I couldn't let her know I was coming," my father said. "I got directions and drove out there. She has a trailer by the road, at the edge of a big field. I knocked on the door, and after a minute she opened it. She's in her thirties, overweight, with a pretty face. She seemed a bit wary, but she invited me in and offered me some coffee. The trailer was pretty crowded. There were plants everywhere, in jars and coffee cans, standing under the windows, lined up on the floor."

There was more noise from the kitchen, a sort of subdued shout. I looked again at my mother, but she was smiling at my father.

"I thanked her for setting up the program and congratulated her on how well she'd done it. She looked at me for a moment, and then she thanked me, but she didn't smile. Then I told her about the grant; I was very pleased about it. I watched her face, waiting for it to change, but it didn't. When I finished, she didn't say anything, she just sat there. I thought she hadn't understood me, so I explained it again. She had small, very bright blue eyes, very steady. She sat with her hands tucked tightly between her legs. When I finished the second time, she still didn't answer for a moment. Finally she said, 'I don't want the money.'"

Something, again, in the kitchen. I looked at Sam. His face was solemn.

"She said, 'I started this program, and it feels like it's mine. But if I take money from the state, it will be the state's program. I'll start worrying if I'm doing it right, or if I should ask some-one how to do it, and I'll worry that someone will come in and start telling me how to run it. So I don't want the money. I'd rather do it on my own.'"

Grandpère was watching my father. He was sitting in a high-backed wing chair facing the fire, and I could see the firelight on his face. "And what did you say to her?" he asked. His face looked warm, as though he were about to smile, and it made me feel safe, watching my grandfather look that way at my father.

My father shook his head, rueful, smiling slightly. "There was nothing to say. It was her program. I wanted her to have the money, but I couldn't make her take it. And I admired her for refusing it. When I was thanking her and congratulating her she hadn't said anything, she'd just looked at me. It had made me uncomfortable at the time, and afterward I'd wondered if I hadn't been doing, myself, just what she was talking about, trying to intrude onto something that belonged to her and the children she'd helped, instead of being helpful." My father shrugged his shoulders. "There was really nothing I could do. I told her I understood her position, and that if she wanted help we'd give it to her in any way we could. I thanked her for the coffee and left. She was a very impressive woman."

"My goodness," said Grandmère, smiling. She shook her head. "A lady of principle." She looked at me and patted my hand. I smiled back at her.

Now the noise seemed too loud and too persistent to ignore. My father said to Grandpère, "Do you hear something in the kitchen?"

Grandpère's face had changed; he looked serious. He set his glass down on the little table next to the sofa. "I wonder what's going on in there," he said. "Sometimes Bud outdoes himself at Christmas revelry." He stood up.

I looked at Sam: Bud! The fabled Bud!

"I'll come with you," my father said and stood up. Sam stood up too, but my mother shook her head.

"I think you children should stay in here with us," she said.

The two men walked through the big arch into the dining room, toward the long portrait of Grandpère in his "pink" hunting coat. They pushed open the pantry door, and as it swung wide we could hear a voice, suddenly loud; then as it swung shut the voice was muffled again.

Grandmère and my mother looked at each other. Grandmère looked worried; her mouth had lost its smile. "I hope Bud isn't making trouble again," she said, "it's so hard on Molly when he does that." She didn't move. The living room was quiet. The fire hissed and murmured, and its light flickered on the silver ashtrays. On the mantel was a round clock with a white face, with a black sphinx lying on either side of it. In the silence we could hear its steady ticks. The Christmas tree towered, glittering, in the corner. My arm was getting hot from the fire, and I moved closer to Grandmère. She patted my shoulder, pulling me toward her.

There was a roar from the kitchen. *"You think I don't know that?"* It was a man, shouting, wild. Sam and I looked at each other. We heard Molly's voice.

"Bud, don't, for God's sake. For God's sake."

Sam and I stared at each other. We would never have wanted to hear that tone of voice from Molly, pleading, imploring.

Then we could see them. They had pushed open the door from the pantry, and we could see them, at the far end of the dining room, standing beneath the big portrait. There were four of them: Bud, Molly's husband; Molly, strange in a blue dress; and Grandpère and my father, in their dark tweeds. Bud had pushed through the door, and all the others had followed. He was a big man, not as fat as Ree-ard, but tall and heavy. His shoulders looked as though they had had air pumped into them. His face was swollen and red, and his small blue eyes were inflamed and pink. Molly, our Molly, the absolute ruler of the kitchen, was hanging on to one of his shoulders and weeping.

"Get out of there, Bud," she said, frantic. She was pushing at him. "Come along, get out of there. Come back with me."

Bud ignored her. He was staring at my grandfather. "You think I care about your fancy manners?" he asked. His voice sounded strangely slow, as though he didn't know how to use his mouth. "You think I care about your fancy place?"

"Ah, get out of here, Bud," Molly said, her voice rising. "You're not yourself. You're not thinking. Come along with me."

Her voice was high and frantic.

My grandfather said nothing. He was watching Bud, his head slightly lowered, his chin drawn in. His hands were down at his sides. He said nothing, but his eyebrows were low and drawn together.

"Here's what I think about your fancy place," Bud said, leaning into Grandpère's face. His hulking shoulders swam closer. Molly scrabbled at him.

"Bud!" she said. "Leave this! Get out of here! Leave Mr. Weldon alone, for God's sake."

But Bud was in the grip of something stronger than Molly. He leaned into my grandfather's face, his own red face glowing, his little pink eyes lit up, as though waiting to see what would happen. Then I heard a noise from him, a disgusting noise. I couldn't see what had happened, but I saw Grandpère blink and his head jerk slightly back.

"That's enough," Grandpère said. Now he was very angry. "I will ask you to leave this house, sir."

Molly began to make a strange sound, jerky and high. "Don't do this," she said, and she beat her fist against Bud's shoulder.

"I will not leave this house," Bud said loudly.

"I am going to telephone for the police," Grandpère said. He stood straight and stiff, his chin now lifted, his head high. A kind of heat, a fine outrage, came from him in waves, so powerful that it seemed almost as though he were doing something violent, though he did not move. "Go back into the kitchen and wait for them to come. Leave the room, sir," Grandpère said, and the way he spoke was so stern and so menacing that I wanted to leave, myself, to get away from it. *"Leave this room,"* he said, again.

Bud smiled, his swollen face splitting in a manic grin. "I'll leave when I'm ready to leave," he said to my grandfather.

Grandpère, without turning his gaze from Bud's face, spoke to my father. "Robert, go and telephone the police. I'll stay here."

My father hesitated for a moment—he didn't want to leave his father, we could see that—and then he turned and came urgently through the dining room, toward us, his face tense, before going into the hall to the telephone.

"Yes, get your son to do your work for you," Bud said sneeringly, putting one hand on Molly's shoulder. "It's a nice way to live." He nodded blearily, contemptuous. "Of course, I don't have the opportunity myself. Since my son does your work for you too, driving you around in your shiny car." He nodded again. "My son's no help to his father, no more than my daughter is." Now Bud's face changed, and it became no longer sneeringly triumphant but dark. "My daughter does someone else's work as well. And whose work does my daughter do? What manner of man does my daughter work for? What manner of work is it that she does for him?" He waited for a moment, his face still full of rage, still wild, but now tortured. His rage had somehow turned inward, or had become general; it seemed as though he was angry now at the whole world, though he leaned again toward Grandpère. "My daughter can do nothing for her father. Her time is taken up by looking after someone else's child. And who is that? *Satan's child!*"

The way he said those last two words—furious, anguished—chilled me with fear. Satan's child! Margaret had had Satan's child!

Grandpère looked steadily at Bud, not moving.

"Bud!" Molly was shouting at him now and pummeling. She pushed at him, as hard as she could, but he was huge, massive, leaden.

"She's here with us for Christmas, Margaret's little girl, here with her family, same as your precious grandchildren." Bud raised his chin at Grandpère and then looked, for a moment, toward us. I felt invaded by his eye, and leaned toward my grandmother.

My father reappeared from the hall. "They're on their way."

He spoke to Grandpère, who did not stir, whose gaze did not leave Bud's.

"Now, leave the room, sir," Grandpère said severely.

"I will not," Bud said, raising his chin even higher. "I know you think you're too good for anyone, so maybe you're too good for a fight."

My grandfather said nothing to this. My father, next to him, looked very dark now too. The blood came into both their faces. Our dog Huge was on his feet, his ears pricked, alarmed. My mother put her hand on him.

Molly moved in front of Bud and threw herself at him, shoving him backward. "Get out of here," she cried, beside herself. "Get out of here."

It seemed now that Bud was out of steam, somehow, or energy, and when she pushed at him he was off balance, and took a staggering step back. "Get out of here," she said again, furious, her voice cracking. "Get out, get out, you fool."

She pushed Bud, step by lumbering step, back through the pantry door, and then it swung shut behind them. For a long moment my father and my grandfather stood still, beneath the giant portrait of Grandpère, looking majestic and elegant in his scarlet coat and black boots, holding in his hand the hunting whip, with its long, curled-up leather thong.

I waited for someone to speak. I waited for the next thing that would happen, for the grown-ups to take charge again. I didn't understand these things, and I knew that no one would explain them to me. I knew that all of it—the blue nightgown and the bare feet, Molly's terrible high frantic voice and Bud's glaring pink eyes, even the fat woman in her trailer with all the plants—was part of the language I still could not speak.

Part of what I felt was shame, shame for something I didn't understand. Shame for other people's misery, shame that it had lain naked and exposed before us, shame that we'd seen it. I felt sorry for the wild wretched sweating Bud, pushed back into the kitchen, waiting for the police. I felt sorry for the daughter of Satan, pressing her pale face against the banisters. I felt sorry for Molly, weeping and shoving at her husband.

The only ones I didn't feel sorry for were the woman in the trailer and Tweenie. I liked the woman in the trailer. She seemed strong and free, and I liked thinking of her, plump and blue-eyed and messy, living on the edge of the big field, with her plants in coffee cans lined up below the windows. It seemed that she would escape shame and misery, that she had somehow risen magnificently above them. And of course I still hated Tweenie.

The Face-lift

This happened in San Salvador, not long ago. My friend Cristina was coming back from lunch at a restaurant, downtown, with her mother, Elvira, and her mother's friend, Consuela. They were in Cristina's big car, and they all three sat in the back. The driver was in the front seat alone.

Cristina was dropping her mother and Consuela off first, at her mother's house. Her mother lives on a narrow street lined with high stucco walls and solid gates. Everyone in that neighborhood has big heavy gates, controlled by electricity. The way it works is the car drives up to them and the chauffeur pushes a remote control button, and the gates open inward, and the car drives inside and they close after it. The walls in San Salvador have always been high. In the past there were broken bottles cemented into the top of them, a row of glittering teeth to keep people from climbing over them. Now there are no longer broken bottles on top of the walls, there are electric wires instead. El Salvador has always been like this, but since the revolution it has been worse.

Cristina's car pulled in to Elvira's clean quiet street. All the houses there were tidy, the high stuccoed walls all freshly painted, all the gates stood tightly closed. They drove slowly down the block toward Elvira's house. There was a car parked halfway down the block, which no one noticed then. At her mother's house, Cristina told the driver to pull over to the curb, to let her mother and Consuela out. They didn't go in through the big gates, because Cristina was going on from there. The car was letting the two women out at the little street door, right next to the sidewalk.

"Por aquí, por aquí, por aquí," Cristina said rapidly to the driver. Cristina says everything rapidly, she moves quickly and talks fast. She is quite beautiful, with thick black-brown hair and large, bright dark eyes. She has a round face and a short straight nose. Her eyelids are slightly droopy, which gives her a drowsy, aristocratic look. She was my roommate in boarding school.

Cristina and I went to the same girls' school outside Philadelphia, on the Main Line, but we came from very different worlds. I grew up in the country, in western Pennsylvania. My mother was a librarian at my elementary school, and my father was a doctor. We lived in an old stone farmhouse, rather dark inside, with small windows. I was an only child. Every night the three of us sat down to dinner at the round wooden table in the kitchen. We bowed our heads, and then my mother said grace over the food. Afterward we raised our heads, and it was my job to pour each of us a glass of water. The water pitcher was made of dark blue china. My father spoke very little at meals, and inside our house it was quiet. Outside the house there were smooth rolling fields. At night I could feel the three of us in our small lighted house, alone in all that empty land, set among the dark fields.

I was brought up to be good and obey the rules, and I was, and I did. It seemed impossible to me to violate those beliefs that grown-ups held—that rules were important, that lies were intolerable, that being good was the correct way to be. At school I was good. I wasn't good enough to be a star at anything—I was a mediocre student—but I wasn't bad. The worst thing I ever did was to sneak out on Halloween and go trick-or-treating through the darkened streets of Bryn Mawr, carrying a pillowcase and knocking timidly at front doors. I never lied to teachers, or snuck out to meet boys, or cheated on tests, or snuck in alcohol, or smoked marijuana, or did anything important. Those things were beyond me, somehow, out of my reach. The rules I'd been given held me within their bounds.

But Cristina came from a large family, in a fiery hot place which was unimaginable to me, and she broke any rule she felt like breaking. She kept vodka in our room at school, right on her bureau. It was in a pHisoHex bottle, in full view of all the housemothers. Cristina looked straight into teachers' eyes and lied about where she was going for the weekend. She lied about how she was getting there and who she was seeing. She did all this with a bold and absolute certainty that I admired: she was utterly sure of the rules she wanted to break, and of the things she needed to do. She didn't care about her marks, or about honesty, or about living up to people's expectations. All that was immaterial to her. The things she did need to do were things like going off to Princeton for the weekend. The things she didn't need to do were things like homework.

After we graduated, I went on to college and Cristina went back to El Salvador. In school she had laughed when I asked her about college.

"Are you kidding?" she asked. "You have no idea what it's like down there. No one I know goes to college."

"But what do you do instead?" I asked.

"We do our hair, then we do our nails." She looked up at me and laughed again. "What we do is visit each other. We go and stay with friends in their country places, then they come and stay with us at our beach houses. We go to someone's ranch in Argentina. We go down to Rio, sometimes. We're busy!" Cristina said excitably. "This takes up all our time. Then we get married," she added.

While she was telling me this Cristina was sitting on her bed with no clothes on, a thick maroon towel wrapped around her head. She had a bigger, thicker towel wrapped around her body, tucked in on itself at her left armpit. Her legs were shaved perfectly smooth. She was doing her toes, very carefully and meticulously, and she had little tiny puffs of cotton separating each toe. She had a bottle of scarlet nail polish, and undercoat, and top coat, and bottles of other luxurious things, emollients and oils and lotions. It looked as though a professional had just stepped out of the room for a moment, in the middle of doing a job on Cristina's toes.

I never did my toenails at school. Even today, I've never done my toenails. My feet are large and rather homely. Putting scarlet shimmer on my big square nails would be an error, and I can't help knowing this. I loved the way Cristina put scarlet shimmer on her nails, everywhere, wherever she wanted.

Cristina got married two years after we graduated from boarding school. She asked me to the wedding, but it was during my final exams, and I couldn't go. In fact I never went down to see her. We wrote to each other for a few years, but Cristina is not so interested in writing. After the letters stopped she sent Christmas cards, and each year I would examine the family photographs: there was Cristina, looking wonderful, tanned and gleaming, with her delicious smooth caramel skin and her thick dark bronzy hair and sleepy eyes, standing beside her husband, who was very handsome. Cristina had always said she would marry only a handsome husband, and so she did. His name was Carlos, which she pronounced "Car-los," with that wonderful sort of gargle just before the "l." Car-los had dark skin, a square face, dashing low eyebrows, big brilliant black eyes. The children looked like Cristina, exactly. Two girls and a boy. I watched them on the Christmas cards, turning more and more like Cristina each year, their chins pointed, their small perfect bodies supple and alert, their features neat and animated. I knew their names: Analisa, Jorge, Elenita. Sometimes, when I was thinking about Cristina, I would say those names in a whisper to myself: Analisa, Jorge, Elenita. They had such a crackle, such a lilt. That seemed to be the way Cristina's life was.

After college I got married, and in the beginning I thought I would have children, too. I sent Cristina Christmas cards, sometimes seasonal pictures of reindeer or snowy forests, and sometimes snapshots of Mark and me. Every year I hoped I would be able to put a note on our card: "Next Christmas there'll be three of us!" I imagined writing the notes. I imagined different ways of making my announcement, something lively or funny or clever. A photograph of the two of us with a note next to it: "How many people are in this picture? Wrong."

Cristina didn't come to my wedding because she was pregnant with her first child. She was too big to travel, she told me. She couldn't move, she told me. I smiled as I read this, trying to imagine Cristina big as a house, lying like a languorous whale on a long sofa out on the veranda, long-leafed plants in giant urns at each end. I liked the image of her sleepy and swollen. This is what it's like, I thought to myself, with a little thrill of anticipation. Soon I would know about all this: morning sickness, fatigue, swollen ankles.

When I learned that she had become pregnant again, three years later, I felt a jolt. It seemed unfair, that she should be pregnant for the second time before I was for the first. Then it happened for the third time. I saw her swollen belly on the Christmas card photograph of that year, with a casual hand laid on top of it, and I felt betrayed and abandoned, as though some promise to me had not been kept. I loved Cristina, and I didn't begrudge her having children. It was just that each time she did, I felt more severely the absence of my own.

Cristina always asked, on her Christmas cards, when I was going to come down and visit them, and I thought for years that I would. But there never seemed to be a time for me to do it, and so I just kept Cristina and Carlos and the three tiny Cristinas in my head. I imagined them, living luxuriously, in a low colonial city, stone buildings, wide colonnaded avenues, palm trees, those scarlet flowers erupting everywhere.

When I heard about the revolution, about assassinations and hostages and *desaparecidos,* I worried. I wrote Cristina twice, but I heard nothing from her. I hoped they had moved to Guatemala, where Carlos had family and business interests, or somewhere else out of danger. Both Carlos and Cristina came from very rich families, and it seemed that everyone they knew was rich. That—being rich—had seemed originally like a great shining carapace of protection over them, shielding them from everything: from having to go to college, waking up in the night with a crying baby, having to carry money, having to stand in line at the supermarket, having to find a parking place. But during the revolution down there, being rich took on another aspect. Then it seemed like some dangerous heat you gave off continually and involuntarily, which made you terrifyingly vulnerable, a target for those hot blasting heat-seeking missiles which followed you through the air no matter how you twisted and turned, no matter what you tried to do to save yourself.

I hoped that Cristina and her family were somewhere safe, and I found out later that they were. They had gone to Guatemala, I heard, and then one year they turned up in New York, the whole family, for a week before Christmas. Cristina called me, and we met for lunch. She looked just as wonderful as she always had, vivid, exotic, her clothes a little brighter than a New York woman's, her jewelry a little more brilliant. She held my shoulders tightly in her hands and kissed me on both cheeks.

"Julie!" she said. "You look *wonderful!*"

I don't look wonderful, I know that. I'm plain, with pale freckled skin. I've put on a middle, and I wear my skirts below the knee. My hair is just as it was at boarding school, shoulder length, and held back from my face with a tortoiseshell band. Even when I remember to wear earrings, as I had that day, it looks as though I've borrowed them from someone. I've always looked like this. I never had the nerve to wear clothes that were tight and spangled, jazzy and stretchy. When I was at school, it seemed to me wrong to wear clothes like that. It seemed then that there was a moral choice to be made, and I felt somehow that I was coming down on the right side. I think I believed in some long-term goal, as though later on I might get an award for Discreet Dressing. Now it's too late for me to change; this is the only way I know how to look.

I'm divorced now. Mark has remarried and lives in San Francisco, where he works for a software company. He has two children, boys, I think. I haven't heard from him in years. There's no reason for us to talk, ever again, really. Nothing connects us now but pain. Looking back at that time we were together is like looking into a black tunnel of grief, tumultuous, endless, without solace. Just thinking of his name brings back the memory of that misery.

I'm used to living on my own, though it's not what I'd hoped to do. I live in a small apartment in Murray Hill. I run a family arts foundation that specializes in music education, and we give away fifty thousand dollars a year, in small grants. We review the recipients very carefully. We visit the site, we interview the participants, we talk to other people in the field for references. It's important to me to feel that we are rewarding the people who most deserve it. I want to give them their due.

I've always tried to be fair, and to be responsible. I thought that was the way the world worked, that it was the way everyone worked. I was always amazed, at school, that Cristina got away with what she did. There were times, even though I loved her, when I have to confess I almost hoped that Cristina would get caught at something. There were times when I resented her amazing bravado.

I remembered her, one Friday afternoon in junior year. Cristina stood coolly in the handsome front hall of the school, on the Oriental rug, next to the big Spanish chest. She was wearing a new orange suit and waiting for the taxi to come and take her to the train with her suitcase.

"Now, let me see, Cristina. This is your uncle's name, Alfredo Pacheco?" Mrs. Winston, the housemother, held Cristina's weekend form, which Cristina had duly filled out. Mrs. Winston was a pleasant woman, tall and lean and attractive, with black-rimmed glasses, perfectly curled-under gray hair, and a perfectly straight back.

"That's right, Mrs. Winston," Cristina said. She smiled dazzlingly at the housemother. Cristina's shoes and pocketbook matched, both dark brown. Her hair was glossy and full of bounce. She had a brown-and-orange silk scarf at her throat.

"And he lives in Philadelphia, at this address?" Mrs. Winston looked down at the form.

"That's right," said Cristina. "I put down his phone number. That's where I'll be." She was going to Princeton for House Parties Weekend.

"All right," Mrs. Winston said, looking again at the form. "This looks fine." The taxi drew up to the door, and Cristina picked up her suitcase. "Have a nice time," Mrs. Winston called, and Cristina waved as she got into the car. She looked out at me and waved again, her smile to me slightly different. She never got caught, I never went to House Parties Weekend.

But I loved Cristina. In New York, that day, when she grabbed me and hugged me, I was caught up again by her energetic intimacy, won by the charm of her presence.

"Tell me everything," Cristina said, sitting down again, "and let's get something to drink. Or at least I hope you'll have a drink? Everyone has stopped drinking. And smoking. Do you mind?" She looked at me solicitously, holding up a cigarette.

"I don't mind," I said, "but the restaurant won't let you." We were in a small Italian place in the East Seventies, just off Madison. She couldn't smoke there, or in any restaurant; it's illegal now in New York City.

Cristina waved her hand. "Oh, they don't mind if I smoke," she said. "I've already talked to the waiter." There was an ashtray next to her, and she flipped open her lighter and lit up. I was surprised by this. I had never seen anyone smoke in a restaurant since the law was passed, and I looked nervously over at the waiter, but he passed right by our table with a bottle of wine, indifferent to our illicit behavior. I wondered if there were any rules at all that Cristina had to obey.

"But what's happened to everyone?" Cristina asked, drawing hard on her cigarette, sucking in her cheeks for a long disreputable pull. She exhaled, shaking her head and expelling a bluish mist. "I go away for a couple of years and all of a sudden the entire population of New York has turned into goody-goodies. What is it?" She grinned at me. "I bet *you* don't smoke, do you," she said, cocking her head.

"No," I admitted, "but I never really did."

"No, that's right," Cristina said, remembering. She leaned back in her chair and took another long luxurious drag on her cigarette. She grinned again. "You never did. You never broke any of the rules. You made me feel like such a bad girl! I felt like a felon!" She laughed and shook her head. "But now you're a big success, eh? I hear you're the head of your foundation! *La Exigente!*"

That's how Cristina talks, all exclamation points and big scarlet smiles. Anything is more fun when she tells it. And listening to her, and watching her smoke, I found myself being torn, as I always had been, between falling in love with her all over again and wishing grumpily that somehow she wouldn't get away with everything.

"You look wonderful," I said, which was true.

Cristina pulled in her chin and gave me a knowing look. "*Please,*" she said extravagantly, rolling her eyes. She put down her cigarette and turned sideways, thrusting her head forward and stretching out her neck. There was a tiny swag of skin that hung below it. Cristina patted the top of her hand against it. "What about this horror? But it's going," she announced. She turned back to face me and touched the line between her eyebrows. "And this."

I dropped my voice. "You're having your face done?" I asked, impressed.

Cristina shrugged elaborately. "I wouldn't call it *done,*" she said. "Only the chin, the eyes, the line in the forehead. A few little alterations, but hey! Nobody's perfect." She picked up her cigarette again and added, "Except this surgeon, I hope. He's meant to be a genius. He's in Brazil." There was another pause, while she grinned, then she added, "I'll probably come out looking like a monkey."

I confess that I felt a tiny surge of moral triumph when I heard about this, having a face-lift. Because I thought that scarlet nails were one thing, but a face-lift was something else. A face-lift, I thought, was wretched excess, and I thought that now she'd gone too far. It seemed to me there was a fundamental difference between makeup and surgery, and self-respect should prevent us all from the latter. There was a line to be drawn, and it had to do with integrity and honesty and probity. Face-lifts were definitely on the other side, the far side, of that line. It was clear to me that women debased themselves, trying to fight the biological fact of ageing. It seemed that women who struggle are acting foolish, and women who don't struggle are acting dignified and self-confident. So when she told me what she was going to do I felt a thrill, as though, at last, I had finally bettered Cristina at something. I felt a jolt of self-righteous pleasure.

"I'm going to do it soon," said Cristina. She took another long pull. "I want to do it before I go back to San Salvador. You know we're moving back, everyone's moving back there."

"Is it safe?" I asked.

"Well. There are armed holdups, hijackings and murders, but no rapes. Which is to say it's safer than New York City." She smiled dazzlingly at me again and then shrugged her shoulders. "It's home. It's where I grew up. The revolution is over. Everyone is going back."

Cristina's troubles were through. She was going back, after the revolution, with all three children and her handsome husband, and she was still rich. And in another few weeks she'd look twenty-eight again, instead of forty-two. And I found myself wondering if she would go on forever getting away with things. But I knew this was mean-spirited, and I dislike that side of myself. So what I said to her was that I was glad she could go home now. And I meant what I said: I do love Cristina, and I don't like my uncharitable side.

I told her it was wonderful that the danger was over.

"Well," Cristina said and paused again. "It's not really over. It's never really over, right?" She stubbed out her cigarette and gave me her big flashy smile. "And who cares?"

That day in San Salvador, Cristina told the driver to pull over to the side of the street, behind the car that was already parked there. The driver, for some reason, was taking a long time to pull in behind the other car, which was where he had to go to be right next to the street door, so that Elvira and Consuela could step across the sidewalk and go right into Elvira's house.

"*Ándale, ándale, ándale,*" Cristina said rapidly, leaning forward to the driver. He started to say something to her, but her mother did at the same time, and Cristina turned back to her mother. Their car pulled in behind the other and stopped. Consuela, Elvira's friend, opened her door, but without getting out; she was waiting for Elvira, who was asking Cristina about a piece of silver she was going to return.

"Okay, okay, okay," Cristina was saying, very rapidly, "okay, Mama, you're right. *Claro que sí.* I'll do it tomorrow. I don't know why I didn't do it before. You're right, the sooner the better. Okay," she said again, and right then all three women realized that something was happening.

The door that Consuela was holding nearly shut was pulled suddenly open, and Consuela herself, gray-haired, in her sleek gray dress and holding a black bag, was yanked out by her arm, and she fell, frightened, onto the grass strip along the sidewalk. The man in the doorway was leaning into the car, holding a gun that was bigger than his face, and he grabbed at Elvira, pulling her out as well. All the time he was talking fast, fast, fast.

Get out, he was saying, get out or I'll kill you, get out, he said to the driver, I'll kill you all, get out, get out, get out. He kicked Elvira as he pulled her out. She staggered a bit and then sat down unintentionally on the grass next to Consuela, who was leaning over, holding her knee. There was no one on the street, the sidewalks were empty. All the houses were hidden behind the high walls, the closed electronic gates.

Get out, get out, get out, the man said, pointing the gun at the driver. The driver turned his face away at once, as though that made him safer, and he ducked down and climbed out of the front door on his knees. All these things happened so quickly, the two older women sitting heavily on the grass, the driver in his dark uniform crawling on his knees along the hard concrete road.

The man was wearing a dark shirt and pants, no jacket. He had dark skin and black hair and his face was pockmarked and his black eyes were enraged, as if hatred and wildness were the only things inside him. He pulled Cristina out of the back seat last, and he held on to her arm so she stood next to him on the grass. He held her tightly as he pulled open the front passenger door. He was watching Elvira and Consuela then, and he pointed his gun on them. I'll kill you, I'll kill you, he promised, over and over and over, and his voice was filled with such wildness, such heat, such fury that no one doubted him. He slid into the front seat, pulling Cristina in after him, still keeping his gun pointed at the two older women. Don't move or I'll kill you, he chanted.

Then it was like a movie, everything happening without you being able to stop it, him moving into the car, the chauffeur crawling further and further away along the street, Cristina's eyes brilliant as the man held his elbow around her neck in the front seat, and just as in a movie everyone could see how things were going to unfold, that this was how it happened, how one became *desaparecida*. Cristina could see there was no help for it, she saw herself part of this scene, getting into the car with this man and his gun, leaving her mother and her children and Carlos, as the man was muttering in a steady violent stream that he would kill them all.

And then something else happened. Elvira, who was now struggling to stand up, realized that Cristina had been pulled back into the car with the gunman, and she turned and ran the few steps across the grass to the car and threw herself over its hood, her gold earrings glinting against the hard shine of the black paint.

"*Don't take her!*" screamed Elvira. "*Don't take her, she's a mother! Es una madre! Tiene tres niños! Take me!*" Elvira screamed, throwing her thin old woman's arms against the hood, banging on it in a horrible, unsettling, embarrassing way. "Take me!" she screamed, her voice high and demanding. "Take me!" she insisted. "Don't take her! She has three children! Take me!" And she clambered, sprawling, like a heavy sack, in her beautiful gray wool dress, over the hood, beating at it with her bony old fragile fists, her gold bracelets jangling in an excruciating way on the metal, and her wild screaming face looming into the windshield.

The gunman was trying to organize himself, holding on to Cristina with his arm hooked around her throat, trying to hold the gun cocked in the air and pull the driver's door shut and find the key and turn it in the ignition and ignore the horrible screaming of the old crone who was flailing her arms on the hood in front of him.

He leaned out the window to shout at her. "We don't want an old woman," he yelled contemptuously. "We want the young one."

When he said that, Cristina said, it was as though everything stopped for her, just for one moment. Everything went slowly and perfectly into crystal in her mind. She heard the gunman call out what he wanted, and she could see what would happen next, she could see the car driving off, with her mother weeping and flinging her hands up in the air. She could see herself being driven off to where the gunman's friends waited, she knew the pain that was waiting for her there among them. She could see that she would die, that they would kill her. Whatever they wanted, she meant nothing to them, and once her body was still they would throw it from the car. It would be found by the side of some road, and later it would be taken, bruised and discolored, to her family. Then her mother would weep in earnest. It was that thought, the thought of her mother when they found her body, and her children sinking down afterward, moment by moment, into the profound darkness of grief, that changed everything for Cristina.

As the gunman was holding her close to his body, his mind distracted, leaning out of the driver's window to shout at her mother, who was screaming in at him through the windshield, Cristina raised her arm up and brought it down as hard as she could, the point of her elbow driving down as hard as she had ever imagined doing anything, deep into the soft place where the gunman's legs met his body. What she did was smooth and exact, as in a dream, as though she had practiced that one stroke all her life, in preparation for this moment.

The gunman's face dropped like a stone toward the place where her elbow hit him. His whole body seemed to turn in on itself, as if it had now some secret business, rolling tightly and deeply into itself with a grunt. And even before the gunman's head started going down, almost before she felt him start to crumple, Cristina found herself moving, sliding across the front seat, opening the door and spilling herself out onto the grass.

Out on the grass things had changed: Elvira was pulling herself off the hood, Consuela had managed to stagger to her feet, and from the corner of her eye Cristina could see the houseman, alerted by all the commotion, by her mother's furious pounding and her demands, standing in the open doorway of the house.

"*Porfirio!*" Cristina yelled to him at the top of her lungs. "Call the police! Kidnappers! Thieves! Call the police!" Now it was her turn, now she was yelling over and over, anger and wildness in her voice, and the gunman clambered out of the car and began running toward the other car, which was idling in front of him. Now the chauffeur thought he was being pursued, and so he lay down on the street without moving as if he were already dead so he wouldn't be shot. The gunman pulled open the back door of the other car and jumped in, and before the door was even shut again the car fishtailed and skidded and roared, and gunned off down the street. It was a red sedan, an old beat-up American car. They never found it.

Cristina told me all that while we were having lunch. The restaurant we were in was chic, and full of women with streaked blond hair, wearing tight snappy suits and gold earrings. The Italian waiters wore white aprons over black pants and white long-sleeved shirts, with the sleeves rolled up.

Cristina told me the story the way she tells everything, with exclamation points and pauses, rolling her eyes. She told it as though it were both extravagant and hilarious, and as though those are the only things she chooses to register. As though the gunman, holding her desperate throat in the crook of his brutal arm, were funny; as though her three children, poised on the verge of endless grief, were funny; as though her mother, beating her frail old arms on the car's hood and shouting crazily into the windshield, were funny; as though her own brilliant and daring and courageous escape were funny; as though the whole world were spread out before Cristina in a series of wild and uproarious adventures, which she chose to see as absurd, though she knew exactly how dangerous and serious they really were. She talked as though boldness and certainty and a fearless readiness to break any rules, any rules at all, were all normal traits, common, insignificant, negligible. She talked as though challenges were there for her amusement, as though they were simply things for her to rise astonishingly up to, like a swimmer lofting herself miraculously over the crests of great waves.

And I forgave Cristina the vodka, the House Parties Weekends, the smoking, the face-lift, the children. I forgave her everything.

Assistance

Adele had not had a good night. She had gone finally to sleep around midnight but waked up again at two-fifteen. This was not a surprise: Adele always had trouble sleeping at her parents' house.

Adele was forty-eight years old and lived alone. She had been divorced for twelve years, and her son, Philip, was at college in California. She lived in the top floor of a brick house on West Fourth Street in Greenwich Village, overlooking other people's gardens. Her apartment was small but sunny, and in the mornings she watched the neighborhood cats parade slowly along the walls dividing the gardens. Her life was quiet, and she worked at home: she translated novels from the French.

Adele liked all of this. She liked her solitary life, with her view over the back gardens, and she liked the silence and rigor of translating. She liked the notion that she was effecting a linguistic transition, making something possible that was otherwise impossible, creating a calm and useful channel of understanding between two vast and powerful oceans.

Adele had driven down to Chestertown, on the Eastern Shore, where her parents lived. Her father, Sam Bolton, had been a hand surgeon at Johns Hopkins for nearly forty years. He was now ninety, and her mother, Bess, was eighty-seven. They were both still mentally vigorous, but physically they were becoming rather frail. Sam had had his second hip replacement operation two months earlier, and Bess's trouble with her knees was getting worse. Since Sam's operation, Adele had been coming down every few weeks to help out.

Beforehand, Adele envisioned each of these visits as orderly and productive. She saw herself as competent and sensible, helping to translate her parents' old life into this new unlearned one that lay ahead. But this was not the way the visits turned out. Going back to her parents' small house was like entering a foreign force field, where the normal rules of transaction—logic and reason and predictability—seemed suspended. It was a strange, disorienting, gravity-free realm where the air sang and jangled with dysfunction, where her own competence somehow evaporated, and giddy chaos threatened.

From two-fifteen until four-thirty Adele lay awake, reading, in the blond-wood contemporary bed her uncle had given her mother when he got rid of all his Swedish modern in the nineteen seventies. The austere bed looked out of place: the room had lavender walls and white ruffled curtains, and was full of dark Victorian furniture from Adele's grandparents. The mahogany sleigh bed had gone to Adele's older sister in San Diego when the Swedish bed arrived. Adele's mother draped a length of thin lavender cloth over the wooden headboard, in an effort to make the new bed blend with the room. It was unsuccessful. The angular blond-wood bed, with its loose lavender hood, looked merely bizarre, as though it had been set there among the ruffles and mahogany according to some alternate universe theory of decoration, inaccessible to us.

At four-thirty Adele gave up and took a sleeping pill, so that when she woke again for the day it was late, past nine, and she was groggy. She could hear her parents, keeping their voices down for her sake, but already started in on the day's arguments. Sam was downstairs in the kitchen, and Bess was on her way down after him. The house was small, and the guest room door was next to the stairs. Adele heard her mother carefully maneuvering herself onto the electric chair that shuttled majestically up and down the staircase.

"I've *already* called him," Bess said in a low, strained voice, trying to make her words carry down to the kitchen on the floor below, without waking Adele in the next room. "I just think we should *see* if there's too much in it."

"What do you want me to do?" Sam called out from the kitchen. His voice was loud and antagonistic. At the hospital he had been the head of his department for nearly twenty years, and he did not take direction well. Adele could hear the stair-chair arms clicking into place as Bess settled herself into the seat.

"What do you want me to do?" Sam shouted again, still louder, and now impatient. Adele heard the electrical click of the switch, and then the low masterful hum of the stair chair as her mother began to descend.

"What do you want me to *do*?" Sam called for the third time, his voice full of exasperation.

At the bottom, there was another click as the stair chair stopped, and the heavy arms clunked up and then thudded down again as Bess climbed out. Bess began walking slowly toward the kitchen. She spoke when she got close enough so that she didn't have to yell, but her voice was now exasperated too. She spoke to Sam so slowly as to be almost insulting.

"I *told* you," Bess said. "I think there's too much food in the refrigerator, and that's why it's making that *noise*. I've called the *repair*man, but before he makes a special trip I want to take some of the things *out* to see if that's what's causing it."

Adele sat up in bed. Since her father had come home after the operation, a group of friends and neighbors had taken turns bringing dinners to her parents. There was a list stuck up on the refrigerator door, with names and dates, so Sam and Bess would know who was bringing the meal that night. The friends took considerable trouble with the meals, fixing things that were interesting and often exotic, but neither Sam nor Bess ate very much, and they didn't like fancy food. After several weeks of this, the refrigerator had become crammed with half-full plastic boxes half-covered with foil, bowls of limp vegetables covered in pale sauces, pans with small hard tracts of curried chicken or baked lasagna, all of their surfaces now darkened and desiccated by the chill darkness of the refrigerator.

When Adele came downstairs her mother was sitting by the telephone in her pink bathrobe. Her long wispy hair was pulled back to a fraying bun. Sam, in bathrobe and slippers, was standing at the refrigerator. Several cartons of milk stood on the table. He was lifting a jar of mayonnaise from the refrigerator, and frowning.

"Let's just see what happens," Bess said to him.

"Mother," Adele said, coming into the room, already annoyed, "the refrigerator doesn't get overstrained because you have a lot of leftover food in it."

Neither of her parents answered.

"The refrigerator just keeps a particular space cold," she went on. "A certain cubic area." She was proud of coming up with *cubic*. "It doesn't matter how much stuff is in it." She said it with certainty, wondering as she spoke if it were true. But surely it was. "It doesn't make any difference to the refrigerator. Well, unless you put hot things in it, a casserole right from the oven, or something."

"Putting things in the refrigerator from the oven?" Sam turned around and stared challengingly at Adele. His white hair stood straight up at the crown of his head. He wore wrinkled cotton pajamas, and a handsome Black Watch plaid bathrobe that Adele had given him for Christmas.

"If you did," Adele said, aware that she had allowed a dangerous digression into her argument.

"Why would we put things into the refrigerator straight from the oven?" Sam asked. He sounded disgusted and cross, as though Adele had accused him of it. "What would be the point of that?"

"I mean," Adele said doggedly, "that your refrigerator isn't making a noise because of what's in it." She paused. The refrigerator was not, as far as she could tell, making any unusual noise at all. It was humming innocuously. They all listened.

"Just put them on the table," Bess said to Sam.

Sam put the mayonnaise jar next to the milk cartons. Adele leaned over and looked at the dates on the milk cartons. There were six of them, in varying states of fullness.

"Mother, half of these are already outdated," she said. "Do you want me to throw them out for you? That way—"

"Now, you just let me take care of the milk cartons," Sam said in a patronizing way. He was the one who drank milk. "I keep track of these things pretty closely."

Adele looked at Bess, who rocked slightly in her chair and said nothing. "So the repairman is coming?" Adele asked.

Bess nodded uncertainly. "I called him. I don't know when he's coming, but I called him. But it may be all those milk cartons, you see."

"But what's the noise?" Adele asked. "I don't hear any noise."

"Well, it *was* making a loud noise, earlier," Bess said defensively. "That's when I called the repairman to see if he'd come and take a look at it. He's the one who fixed the heater in your father's study."

"Wasn't broken," Sam said in a triumphant undertone. He lifted out a casserole with an uneven covering of aluminum foil.

"Well, made it work again," Bess said.

The kitchen was small and square, with yellow walls and white metal cabinets over the sink and the counters. Most of the room was taken up by a long pine table, its near end by the sink and the door to the dining room. The near end was where they ate; there were three dark blue woven place mats set on it continually. The far end of the table was by the telephone and the back door, and it was covered with piles of mail and catalogs. Now the near end of the table was crowded with half-full milk cartons. In the middle of Adele's place mat was a large mayonnaise jar.

"Well, I'm going to have some breakfast," Adele said. "Can I fix anything for either of you?"

"I've already made my breakfast," Sam said. "Your mother's not hungry. Like some toast?"

"Don't you want anything, Mother?" Adele asked. Bess shook her head. She had always been thin, and lately it seemed that she had begun to slip deliberately toward insubstantiality, her skin paler and paler, now almost translucent.

"I'd love some toast, thanks, Daddy," Adele said. "Is there any decaf coffee, Mother?"

"I think so," Bess said. "I try to keep everything my children want. I think it's in there."

All their food was stored in a narrow standing metal cupboard, painted pale yellow to match the walls. In the top shelf of this Adele found a small ancient jar of instant decaffeinated coffee; the new jar she had bought during her last visit had disappeared. There were several spoonfuls left inside the old one. The grains had begun to liquefy into a deep brown sludge, and she had to scrape to get them out.

Adele moved the mayonnaise jar and set her place at the table, putting down a flowered plate, an orange-juice glass, a napkin, and silverware next to the giant stand of outdated milk cartons. The toaster gave a resentful whir and smartly popped up two slices of bread. The toast was charcoal brown, nearly black. The toaster always did this, no matter where the control lever was set. Sam took them out and put them, unbuttered, on Adele's plate.

"There you are," he said. Sam's place was unthreatened by the tide of milk cartons, and he sat down to his boiled egg. He cracked the shell of his egg with his knife.

"Don't you want a piece, Mother?" Adele asked. "I'll butter it for you."

"Well, maybe I'll have a half," Bess said.

She made her way cautiously from the chair by the telephone to the table and sat down with the others. Adele buttered her a piece of toast.

"If you want me to," said Adele, "I'll go through all those things in the refrigerator with you. I'm sure there's stuff we can throw out." She handed her mother the toast.

"The trouble with those meals is they had too much seasoning," Sam said. He scooped the soft innards of the egg out into his bowl, where they collapsed, loosing a dense orange tide. "Too spicy. Kept me awake."

"Couldn't you ask the people not to use spices?" asked Adele reasonably.

"They don't listen," Sam said, with a thin intolerant smile.

"There," said Bess loudly. They looked at her. She held her index finger up, her head high and tilted. "Listen. There it is again."

They all looked at the refrigerator. Its door was covered with yellowed and fraying newspaper clippings about family members. "Local Resident Finds Giant Mushroom" was the biggest headline. They sat and listened. The refrigerator was definitely making a loud noise. Things had changed, internally, and it had moved into some new and interfering gear. A hostile rattling sound came from the motor.

"You see," said Bess.

"It's not the milk," Adele pointed out.

"Maybe you should take some more things out," Bess said to Sam. Sam rose from his chair and shuffled to the refrigerator.

"It's not the things in it," Adele said, exasperated. "If it were, taking them out would have helped."

"What?" Sam asked, turning to look at her.

"If it had been the milk, then since the milk is all on the table the noise wouldn't be coming again now," Adele said. She was aware that she sounded unclear.

"But it is coming again now," said Sam. He was frowning.

"Right," said Adele, "but that means—"

"Take some more things out," Bess said to Sam. The table was filling up with containers covered with aluminum foil, small plates of three or four shriveled carrots, pots with their lids on.

"But don't you want some of these things thrown out, Mother?" Adele asked. "I looked at them yesterday, and these are really mostly inedible."

"Oh, I don't know about that," Bess said firmly. She picked up her toast and took a small bite.

"I think your mother knows what she wants to keep and what she doesn't," Sam said. The table was now completely covered with containers of old food. He sat down again and began to tear bits of crust from his toast, sprinkling it onto the orange-and-white sea. There was a silence while they ate.

"I think I'm going to write another letter to the town board," Sam said, frowning. He spoke loudly, over the rattling roar from the refrigerator.

"What about?" asked Adele. Her father was fond of writing letters to people in which he told them what to do.

"About that stop sign at the intersection of Beech Tree Lane and Route Thirty-five. I've told them before, but they still don't seem to realize how badly designed that intersection is."

"Did they answer your letter from before?" Adele asked.

"They answered it, but I don't think they gave it the serious consideration that it deserves. I don't think they were really paying any attention to it," Sam explained. His toast was now crust-free, and he began to stir the torn-off bits into his egg.

"You did write them twice," Bess pointed out.

Sam looked up at her. "But they haven't properly responded," he explained.

"But they did answer you," Bess said.

"I've *told* you," said Sam, "I don't think they understand the situation."

"Well, you did tell them," Bess said.

"I *know* that," Sam said fiercely. "You just told me that."

"I know I told you that," Bess said. "I'm just saying—"

"I know what you're saying," Sam said.

The telephone rang, and Adele sprang up. She made her way to the far end of the table, reaching it before her parents could. Bess watched Adele as she talked. She was waiting to be handed the phone.

"Yes," said Adele, not looking at her mother, "yes, it is. This is her daughter."

"Tell him about the noise," Bess said.

"There's a town board meeting on Tuesday," Sam said. He took a bite of his egg-and-toast mixture. "I'd like to get my letter to them before that."

"That's right," said Adele. "It's making a loud noise, that's the problem. Kind of a rattle."

"I've told him that," Bess said. Adele turned, so that she was facing sideways to her mother.

"If I mail it today it will be brought up on Tuesday," said Sam.

"I don't see why you're writing to them again," Bess said to Sam, now distracted. "You've already told them what you have to say."

"Well, here. Listen to it," Adele said. She held the telephone out toward the refrigerator, which had ratcheted up again and was drumming loudly and at high speed. "Can you hear that?"

"I've *told* you why I'm writing to them again," Sam said irritably.

Adele put the phone back to her ear. "Could you hear it?"

"I still don't see why," said Bess.

"Well, it's very loud," Adele said. "Yes, we'll be here. We'll be here all day."

"Is he coming over?" asked Sam.

"Right away," said Adele.

"All right, I'm getting dressed," Bess said, getting up. Her toast lay on her plate, a small bite taken from it.

"Don't you want the rest of your toast?" asked Adele. She now felt guilty about not giving the telephone to her mother.

"I'm not really hungry," Bess said.

"What about you, Daddy?" asked Adele, trying to make up. "If you want to go up and get dressed, I'll do the dishes."

"That's not the issue, is it," Sam said, smiling dangerously at her. "What I'm doing here is eating my breakfast, not washing the dishes."

When the repairman arrived, Sam and Bess were back downstairs, now dressed. Bess was in the kitchen, in the rocker by the telephone, and Sam was at his desk in the dining room, writing to the town. Adele opened the back door to the repairman.

"Come in," she said, "Thank you for coming so quickly. The refrigerator's right here." The refrigerator was humming quietly. Inaudibly; it was hard to hear that it was on at all.

"It was making quite a lot of noise before," Adele said, embarrassed. "Could you hear it?"

The repairman was tall, with a pleasant round face and burned-looking pink cheeks. He wore a green shirt with the name Jerry embroidered on the pocket. He put down his toolbox in front of the refrigerator.

"Let's just see what the problem is here," he said, not answering Adele.

Bess leaned forward in the rocking chair. "We've had too much food in there, I know," she said apologetically. "It's because of my husband's hip operation."

Sam appeared in the doorway, a letter in his hand. "Well, I've finished this," he said. "I'd like to take this in to the post office to mail."

The repairman stepped in front of Sam to get at the back of the refrigerator. He wrestled it gently out from the wall.

"Why can't we just put it in the mailbox?" Adele asked. "I have a stamp. I'll take it out to the box for you, if you want."

"No, I want to mail it at the post office," Sam said. He wasn't yet able to drive himself yet, after the operation, so Bess had been doing all the driving. "You about ready?" he asked Bess. She had been watching the repairman and not listening.

"I said, 'Are you about ready?'" Sam repeated, louder.

"Ready for what?" Bess asked in alarm.

"To take me to the post office to mail this letter," he said.

"Could it wait? I just want to see about the refrigerator," Bess said. The refrigerator shuffled further out from the wall, toward the crammed table.

"What's the matter with the refrigerator?" Sam asked, turning to look at it.

"The noise," Adele said.

"Oh, yes," Sam said. He stood in the doorway for a moment, watching Jerry, then he moved past the refrigerator and down to the other end of the table. He pulled a chair out. "I think I'll fix this telephone while I'm waiting," he said.

"What's wrong with the telephone?" asked Adele. "I just used it. It seemed fine."

Sam did not answer. He sat down at the table. The repairman came out from the back of the refrigerator and knelt on the floor in front of it with a screwdriver.

Sam picked the phone up and set it down. "It wobbles," he said accusingly. "When you set it down it wobbles." He demonstrated, setting the phone down on the table. The phone rocked slightly. He turned the phone upside down, and he and Adele stared at its bottom.

"It's missing a foot," Adele pointed out. "That's why it's uneven."

"I know that," Sam said. He set the phone back down and stood up. "I'm going to get something to fix it." He went into the dining room.

"Are you having any luck?" Bess asked the repairman. He was leaning into a mysterious opening he had created at the front of the refrigerator, below the door.

"Well, we haven't solved the problem yet," Jerry said.

"Got it," Sam said, reappearing in the doorway. He sat down again and turned the telephone over, setting it down upside down. He had a box of binder-hole reinforcers, small white gummed circles. Slowly Sam took one out, licked it, and stuck it carefully onto the site of the missing foot. He took out another one, licked it, and stuck it painstakingly on top of the first, building up thickness, layer by layer. Each time he pressed another small white circle onto the plastic underside, he banged the telephone against the table.

"Well, let's not keep banging the phone around," said Adele. "I'll unplug it," she said. She found the small square plug on the side and disconnected the cord from the phone.

"Here's the problem," Jerry said, backing away on his knees from the refrigerator.

"What is it?" Bess asked, smiling at him.

He held up a yellowed newspaper clipping. "Sam Bolton Hits Seventy-five, Still a High Scorer on his Hockey Team" was the headline.

"Oh, my goodness," said Bess, holding out her hand for it.

She shook her head. "I guess I wondered where that was. We had it up on the door, stuck on with a magnet. And that's what was making all that noise?"

"Yep," Jerry said. He was back inside the black hole again, replacing everything.

"Look at this, Sam," Bess said.

The telephone rang, but for some reason not the one in the kitchen. It sounded shrilly in the living room. Sam ignored it, still licking the white circles, then pasting them on the bottom of the base.

"Excuse me, Daddy," Adele said. She tried to take the telephone from him to answer it, but Sam, who had not heard it ring, looked up at her in irritation and would not release it. "Excuse me, Daddy," she said again, "the phone is ringing." They wrestled briefly.

"The phone is ringing," Bess said loudly to Sam.

Sam relinquished it, and after the second ring Adele picked up the receiver.

"Hello?" she said. The line was dead. The phone rang for the third time, still in the living room, and Adele remembered that she had unplugged the cord. She looked for it, but it was no longer on the table. She realized that it must have been knocked to the floor, and, rather than scramble for it and try to fit it back into the tiny aperture before the caller hung up, she decided to answer the phone in the living room.

As Adele stood up, Bess said to the room in general, "Would somebody please answer the phone?"

"I'm working on it," Sam said rebukingly. On the fourth ring Adele was making for the door, feeling panicky at the telephone's repeated demand. As she ran past the refrigerator, Jerry stood up, and Adele made a sudden intimate acquaintance with the flowing script over his pocket.

"Sorry," she said, flustered but still moving.

"It's okay," said Jerry.

"Do you think someone could answer the phone?" Bess said loudly.

In the living room Adele reached the phone on the fifth ring and at last lifted the receiver.

"Hello?" she said, breathless.

"This is 911," a man said.

"911?" Adele repeated.

"You called for help," he said, his voice stern.

"No, I don't think so," said Adele.

"Ma'am, I am required to ask you certain questions. You may be forced to say things against your will."

Wildly, Adele looked around, wondering for a bewildered moment if there were something she didn't know about, if she were in fact being held fast by a hard-armed terrorist, a gun at her head, alien forces in command.

"No," she said. "We're fine."

"Who is it?" Bess called in from the kitchen.

"Ma'am," said the man, "I must ask you further questions."

"We didn't call, really," said Adele, trying to sound convincing. "There's nothing wrong. It was a mistake."

"Who is on the phone?" Bess called louder.

"It's 911," shouted Adele.

"If you don't give the appropriate response to my questions," said the man, "then we will send out a car regardless of what you say."

"Who?" Bess asked, mystified.

"911," Adele shouted. "Go ahead," she told the man.

"911," Bess said to Sam.

"What do they want?" Sam said to Bess.

"Can you tell me what your mother's maiden name is?" asked the man.

"My mother's maiden name?" Adele repeated. "Hogarth."

There was a pause. "All right, ma'am," the man said quietly. "We're going to send you some assistance."

"No!" said Adele, struggling to think. "It *is* Hogarth! That's my mother's maiden name. I promise you we're all right. What name do you want?"

"Are you Mrs. Samuel Bolton?" asked the man.

"What do they want?" Sam shouted. *"Why are they calling?"*

"They called because you called them," Adele shouted back. To the 911 man she said, "No. I'm her daughter. You want my grandmother's maiden name."

In the kitchen Jerry said, "I'm all through now, Mrs. Bolton. Is there anything else you need?"

"No," Bess said weakly.

"I did not," Sam called in energetically to Adele. "What a ridiculous thing to say."

"You did too," Adele said resentfully, putting her hand over the receiver. "You kept banging at the phone while you were pasting those things on it."

The 911 man paused cautiously. "We have to be very careful here. If you are Mrs. Bolton's daughter, then will you give me your grandmother's maiden name?"

"I didn't call 911," Sam said loudly.

"Chase," Adele said triumphantly. *"You did,"* she called back to her father.

There was another pause.

"Are you sure you're all right?" The man sounded reluctant.

"I can promise you," Adele said in a heartfelt voice.

Around her the air was singing, jingling, alive with disturbance. It was as though there were two languages here, and Adele could not forge a meaningful link between them. She was helpless, listening to the strange foreign tongue, even speaking in it, but hopelessly unable to transform it into known and useful speech, utterly unable to translate this world into her own.

She imagined the 911 vehicle arriving, armed men in sunglasses and black clothes creeping silently from it to surround the house.

"Everything here is *fine*," she said, trying desperately to make herself understood. "It's perfectly fine. Don't send any assistance. Please."

Choosing Sides

Wednesday is market day in Sainte-Cécile, and Nina and John spent the morning making their way slowly through the crowded streets. It was high summer in Provence, late July. The big sycamore trees, their trunks dappled like giraffes, were in full leaf, shading the boulevard that circled the center of the small town. The market was spread out in the big main square by the church, and in the quieter, shady one by the *mairie,* and along the main interior street.

Sainte-Cécile is in a farming region, near Arles, and the market was made up mostly of local offerings: neat bunches of dried lavender, handmade soaps, piles of loose fragrant herbs, rough pottery bowls and jugs, cheap clothes made from Provençal cotton prints, in blue and white, red and mustard yellow.

Nina walked in front. She could feel John behind her, losing patience with the heat, the crowds, the array. They were both tired from the trip here. Nina paused at a table covered with an oilskin Provençal cloth and set with bowls of white peaches.

"Madame?" The man behind the table smiled at her. He had

a dark weathered face, grizzled hair, and a pirate's gap between his front teeth. *"Prenez-un."* He offered her a small bowl holding a spray of glistening slices. The flesh was cream-colored.

"If you take one, you'll have to buy a peach," John warned her.

Nina didn't answer him. She smiled at the shopkeeper and reached out for the bowl.

"Merci," she said. She took two slices and handed one to John. She watched him as they bit into the slices. The peach was succulent, luscious. Nina turned back to the shopkeeper, who stood back, cocking his head pleasantly.

"Cela vous plaît?" he asked, smiling. His eyes, in his dark sunburnt face, were surprisingly pale—blue, or anyway hazel.

"Oui, beaucoup," Nina said, taking out her change purse.

She liked the question in French: "Does it please you?" It seemed to suggest that the world was spread out before you for delight. Nina had been brought up in English, with a more austere and puritanical view, in which her being pleased was not paramount. *"Deux pêches, monsieur, s'il vous plaît."*

The man bowed his head in response and leaned over to choose two fruits from the full bowl. He lingered, as though he were selecting jewelry.

Nina paid and thanked him. She handed a peach to John, turning away from the table. "Ninety cents," she said to her husband. "How bad is that?"

John shrugged, taking his peach, and they turned back into the crowd. It picked them up and shouldered them along the narrow street, past a group of young South American men, street players: high cheekbones, dark skin, woven hatbands, a bright-covered CD in a basket at their feet.

"South America," Nina said to John, after they'd passed. "How did they get here, to Sainte-Cécile, on market day?"

Nina and John had gotten to Sainte-Cécile by taking the night flight from New York to Nice, as they always did. They had arrived only yesterday and were here for two weeks. They were meant to be here on vacation, but what they were doing so far was arguing about their son.

"How much more of this do you want to see?" John asked from behind.

"I don't care," said Nina. "We can leave now if you want."

Having won, John turned generous. "I don't mind staying," he said untruthfully, "I just want to know for how much longer."

"I don't care," Nina repeated. "I've bought soap and lavender. That's all I want. Let's go back and have lunch."

Sainte-Cécile was a small, pleasant, bustling town, its main streets lined with tall eighteenth-century houses. On the side streets were smaller buildings, their stuccoed walls painted in hot-country colors: ocher yellow, pale coral, dusty reddish brown. Geraniums cascaded luxuriantly from window boxes. The inner streets were so narrow that even the tiny European cars could barely get through, and only the locals tried.

Nina and John had first started coming there because of Claire, a French friend from Nina's junior year abroad. For a decade they'd rented a house here for a month in the summer. Nina had hoped their son, Tim, would make friends with Claire's son, Gilles, though this had never really happened—Tim had never learned as much French as Nina had hoped.

French was a language Nina loved. It was like a beloved country, the language beautiful in her mouth and her ear, liquid and supple, lyrical. It was more physically demanding, and required more muscular precision, than English, which could be spoken lazily, with the mouth half-closed, the lips nearly flat. In French, the mouth, the lips, the tongue all worked acrobatically to produce those exquisitely precise syllables and intonations. And it wasn't just the sound of the language: in French, your mind was meant to work constantly as well. You were expected to have strong opinions, and to state them. You were expected to raise your voice, to disagree. Nina, who had been brought up, in English, to be tactful and diffident, her voice low and modulated, felt bold and potent in French.

Claire was Nina's passport into that country; they spoke to each other only in French. The two women shared the same birthday, and, oddly, the same maiden name—Vincent—though it sounded very different in the two languages. They looked nothing at all alike—Claire had dark hair and eyes, honey-colored skin, and a narrow, intelligent Gallic face; Nina was fair and blue-eyed, with a broad forehead—but they called each other the Twin, "La Jumelle." Nina liked this feeling of kinship. She felt that Claire was her French self—pragmatic, direct, forceful. Claire was living Nina's alternate life for her. Here in this flat aromatic landscape, with its hot baking summers and cool mild winters, its bright colors and aromatic scents, Claire was doing everything Nina was not.

Claire and Nina had gotten married the same year, and three years later their sons were born, twenty-four hours apart. After that, their paths had diverged: Nina was still married (John a partner at Debevoy's), but Claire, who taught French literature at the university at Aix-en-Provence, had divorced Jean-Louis, her architect husband, eight years ago. She took up then with handsome Daniel, who had narrow bright green eyes and a shock of thick reddish brown hair. He did not work, and spent most of his time riding his motorcycle. He had a slow, intimate smile, a flat, hard stomach, and was sixteen years younger than Claire. They had spent their first summer living amicably together with Jean-Louis, before they found a house.

Claire had told Nina about all this, easily, without a soupçon of embarrassment, without any shame at her divorce, or awkwardness at the age difference, or any hint that there was anything odd about the ménage à trois. Claire acted as though life was to be lived exactly as she wished it. Nina, who felt hemmed in by a jostling throng of rules and expectations, could not imagine telling her friends in New York that she had taken up with a jobless motorcycle rider more than a decade her junior, let alone asking John if they could all share a house after the divorce. She was proud of her *jumelle,* proud that her other self was so bold and unconventional. She loved hearing Claire's glittering complicated stories—the stories of her own other life.

John and Nina had stopped renting their house when Tim stopped coming with them. They were staying this year at the Hôtel des Alpilles. This was a handsome old manor house just outside of town, at the end of a sycamore-lined drive, among wide green lawns. Inside it was cool and dim and pleasantly *ancien:* mirrors with faded gilt frames, a long dark wooden Provençal sideboard. The hotel was run by two middle-aged sisters, and when Nina and John came in, the plump one, with the thick square glasses and short brassy hair, sat at the desk.

"*Bonjour, monsieur-dame,*" she said at once, with the automatic courtesy of the French. She smiled crisply.

"*Bonjour, madame,*" Nina answered. John nodded.

They started up the stairs; there were only two floors, and no elevator. Their room was on the corner, looking out toward the pool. This was rectangular, set abruptly into the lawn without paving. Beyond was a small patio and a snack bar, serving salads and sandwiches.

In their room, Nina took off her sandals. The sisal rug was scratchy against her bare feet. She put her peach on the desk by the window and folded her arms on her chest. She was tall, almost as tall as her husband, and lanky, with knobby knees and elbows. She had been blond as a child, but her hair was now fading to an indeterminate gray.

"The thing is," she said, looking out at the pool. "The thing is." She stopped.

"The thing is," said John, "you think he should marry her and I don't. And he doesn't. If he doesn't want to marry her, he shouldn't. How can you tell him to marry someone he doesn't love?" John was going through his pockets, putting his wallet and change and sunglasses onto the bureau. He turned around to her. "You sound like a nineteenth-century marriage broker. Or a priest. I can't believe what you're saying."

Nina unfolded her arms and sat down on the bed. "I know," she said. "I know you're right, he shouldn't marry her if he doesn't love her. But then why did he stay with her for so long, if he didn't love her? *Three years,*" she said, disapprovingly. "Living together. What was he thinking of? It was better in the nineteenth century. Trollope says, 'One turn about the conservatory at a dance,' that's all you need, to know if you want to marry someone. Living with someone for three years—what does that tell you? About how Tim feels about her?"

John pulled his shirt off over his head. He'd been lean when they married; now his high firm chest seemed to have slid down to his waistline, and his shins seemed somehow more prominent, the bone now closely approaching the skin. The hair on his chest and legs was pale. It had been blond, now it was colorless.

"Are you coming down to the pool?" he asked.

Nina looked at him. "I mean, it's sort of too late for him to say he doesn't love her. In the nineteenth century they'd be married now."

"In the nineteenth century people made miserable marriages. That's why divorce became legal." John stood by the door, holding a towel.

"So, nowadays, everyone lives together beforehand for years, and then they still get divorced. What have we gained?"

John shook his head and opened the door.

"Go ahead," said Nina. "I'll be down in a minute." He closed the door behind him. Nina sat without moving. The bedstead was dull brass, and against it, high lumpy pillows were piled under a woven white bedspread. The tall windows had interior shutters that could be folded shut against the midday heat. They hadn't remembered to shut them before they went out that morning, which had been a mistake. The hot air had crowded into the room. Nina stared outside toward the lawn, though from here she could see only cypress trees.

The first time Nina had seen the baby had been on the sidewalk outside the hardware shop. She had known about it by then, of course. People had told her. Hilary had even called once, herself, but at a certain point Nina had stopped taking Hilary's calls. Then Hilary's mother, Elaine, had called; the conversation had not been a success.

"Nina? Elaine," Elaine began briskly, like a supervisor. At the tone of her voice—officious—and at the way she said Nina's name—peremptory—Nina's blood began to pound, and suddenly her thoughtful, reasonable, understanding self vanished.

"Hello," Nina said. Something chemical had happened, and she felt herself vibrating with antagonism—toward Elaine, her tone of voice, the fact that she'd had the audacity to call.

"I thought you and I should talk to each other," said Elaine. "I think maybe we should deal with this directly."

Elaine spoke with a nasal sort of Long Island drawl which Nina, who had grown up in Connecticut, found insufferable. Nina said nothing; there was a pause.

"I mean, we have a serious problem here," Elaine said.

"Actually," Nina said, refusing to be drawn in, "I don't think *we* have it."

There was another pause.

"Well," Elaine said, "it *is* Tim's child." She spoke imperiously, as though she were in charge of everything.

"I'm sorry," Nina said, "but how do we know that?"

She'd really only meant to stop Elaine from being so imperious; as soon as she'd spoken she knew she'd gone too far.

Now the silence was furious.

"We know it's Tim's child because Hilary says it is. They were *living* together. She wasn't *seeing* anyone else. She hadn't seen anyone else in *years*. Do you want a *blood* test?"

Nina waited again. She tried to make her voice neutral.

"Elaine, did you and Hilary ever talk about an abortion?"

This was unfair, she knew, as well as openly hostile, because Nina had heard from Tim that they'd talked at great length about an abortion. Elaine had urged her daughter to have one; Hilary had refused. Hilary had refused over and over, each time her mother had brought it up, week after week after week, until it was too late.

Elaine said grimly, "The baby is here now. This is what's happened, Nina. This is what we need to talk about."

Nina resented Elaine's saying her name, hated the way it sounded in Elaine's insufferable accent. Still, if Elaine had stopped right then, Nina would have given way, because it was true, the baby *was* there. But Elaine went on.

"Responsibility. That's what we need to talk about, Nina."

And at that, at Elaine's bullying, hectoring manner, Nina balked.

"Elaine, Hilary has made her choice. And Tim has made his choice," she said. "We can't change any of that."

"Is that all you have to say?" Elaine asked. Her voice now was furious. "Is that your *position*?"

Nina could hear Elaine winding up to deliver a tirade.

"I'm afraid it is," she said. "I'm afraid it is all we have to say." She was bringing John in for support. "I'm sorry it's gotten so complicated."

"'*Complicated*,'" Elaine began energetically, but Nina cut her off.

"I'm sorry," she said, "but I don't think it's going to be productive to discuss this any longer." Then she hung up, her heart pounding at her own abruptness. Also, she'd sounded just like John, really, which surprised her. What she'd said wasn't even what she thought.

The problem was that she didn't really know what she thought.

Some months after he'd found out about the pregnancy, Tim had moved out of the small apartment in Brooklyn he was sharing with Hilary and moved in with a friend. Hilary, who didn't have a job, and now didn't even have a boyfriend, let alone a husband, had left too, and moved up to Connecticut to live with her mother. Who didn't have a job either: Elaine lived on the alimony from several husbands, though she claimed to be a decorator. It was all really a mess.

"We weren't *planning* to have a baby," Tim had told Nina. He'd sounded tense but determined. He'd come out for the weekend; it was before the baby was born. Nina came down on Saturday morning to find him alone in the kitchen. She wanted to talk, though it was clear that Tim did not. He was ready to leave the moment he saw her. Nina held him still with questions; he answered with his hand on the doorknob.

"But if a baby comes . . . ," said Nina.

"She never told me about it," Tim said, his face turning angry. "All of a sudden, one day she's pregnant, and then, boom, our whole lives are changed. All of a sudden I'm told I have to get married, I have to do this and I have to do that, whatever she says. We'd never talked about it, we'd never planned it, and it wasn't my decision, it was only hers. It wasn't a decision that she should have made by herself."

He let go of the doorknob now and folded his arms defiantly on his chest. Tim was twenty-three, still in business school. Hilary was only twenty-two, just out of college. They seemed so young, so unready—though Nina had been only twenty-two when she married, she reminded herself. But it was different now; this generation, wary and preoccupied, married late.

"I'm not getting married just because she tells me I have to," Tim said. His head was lowered and truculent, his mouth pursed. He was tall, like John, with a wide flat face and bright blue eyes. His body was solid: he was now full-grown, as big as he would ever be. But the truculence, the pursed mouth, the lowered head, reminded Nina of the lanky, obstinate teenager, testing his awkward strength against the world, his parents. His voice was swollen with something—aggrievement, self-absorption. Hearing that note—the whine—made Nina impatient; she wanted to tell him to grow up.

"What I mind is her deciding without me," Tim said. His voice had quieted. He looked up at his mother, hurt in his eyes.

At that, Nina had felt a sudden loyal flare of anger against the young woman. Tim was right, she thought, that was fair. Nina had, until then, always liked Hilary: the long fall of silky blond hair, the languid eyes, the sweet smile. Hilary had sat at her table many times; Nina had believed she'd loved Hilary. Hadn't she? She'd been prepared to love her—or was it all provisional? Did you like your child's mate only as long as your child was happy? If the mate made your child unhappy, didn't you turn against the outsider? Didn't you close the gate, draw the wagons in a circle, close out the interloper? What if the interloper had given birth to someone who belonged inside the circle?

Now, in the hotel, Nina took off her skirt and folded it on the chair. She struggled into her bathing suit—were they made tighter now? Or were her arms weaker? It had not been a struggle to get into a bathing suit when she'd been twenty. She stepped back into her sandals.

In the pool, John watched her approach from where he was floating in the deep end, the water slapping up toward his chin. In the shallow end a group of dark-eyed French children were playing; a spray of silver drops splashed boisterously onto the grass. Nina waded carefully down the steps and began a cautious breaststroke toward her husband, squinting her eyes against the children's splashing. She could see from John's expression—watchful, forebearing, tentatively friendly—that he was ready for a truce. She swam up to him and stopped, treading water, feeling the loose surge against her body.

"Nice, isn't it?" he suggested, about everything: the line of feathery sycamores along the drive, the beneficent sun overhead, the wide green lawn stretching out to the orchard beyond.

"Very nice," Nina agreed, looking around, smiling. She too wanted a truce. "What do we do about the baby?"

John sucked in his breath, opening his mouth into a wide O. Raising one arm over his head, he threw himself sideways, into the chopping surge, and began to swim away. Nina, watching him, felt his wake drift against her limbs. At the far end he stood and walked deliberately up the steps without looking back. His bathing suit had slid downward around his hips, without a waist for it to clasp, Nina noted disloyally. He hitched it up from the front as he mounted the steps.

The baby had been in a dark blue carriage, parked outside the hardware store, next to a bright red wheelbarrow and a shiny garden cart. That was what had made Nina look at it— the three brand-new vehicles, lined up side by side—it was a sort of sight gag. She glanced idly into the baby carriage, to see if it was for sale.

It was occupied.

The baby lay under the deep shadowy cave of the canopy. Nina, leaning in, was drawn out of the harsh bright sunlight, the noise of passing traffic, the quick staccato footsteps of the passersby. In this dim sheltered space the baby was small and quiet, lying flat and tranquil on the smooth white sheet, her eyes points of liquid light. She was very young, her body was not yet plump. She was lean but solid, dense, like a loaf of bread, a tiny motionless island beneath the blanket. The small head was furred with fine blond down, the skin pale and translucent. The arms were free from the covers, and the tiny starfish fingers moved gently about, testing the air. The body seemed barely large enough to hold life. As Nina looked down into the shadows at her, the baby blinked, moved her chin, then focused her calm blue radiant gaze on her grandmother.

It was a shock. Nina knew suddenly who this was, she could feel awareness run up through her like a breath through her chest. For a moment Nina hung motionless over the carriage, fixed in that wise blue stare, trying to memorize the broad pale forehead, the small delicate mouth, the sense of peace in that dim sheltered space. She knew that at any moment she'd be discovered. Heart beating, she turned and left, quickly, not looking at the shop door. She walked rapidly on down the street, hearing her own heels echo on the sidewalk, her head lowered, feeling like a thief. Well: she had stolen something. That illicit moment alone with the child.

John hadn't seen the baby. She'd told him, but he'd only shrugged his shoulders: it would be different if he'd seen her. As he certainly would, since Elaine and Hilary lived only one town over from them. They'd see each other inevitably, and what would happen then? What was the baby to call them, as she grew up? How would they be introduced? The baby was called Emily.

"Emily," Nina said out loud in the pool. "*Emilie.*" It was just as pretty in French. No one heard her, the French children were shrieking, and John was stalking across the lawn to the chair where he'd left his towel.

At lunch they sat at a table shaded by an umbrella.

"I know you don't want to talk about it," Nina said.

"You're right about that," John said.

"So, just tell me what you think should happen in five years? How do we deal with this for the future?"

"The point is that this is something Hilary has decided," John said firmly. "She had all sorts of alternative options available to her, and this is what she chose: to have the baby without being married to Tim, and without his agreement or support. What are we supposed to do? Adopt it?"

"She's a girl," Nina said. "Not an it."

"You answer me for a change," John said.

"No matter what we do, or what Hilary did or shouldn't do, this is our grandchild," said Nina.

"Well, I feel as though our son has been manipulated and tricked, and I don't like it," John said. "And no, you're right, I don't want to talk about it."

"Why is it always the men who are manipulated, and not the women? Why didn't he manipulate her, by moving in with her and acting as though he wanted to spend the rest of his life with her?"

John concentrated, frowning, on his *frites*.

"It made a lot more sense before the sexual revolution," Nina said, "when girls didn't have to sleep with everyone they went out with. Sexual liberation turned out to be a very poor deal for women. Now they have to whine and beg for marriage."

"Your point is?" John asked.

"I don't know what my point is," Nina said, giving up. "I don't know what we should do. But she's our granddaughter."

John did not answer. He went on chewing, his eyes focused on a cypress tree on the other side of the lawn.

That night they were seeing Claire for the first time; she'd asked them to dinner. Her parties were large and casual, and it would not be the moment to tell her about Emily. Nina would wait until they saw each other alone. Claire's opinion, whatever it was, would be instantaneous and absolute. She would view Nina's uncertainty with incomprehension. *"Mais chérie,"* she would say, *"c'est évident!"*

In the evening John and Nina drove into the hills, through the transparent dusk. The air was turning dim; darkness was washing over the crepuscular landscape. The olive trees were becoming dense and mysterious. Claire and Daniel lived up in the Alpilles, on a quiet back road near the lake. Their long dirt driveway was rutted, and big clumps of lavender stood on either side of it. The soft shrubs crowded against the car, breathing out their sweet sharp scent.

Claire was out under the trees.

"Nina, John," she cried, when she saw them. *"Vous êtes arrivés! Quel plaisir!"* Crisply she kissed them on each cheek. She held on to Nina's shoulders, smiling at her. *"Tu parais merveilleuse, comme toujours."*

"Toi aussi," Nina said, smiling back.

Claire was thin and tan, with thick short hair. She wore a narrow long skirt and a tight off-the-shoulder sweater that showed off her strong throat and the bones of her shoulders. She held a cigarette: Claire smoked constantly, drawing in the long hot breaths with authority and satisfaction, as though there had never been such a thing as medical research, or the word *cancer.*

"Alors, que voulez-vous boire?" Claire walked them toward a table with wine; they found glasses and began to mingle. There were some expat Americans, some French writers, musicians, artists—Claire's circle was eclectic. Handsome Daniel came up and smiled into Nina's eyes. Gilles, Claire's son, tall and burly, was moving through the crowd, and someone's small child, only two or three years old, squeezed her way between people's knees. Nina began talking to a violinist who played at the Avignon festival; John stood with a short tanned woman with wavy blond hair.

Dinner was outside, and they sat at two round iron tables dragged together. People served themselves to a rich aromatic chicken stew, then sat anywhere. Stars began to prick the deep blackness of the Provençal sky. Daniel came out with a box of matches and the candles sprang into being; light flickered on the animated faces. Everyone argued about everything: food, theater, movies, politics. *"Mais non, mais absolument pas,"* people said to each other, voices and eyebrows raised. *"Mais si, mais si."* Only in French was there a special word for contradicting someone, *si,* the extra-assertive yes-after-someone-has-just-said-no.

Afterward, Nina helped clear. Carrying a stack of plates, she followed Claire into the tiny kitchen. The house was small and spare and casual. Stuck onto the refrigerator were photographs of people asleep—friends curled on the sofa, stretched out on the lawn, Daniel in a hammock, Claire on an airplane.

"Where shall I put these?" Nina asked, looking at the photographs.

"Wherever you can," Claire answered, balancing her own stack on the old iron stove.

"I like the musician," Nina told her. She set her plates in the sink.

"He's the friend of Michelle," Claire answered. She took down a salad bowl from the open shelves over the sink.

"Who's Michelle?"

"She's the one who was talking to John before dinner." Claire turned and looked at her. "You haven't met her? I haven't told you about Michelle?"

Nina shook her head.

"*Eh bien,*" Claire said. She set down the bowl and leaned back against the big porcelain sink. She lit a cigarette and shook the match out with a quick authoritative snap.

"Michelle is an old friend. She used to live in Lyon, but a few years ago she called me." Claire took a long deliberate drag on the cigarette and exhaled a smooth white plume. "She was in despair, she said. She was forty-three, with no husband and no children. She desperately wanted a child, but she didn't even have a boyfriend." Claire shook her head.

"So I said, come down here. There are lots of men. If you want a baby, we'll find you a father." Claire shrugged. "So, Michelle arrived. At first she stayed with Jean-Louis, my ex-husband. You know Jean-Louis is gay?" She added this parenthetically, and Nina, who had wondered, nodded. "Daniel and I were still fixing this place up, and we didn't have room for her. That summer, Gilles and a friend were also staying with Jean-Louis. They were both nineteen." Claire took another long drag on her cigarette, exhaled. "So. That summer, Michelle became pregnant." Claire shrugged neatly, to show the speed and elegance of the solution. "Perfect. Just what she'd wanted. But"—she paused—"after a few months, Jean-Louis called me and said, 'Michelle doesn't dare tell you.'" Claire looked at Nina. "I said, 'Tell me what?' He said, 'She says the father is either Gilles or his friend.' She'd spent one night with each of them."

Claire pursed her lips and shook her head. "I said to Jean-Louis, 'Fine. Tell her she wanted a baby, now she'll have one. It doesn't matter whose it is. It will be hers.'"

Claire shrugged again.

"A few more months go by, and now she's eight months pregnant. Jean-Louis calls and says again, 'Michelle doesn't dare tell you.' I said, 'Tell me what?'" Claire shook her head. "'Michelle is sure it's Gilles.'" She paused. "'She wants a blood test.'"

"Oh, my God," Nina said. "What did you say?"

Claire stood up very straight. "This time I called her myself. I said, Michelle, the child is yours, and that's all there is to it. You wanted it, and now you'll have it. Gilles is nineteen years old. This has nothing to do with him, or with his life. You have no business drawing him into it. He has a whole life ahead of him—he'll get married, he'll move away—and it has nothing to do with this child."

Nina remembered suddenly. "That little girl who was here tonight?"

Claire nodded composedly. "Denise."

"And who does she look like?"

"*Exactement comme la mère,*" Claire said firmly.

"Where is she?"

"Asleep on my bed."

"But she's here? With Gilles? And you?"

Claire looked surprised. "*Bien sûr.* Michelle is my friend. Of course I love Denise. I see her all the time. I babysit for her." She put out her cigarette in the sink, twisting it against the porcelain, then tossing it in the trash. She folded her arms and looked at Nina.

"But she is not my granddaughter," she said. "Even if there were a blood test, and it showed that Gilles were the father, she would not be my granddaughter." She paused for emphasis. "If Gilles marries, and if he and his wife cannot have children, and if they adopt a child from China, *that* will be my granddaughter. Denise is the daughter of my friend."

There was a pause.

"And what does Gilles say?" asked Nina. She was spellbound by the story, its opulence and vitality.

Claire shook her head. "He says nothing." She shrugged again, slightly, her smooth shoulders polished by the light. "What is there for him to say?"

Nina did not speak. She thought of the small figure of Denise, dodging confidently through the forest of adult legs, asleep trustingly on Claire's bed. She thought of the forty-three-year-old Michelle, sliding down between the sheets with the teenage boy. She thought of Daniel, with his hard flat stomach and purposeful looks; she thought of Claire moving amicably out of her marriage to Jean-Louis, remaining his friend. She loved this story, she loved the freedom and forcefulness—the absolute certainty—of Claire's attitude.

It seemed that none of the rules Nina had been taught applied here. Convention played no part: loyalty, pragmatism, tolerance, but not convention. There were no rules—was that it? Certainly it was clear that you could make your own. It was clear that it was up to you to decide who your granddaughter was.

Family: What makes it? Who's to say? It's whatever you de-

cide. Her mind moved back to the memory of the small body in the cool shadows of the carriage, to the deep shared silence of the moment as she gazed down into the calm eyes of her grandchild. Peace welled up at the thought.

She's mine, Nina thought. With the words, certainty swept across her, like the slow wash of a wave. *She's mine.* Tim and John could do as they wished, but she wanted this child in her life. She would make friends again with Hilary—who had been brave, she now thought, to carry through with this alone—she would put up with Elaine. None of that mattered. That small solid form, bundled in pale pink—the magical unfolding fingers, those calm blue eyes—was hers. Tim's small daughter had claimed her; they had claimed each other. She was taking Emily's side; you could choose.

Emily: she said the name to herself. *"Emilie,"* she said out loud.

Claire leaned back against the sink. Her eyebrows raised, attentive, she waited for Nina's story.

At the Beach

My wife put Jennifer into the car seat in back, and then she climbed into the front seat next to me. Her hair was in a long braid, and she wore a flowered sort of beach dress over her bathing suit. She shut the door without speaking.

"All set?" I asked. It was a general question, but Diana didn't answer or look at me, so I looked at Jennifer in the rearview mirror as though I were talking only to her. "You all set back there, young lady?"

"Yes, I am, Daddy," Jennifer promised.

I had known Diana wouldn't answer: she hadn't spoken to me in nearly two days, since Thursday night. Or looked at me, really. I couldn't remember a fight that had gone on this long.

We were in the car for only a few minutes; we were only a mile or so from the beach, down small sandy back lanes. It was already hot, and the sky was very blue, and cloudless: a perfect beach day. When we reached the parking lot it was full, of course—this was eastern Long Island, August. Row after row of cars were parked in the sandy lot, surrounded by dune grass. I wondered if I'd have to park illegally, along one of the side roads, and risk a ticket, but as I turned down the last row I saw the taillights of a little red car turn bright, and I stopped just in time.

"Luck-ee," I said. No one answered me, and I began to whistle, pretending that I didn't notice this lack of response, as the little red car slid out in front of me. When it had pulled away, I pulled neatly into its slot and turned off the engine.

"Here we are, kiddos," I said. I looked into the mirror again to find Jennifer watching alertly. She had wide blue eyes, and pale skin that looked so fresh it was impossible to believe it could be four years old. It looked just born, smooth and sweet. I smiled at her and winked. "Hi, kiddo," I said.

"I'm not *Kiddo,* Daddy," she said reprovingly.

"Oh, well, *pardon.*" I said the word in a French accent. "Who are you, then?"

Jennifer hesitated for a moment. "I'm—Bathshena," she declared, closing her eyes regally.

"Oh, I see," I said. "Well, I'm very glad to meet you, Bathshena." I bowed my head to her politely.

Diana ignored us, climbing out of the car and leaning into the back to help Jennifer with the car seat. "Let's get you out of this," she said to Jennifer, as though they were alone in the car.

There was a path through the dunes, and as we walked along it the tall green beach grasses moved in the sea wind against our bare legs, light and slithery and yielding, but sharp, each narrow blade a cutting edge. I carried the hamper and the umbrella; Diana held the beach bag and Jennifer's hand.

"Here's the beach, Jen, here we are at the beach," Diana said. Her voice was bright but it was pitched low, so that only Jennifer would be able to hear it, though I could, just barely. I was walking behind them; there wasn't room for the three of us abreast on the path. Diana kept talking to Jennifer as we made our way along the hot sand.

Usually, when we fight, Diana gets mad and she stops speaking to me. Then I stop speaking to her, and there is a stubborn silence between us, fixed and solid, a wall. But I don't stay angry as long as Diana does. After a few hours my anger begins to drain away, water sinking into sand. The heat goes out of me, the fight loses its point, I can't remember why I was so angry, and then I want the wall down. I want to be in the same world with Diana again. I make an overture: I touch her skin, her smooth shoulder or her cheek. I say something, and then she turns to look at me, and then the walls we have built between us collapse, sliding down into nothing.

But this time it wouldn't happen. I wasn't going to make the first advance. I'm always the one to do it, and why should the burden always be on my shoulders, as though I'm the only one who cares about this marriage, as though it's only my responsibility to make it work? This time I had determined not to do it. It's Diana's marriage too, and this time it was her turn. I was determined to wait for her to make the first move.

That morning I'd been standing in the kitchen, my cup of coffee in my hand, looking out the window. Diana was in Jennifer's room, getting her dressed, and I could hear them laughing about something. They started with low voluptuous giggles, taking turns, their voices sliding into each other, egging each other on, and then becoming long drifts of helpless laughter. The sound was so loose and luxuriant, so swelling and overflowing and delicious that I found myself smiling, starting to laugh, just from the sound of them together. I knew exactly what they looked like: Jennifer rolling on the bed, Diana leaning over her, maybe tickling her small frantic body, the two of them raucous, hilarious, tender, and all those smooth female limbs twisting and intertwined. I wanted to go in and stand there with them, and I thought if I did that Diana would look up at me, her eyes warm and lit up, and the fight would be over, and we'd be together again.

I was looking out the window, starting to smile as I listened. I began to turn around. But then I remembered the night before, and the irritating way Diana had stood at the kitchen counter, drinking from a mug and reading a magazine with her back to me, turning the pages and stirring her tea as though she didn't even know I was in the room. I remembered how stubborn she was being, and how she could only see things from her point of view, and I hardened myself to the laughter. One of us would have to give in on this, and Diana, as always, thought it should be me. I thought of this arrogant assumption and my outrage rose up again and I told myself I would not make the first move, and I stood waiting by the window until Diana brought Jennifer out, dressed.

At the beach we always walked east to get away from the crowds, but of course in August there are hardly any beaches on Long Island without crowds. We walked for a while, until the houses had thinned out, anyway. Where we finally settled down it wasn't empty. There were fifteen or twenty groups of people scattered around on the sand, with folding chairs and big umbrellas and picnic coolers. But we weren't right next to anyone, as the beach was very wide there.

It was beautiful. Pure white fine sand, a long straight line of it for miles: the beaches of southern Long Island are as good as any in the world. You could stand at the high edge of that beach and see the long slow reach to the horizon in either direction, nothing interrupting that brave clean stretch into the far point of distance.

The pitch of the shore sloped down sharply at the water's edge, and the surf was high that day. The waves were big, and they started cresting fifty, eighty, a hundred feet out, and then they came riding high and angry all the way in, curling themselves down in a rolling explosion that thundered along the beach, and the smaller waves rushed mindlessly up along the broad dark patch of sand. Small stones, seaweed, shells washed helplessly back and forth in the shifting shallows. The sound of it all was powerful: the long gathering wait, and then the crash, the rumble, and the small flooding rush. Then a wait, and another crash.

We settled ourselves high up on the beach, away from those pounding waves. We were in a relatively empty patch. The closest people were ten or fifteen feet away; another family, with a small son. The mother was a thin dark-haired young woman in a black bikini. She lay flat on her back, her eyes closed against the sun. The son was nearby, playing in the sand with a plastic tank. The father sat beneath the umbrella, reading a magazine. He was dark-skinned and furry-chested, wearing a white tennis hat with a wavy brim. He stared at us from behind his sunglasses as we set up camp.

I pushed the shaft of our umbrella as deep into the sand as I could, and when it felt solid, I opened it up. The big striped wings lifted creakily above me like a mechanical bird, and a patch of dry shade hovered over the burning ridges of sand. I took out our towels from the beach bag.

"Here's your towel, Miss Bathshena," I said to Jennifer.

Jennifer pursed her mouth, restraining her smile. "Thank you very much, Daddy," she said. She took it from me with a little flounce, her eyebrows lifted, her eyelids lowered. Little girls flirt, even very little girls. And of course I flirted right back with her, how could I not? She was delicious, delectable, my sweet little morsel of a daughter.

Diana was not looking at us, but she was watching, I knew, out of the corner of her eye. She spread out her own towel on the other side of the umbrella from me.

"Do you want to be over here with Mummy, Jen?" she asked. I thought this was mean-spirited of her, enticing my daughter away from me. "Come over here and let me put sunscreen on you."

Clutching her towel in one hand, like a miniature starlet,

trailing it behind her, Jennifer trundled obediently over. She stood meekly while Diana, frowning in the sun, squeezed a white coil of lotion into her palm and rubbed it into Jennifer's soft back, making the angel wings rise and fall with her strokes.

I settled down on my towel. I was sitting up, my arms around my knees, looking around. I set a small smile on my face, general and nonspecific, so that if anyone were to look over at us we would look like a comfortable domestic group, peaceable and united. I saw that we were in an area of all families, and I thought about how my inner sense of direction had shifted. Six or seven years ago, still single, I'd have found myself on a beach full of nubile young women, nearly naked, lying stretched out on the sand in pairs, waiting to be approached. Now things have changed; I don't even know where those beaches are. I don't really care where they are, either, but thinking about that, about my wholehearted and virtuous fidelity to Diana, about my commitment to our marriage, roused my outrage at her again. How could she take this for granted, how dared she? I remembered those beaches, I could find them again.

Here, where we were, there were lots of children around Jennifer's age, staggering around on the sand with buckets and shovels. Down on the long slope of the beach by the water, there were parents sitting with their children, digging at the liquid sand, building fanciful, brief-lived castles.

Diana came over to the beach bag, which was next to me. She leaned down to reach it, and suddenly I felt her body beside me, shading me from the sun. I could feel the cool relief of her presence; I could smell the suntan lotion she used. Right beside me were her long thighs, the warm color of honey, with that smooth shallow groove running down the sides. I knew exactly how they felt to the touch. I looked at them; I remembered them under my fingers.

"Hi," I said to her softly, looking up at her, as though we were lovers.

Just an impulse. But Diana's face was set, it was granite. She didn't answer or even look at me. I could feel determined indifference radiating from her, burning and deadly, like the sun. It shocked me. Up until then I'd been thinking only of myself in this. I'd been thinking that peace was available as soon as I wanted it; whenever my exasperation cooled, it would simply be a matter of my making a move. But now, seeing how set her mouth was, how cool and fixed and neutral her gaze, I felt things starting to slide away from me. It felt like that draining backwash of the surf, that rush which you're powerless to resist, and I wondered if this was the way things were going to be for us. Maybe it was too late for me to make a move. Suddenly it seemed really bad, and I wondered if we'd gone too far. If I'd gone too far, during the fight, if I'd said things that could not now be forgiven. I knew I'd been unkind.

Last night, Diana, in her nightgown, had closed herself into the bathroom before she came to bed. After she'd brushed her teeth and turned off the water, there was silence. She didn't come out, and after a while I became aware of this, and I put down my book to listen: I could hear her weeping. It was very faint, a quiet whispering sound, a staccato series of coughing sighs. A long breathing pause, and then the little coughing sighs again. I'd had to hold my breath to be sure what I was hearing. Later, when she came out of the bathroom, her eyes were changed, hooded and hurt, as they are after crying. She didn't look at me. I lay in bed with my book held up again, looking straight ahead as though I hadn't heard and didn't see. It was her turn to make a move, I was thinking. She got into bed with her back to me, and we went to sleep without speaking. At the time I'd thought angrily, Fine, let her know how it feels, let her decide to end it. But now I thought, What if this time I've lost the right I'd always had to end the fight? Our fights had never lasted this long before. How bad do things get before they're too bad to fix?

I began to wonder if Diana had made some decision of her own, some hostile conclusion that would slowly force me out of our life, into exile, banning me from her forever. I'd always believed that she was in my life for good, but what if I was wrong? What if this fight was the beginning of a terrible unraveling, what if this bright day was something we'd remember forever as a foreshadowing, darkened afterward by pain?

I said nothing more, and she moved away, back to Jennifer. I saw her give Jen a big smile: her face still worked, apparently, only not toward me. That smile grieved me, and I began to be frightened of what might happen. I had a cavelike feeling in my chest, a hollowness that I didn't know how to deal with, so I lay down on my back and closed my eyes and pretended to go to sleep.

Of course you can't go to sleep like that, with the hot August sun beating right down into each of your eyes separately as though it is two mad searchlights. Even with your eyes shut the light drills in at you, turns your eyelids hot and red inside. Still, right then there was nothing I wanted to see, so I kept my eyes shut. I heard Diana talking to Jennifer for quite a long while, and Jen answering. They were kneeling, busy, building a castle together, right there where we were, high on the beach, with that useless grainy collapsing dry sand. I would have gotten up and taken Jen down toward the waves, and built one with the soft liquid sand along the waterline. We would have built a much better castle down there, but I knew it would have been seen as an antagonistic gesture, my taking Jennifer there, away from Diana, and of course I knew Diana wouldn't come with us. I lay in the sun without moving, my eyes shut, listening to the heavy crash of the surf, and the cries of the children, and the ill-bred squalls of the gulls.

I don't know when I first heard the call. Maybe I actually did sleep for a bit, because when I became aware of it I realized I had been hearing it for a while. I didn't know how long. Urgency abounds along the seaside: children scream with sudden intensity, parents shout alarmingly for them to do something, or not do it: it's the turbulence in the air, the surf, the big distances, the shrieking gulls, so many people, running and splashing. Turbulence is all around you, and you respond with shrillness and urgency.

So when I heard the calls, "Annie! Annie!" at first I didn't pay attention. But something in the tone was disturbing, and I sat up, leaning back on my elbows, to watch.

A woman was running along the beach, at the lip of the sand, where it started to slope sharply down to the water. She had dark bushy hair, and sunglasses. She was in her late thirties, with a thick waist. She wore a red bathing suit with a broad blue diagonal stripe across the front. She was running not fast but somehow desperately, and her hands were clenched into fists. On one wrist a gold bangle glinted in the sun. Her feet pounded heavily into the sand. As she ran she kept looking around and around, as though she would run faster, but she didn't know what direction she should take. "Annie! Annie! Annie!"

By now she was abreast of us, and in her voice, it was clear, there was terror. I sat up, roused by that dreadful unbidden stab, and looked around, from side to side. Everyone nearby was doing the same. People were sitting up, getting onto their knees, frowning anxiously, shading their faces with their hands, looking from side to side. But none of us could help—none of us knew Annie.

Behind the woman now came three other women, the same sort of age. One was blond, two dark-haired, and they were all in one-piece bathing suits. They too were shouting "Annie," but it seemed somehow clear that they were friends, not the mother. They seemed more purposeful, and less paralyzed by fear. The friends kept on going, passing the mother, who had stopped. The mother simply stood there on the sand, turning, desperately, in a circle, looking behind her and behind her, and calling out again and again, "Annie! Annie!" in a wild, anguished voice. She didn't look at the surf, thundering in, over and over, below her, but we did. We couldn't help it. We looked, horrified, at the waves, rising slowly up, towering, then crashing down into foam and violence, fearing to see the thing we looked for.

The woman started off again, heading down the beach, running slowly. Her cries carried back to us on the wind. "Annie! Annie!" she called. I looked around our circle: no one was settling back down. Parents called to their children, knelt next to them, stood anxiously, then sat down again, alert and straight-backed. They shaded their eyes and scanned the dunes, they looked furtively at the surf. The children stopped their screaming play. The couple next to us had drawn together. The mother in the black bikini had sat up and moved under the umbrella beside her husband. Their little boy sat still, watching, his tank suspended in the air.

The woman came back past us again, her feet pounding along the sand, kicking it up with each step. She looked at none of us, none of us, none of our children. There was only one shape, one body, that was the right one, and she couldn't find it. "Annie!" she cried. "Annie!" It was unbearable, to hear it. "Annie! Annie!" We could hear how she was beginning to give way. She ran wildly on, past us, back in the direction in which she'd come, still calling out. But before we could even settle down on our knees again, she had made a wide wild loop in the sand and was running back again. Her arms were held out now, stretched open in the air. The gold bracelet glittered.

We were all standing up, now, all of us. All the children had stopped their playing. They had become quiet, and stood by the bare sandy legs of their parents. We were all watching the mother. From down the beach, beyond her, her friends reappeared, the three of them pounding back down the beach, without Annie. They were calling too, still, distracted, frightened: "Annie! Annie!"

The woman was nearly in front of us. We could hear her panting as she ran, we could hear how ragged her voice had become. Beyond her the surf never stopped, those huge green breakers pounding down, over and over. The mother never looked at the water, it was as though that was something she denied altogether. She was tiring, you could hear, and hope was running out.

The family near us had drawn into a little cluster. The father was standing now, with his silent son in his arms. His wife was next to him in the sun, her thick dark hair around her face. She was weeping. She wiped the tears away with her fingers, then she put her arms around her husband and her child, leaning her head against her husband's shoulder. She closed her eyes and opened them again, looking at the mother, who would not stop, who ran and ran, and circled about aimlessly again, pounding past us once more on the sand. "Annie! Annie!" It was a torment.

I looked at Diana, but her face was turned away. We were standing, too. She had Jennifer held close to her, leaning against her. Jen's arms were wrapped around Diana's thigh. Jen was silent and frightened, her thumb drifting fearfully toward her mouth.

Then the mother, running past again, stopped right in front of us, her arms open despairingly. "Annie!" she called again, and then she sank suddenly down onto her knees.

I couldn't bear it. I couldn't bear her giving up, though I could see she'd done everything there was to do—where else could she go? Her friends had come back, their faces twisted and distorted with the sun, the running, the fear. There was nothing more she could do, the mother. She was on her knees in the sand, and she put her hands up to her face, covering it: it was over.

Her friends caught up with her, and stood in a circle around her. One of them, with short tousled blond hair, stooped over her. She put her hand on the mother's shoulder, speaking to her. The other two women still looked around, squinting against the sun. The shorter one folded her tanned arms aggressively on her chest, as if she could somehow take charge. The other woman took off her sunglasses and set them on top of her head. And they both kept slowly turning and turning, looking around and around, scanning the beach. But the mother stayed on her knees, her face covered with her hands. She shook her head back and forth, crying, in a terrible low voice. No one knew what else to do. It was over.

Then in the bright hot glare a moving figure appeared, a little girl in a white bathing suit, coming from the direction of the dunes. She was running through the families scattered across the sand, dodging in and out of them, coming down the beach toward us. As she came closer, the friend with the folded arms said something urgent, and the mother, still kneeling, raised her head. The little girl was running straight for her, and the mother opened her arms. As the little girl reached her, the mother flung her arms around Annie's small body. She closed her eyes and began rocking, back and forth, on the sand. It was over. Now it was over.

The woman next to us started to sob openly. She was holding on to her husband and her son. Around me, the women were crying, covering their faces with their hands. The men were silent and stricken. Everyone could feel the rising terror that had pounded through the mother's heart.

I looked at Diana, and I stepped over next to her, close. She kept her face turned away from me, but it was lowered now, no longer grimly lifted. I put my arm around her, and then I put my hand up and took hold of her chin, and I moved her chin gently around so that her face looked into mine. She let me do it. Her eyes were shut; she was crying. I waited. She took a long gasping breath, and tears flooded down her cheeks. Jennifer, frightened and silent, stood by her leg.

"Diana," I whispered. "I love you."

She did not answer.

"All right, you win," I whispered. "We'll have another. We'll have six more, if you want. Ten."

Now I could see that it was I who'd been wrong, and stubborn. All the things I'd thought so solid and weighty, like granite—why it was too soon for another child, why we must wait, and why the decision must be mine, not hers—were now tiny and flimsy, meaningless. They fell away, water sinking into sand, and I felt ashamed.

I meant it, what I was saying, but it was too soon for Diana to hear it, or to hear anything I said. She was still crying hard, her body was still gusting with sobs. She was still ravaged by that anguish, by the terrible vision of what we all fear most, the lost lost child.

It's fear that takes you over, you're helpless before it. It takes you over, sweeps you into that awful curling rise toward the breaking crash. The roar is loud and terrifying in your ears, and you're reminded how weightless you are, how aimless your movements, how brief the moments before the next crash. How you have nothing to hold on to but each other.

Blind Man

It had been raining earlier, but was now stopping. The windshield wipers began to creak. They were now leaving streaks, instead of cleaning the glass. He turned them off and they quit, sliding weightlessly down into their hidden pocket.

He'd been on this highway for an hour, maybe, though it was hard to tell, they all blended into each other so smoothly: the exit sign announcing the shift onto the ramp's stately decelerating curve; at its end a slow diagonal merge, then acceleration into the new current. It was hard to remember just how long he'd been on this one, exactly when he'd left the last.

He was, anyway, somewhere in Connecticut, on a high bridge over a valley. Below him lay the dense grid of a nineteenth-century mill town. Above the industrial jumble stood a handsome Venetian campanile of dark red brick, a white clock face on each side. Its slate roof narrowed upward to a needle's point.

The bridge stretched from one hillside to the other. The traffic, weaving a complicated pattern, prepared for left-hand exits ahead. The signs for this place, whatever it was, were now behind him. He might never learn its name, or the source of its lost potency, or who had thought to erect a Renaissance tower above the grimy brick labyrinth. All these dismal industrial towns were ghostly now, their energy dissipated, industry gone. All that outrage over intolerable working conditions: now there were no working conditions. Ahead, on the crest of a wooded hillside, stood a large white cross.

He'd been told not to think about it, not to go over and over it, but what else was there to think about? It was what occupied his mind. Trying to think about anything else was a torturing distraction. He was never not thinking about it.

At night he lay in bed beside his wife—also wakeful, also silent, her back to him in the dark—and went over it in his mind. It played there forever, an endless loop.

The soft blossom of smoke, like a sweet cloud of scent, drawn swiftly up through the narrowing shafts into the skull. Sucked down the long hard ribbed windpipe, then released into the spacious crimson chambers of the lungs. Drawn deeper, into the branching, diminishing pathways of the bronchi. Further still, into the depths of the soft honeycomb, the bronchioles, their membranous walls porous and thin. There the barrier between air and fluid was only one slight, slight cell thick. There the mysterious shift occurred: the smoke passed magically through the tissue, into the bloodstream. There it dissolved, becoming part of the smooth surge, pumping rhythmically through the interlacing curves of the vascular complex, flowing through steadily widening channels, headed swiftly and unstoppably for the brain.

He imagined its arrival there as an explosion: the sudden pulsing release of a million stars in the deep black sky of the mind.

He could not hold the two notions together in his mind: the physiological and the individual. The chemical reactions and Juliet.

In the dark, in the close silence of the bedroom, the sheets and blankets became heavy and tumbled. They seemed to pool, carried by some hidden current. They collected in eddies around his legs, tangling his arms in dank swirls.

Each time he remembered, he was shocked by the silence of the fact, its perpetual inertness. There was never any change.

In the morning, he sat on the edge of the bed, the weight of another day upon him, light sifting dully in from under the window shade. He rubbed his face hard, palms rasping against his unshaven cheeks, trying to rid himself of the clinging wisps of the black nighttime world.

The thing was not to think about it. The thing was to be disciplined, to take control.

Though what if he did let go, let himself think about it? What if he just locked himself in the room of his mind and thought about nothing else? Because that was what he did anyway, he hadn't a choice. He was already locked in there, and that was all there was in with him.

Approaching the hillside, the highway passed a grim Catholic church. High on the stone façade was a rose window, too small, and of course dark from the outside.

What he ought to do was review his notes, though just at this exact moment, he could not remember the topic of his lecture. The road ahead was gray, still grizzly with rain. Passing cars made a sissing sound. He was in the middle lane, driving fast, like the cars around him. Being in the midst of this speeding stream gave him comfort. He liked the notion of community, he liked the steady, infinite supply of power beneath his foot. He felt he was getting somewhere.

Being alone was a luxury. The small rented car, for which the university would reimburse him, was anonymous, a haven. The woolly dark red seats, the spotless gray carpeting, the bland mechanical eyes of the dashboard: it was like a motel room. He could do whatever he wanted, speeding across Connecticut among the other cars. He was invisible here, though around him he carried a kind of darkness, a cloud.

A huge truck passed on his left, the size of a small country. The roar was deafening. The silhouette towered alongside him, darkening his sky, streaming on and on. The gigantic wheels spun hypnotically by his face. His small car swayed, buffeted. It would be better not to think about it. Her hair had been in her mouth, there had been strands of it, dark and silky, lying across her open mouth. What else was there to think about?

His lecture, it now came to him, was on the cathedral of Hagia Sophia, the ecclesiastical nexus of Byzantium, symbol of its enormous power, its astonishing beauty, its history of invasion and transformation. He shook his head and thought deliberately of that high empty space, the vast dome filled with silence. The shafts of still sunlight, falling on the ruined mosaics. The wide bare brick floor, worn smooth by centuries of slippered footsteps.

The lecture began with a slide of the exterior. "The dome of Hagia Sophia is only one brick thick. It is a perfect curve, mathematically without flaw. No one knows how this engineering feat was achieved. It is one of the great mysteries of ecclesiastical architecture, just as Hagia Sophia is one of the great symbolic mysteries in the history of Byzantium."

He had given this talk many times, at universities, scholarly institutions, colloquia, and seminars. The first time long before she was born.

He moved sideways, into the fast lane. The little red car rocketed along, the tires sizzling against the damp pavement. Its slight frame seemed sturdy and flexible, like an airplane's, designed to withstand buffeting and winds. Speed seemed to be what held the car onto the road. The roar was loud and steady.

At a flash in the rearview mirror he looked up. Behind him was a big SUV, threateningly close, its headlights blinking an imperative staccato. It was only a few feet from his bumper, he could feel its heavy breath. At this speed it would take only an instant, a tiny split-second shift, for things to go badly wrong. The pace held them all spellbound: his tiny red car, the SUV behind him, the gigantic rumbling trucks.

He put on his blinker and waited for the car on his right to pass. The lights behind him flashed again, impatient, looming closer. He felt a tightening on his scalp. The SUV bore down, closing the brief distance between them. The mirror was filled with the flashing lights. Too soon for safety, he slid sideways, nearly hitting the bumper of the car ahead. As he was still moving, the SUV roared past, barely clearing his car. Spray rose from its tires, coating his windshield with dirty hissing mist. Signal still blinking, he waited for another car to pass and then moved again, into the slowest lane. Abruptly, dangerously, too fast, he slid sideways again, moving off the highway altogether, onto the narrow shoulder. He felt the loose gravel suddenly rough beneath his wheels, the car juddering as it slowed. For a sickening moment it skidded. Then the tires caught, the car slowed and bumped unsteadily to a stop.

He was on a narrow shoulder, barely off the pavement. The car was cramped between a heavy metal guard rail and the road. The sound of the speeding cars was deafening. A giant trailer truck thundered past, wheels sizzling viciously along his window. Within seconds there was another. As each roared by, his small car—frail, he now understood, not sturdy—rocked and shuddered. The grime-covered trucks steamed past. He felt the shock from each one. He set his hands on the steering wheel. Something was flooding through him, like blood clouding into water. He leaned back against the headrest, looking into the traffic vanishing ahead.

The last week: he went over and over it. Juliet in the kitchen one morning, unloading the dishwasher. Bending over, her long dark hair falling weightlessly forward. He'd been at the table, reading. Juliet, a stack of plates against her chest, pushing against the swinging door into the pantry. A wrinkled yellow jersey, cut-off blue-jean shorts. Her limbs were soft, still childish—not plump, but cushiony. Her legs were tanned to a dark honey brown in front, lightening to a paler cream in back, on her calves.

His wife had called from outside.

"Yeah?" Juliet was vanishing into the pantry.

Ann again: something about the hose.

Juliet called loudly back. "What?" She was in the pantry then, stacking the plates in the cupboard. The crockery rattled. It was clear from Juliet's voice—loud, indifferent—that she couldn't hear her mother, didn't care.

Ann's irritation. "Juliet, would you please not walk away from me when I ask you something?" Ann was now in the kitchen doorway.

"Sorry, Mom," Juliet said, reappearing, unruffled. Her round face, her short upper lip and bright narrow blue eyes, echoed Ann's, though the dark straight eyebrows were no one's but Juliet's. She smiled at her mother, at once placating but also, mysteriously, pitying, as though Juliet were in a continual communication with some superior self, far beyond the reach of mortals. "Want some help?" she asked kindly.

They'd gone outside; he'd gone back to his book.

What did it mean, that moment? Anything? He examined everything, now, for clues.

Juliet had been in a kind of disgrace that summer; she was under a certain obligation to be placatory. She had screwed up. She had broken rules; laws, in fact. She had been sent home. She had not finished the college year, she had ended up instead in a group of institutional buildings in another state. Her academic reinstatement depended on good behavior. Her domestic reinstatement depended on good behavior. She was in disgrace.

Though in a way it was he and Ann who were in disgrace, for aren't the parents absolutely implicated in the transgressions of the child? To be honest, aren't the parents, perhaps, more responsible than the child? Didn't they create the world in which the child found these transgressions possible, necessary?

And if you, the parent, have ever allowed yourself small helpings of private pride and satisfaction at your child's accomplishments, if you have ever stood beaming at a graduation in the June sunlight, swelling inwardly over the award for religious studies and feeling that in some unexplained but important way your daughter reflects your presence, that she represents you and your codes, both cultural and genetic; if you have ever felt that your beautiful daughter was somehow flowering forth from you, so then, when another area of her endeavors is revealed— addiction, say, to crack cocaine—you will also feel the heavy cowl of complicity settle over your head.

At the beginning of this summer, when they'd brought her up here, they'd watched Juliet's every move with anxiety. In those first weeks she'd acted stunned, silenced. Not sullen, exactly, simply mute: silenced. She did everything she was asked but without response. It was as though her thoughts were in a different language. She had withdrawn. She was elsewhere. She didn't laugh. She spent hours silent in her room, the door closed. He and Ann, pausing unhappily outside in the hall, tiptoeing on the threadbare rug, could hear nothing from inside. Was she reading? Was she lying on the bed, curled on her side, eyes fixed steadily on the plaster wall?

At meals Juliet ate without speaking, looking down at her plate. They could hear the sounds of her chewing, the faint muscular convulsion as she swallowed.

Once, at dinner, Roger lost his temper.

"Jules, could you pass me those beans?" he asked mildly.

Juliet stopped chewing, the bite of food still evident in her cheek. Without raising her eyes, she handed her father the pink china bowl. She began to chew again, looking down at her plate.

"Juliet," Roger said irritably, "could we please have some

manners here? Could you please look at someone when he speaks to you? It is considered courteous to acknowledge the presence of other people. All the rules of life are not suspended forever, you know, just because you've been in rehab."

Juliet raised her head and looked levelly at him. "Just because I've been in rehab?" she repeated.

"Yes," he said forcefully, deeply sorry he'd begun this. "Manners are the muscular supports of society. They are the embodiment of its moral core. They are the basis for a civil society. You're in a family community here. We all owe each other something. Respect. Courtesy."

"Sorry, Dad," Juliet said, her voice pointedly neutral. *"Here are the beans."*

Roger was already holding the bowl. "Thank you," he answered foolishly. He set it down and served himself to seconds. Somehow he had lost his moral authority. He was afraid of what she might say to him. What was it? What had he done? He thought nothing; he could not bear to learn.

But as the summer went on, the tension seemed to subside. They were up in New Hampshire, in the old shingle house that had belonged to Ann's parents. They had always spent the summers here; Roger's academic schedule allowed for a three-month vacation. Juliet and her older sister, Vanessa, had been here every year of their lives, though starting in adolescence, they'd gone elsewhere as well. Now Juliet was back in the house with her parents, as if she were a child again.

Slowly, during the summer, she had begun to thaw.

One night Ann told them about a zoning meeting she'd attended. Developers had begun greedily to eye the big open mountainsides, and a town meeting was held to discuss planning. Ann thought the Zoning Board's position was meek and conciliatory.

"Jackson Bly might as well have invited the developers to come and stand on his stomach," Ann said. "I couldn't believe what he was saying. I wanted to get up and say, 'Jackson, when we want advice from a hamster, we'll call on you.'"

Juliet was drinking milk, glass at her mouth, and at this she erupted, coughing and gasping, milk flying up her nose. She'd briefly choked, her napkin plastered against her face, white drops spattering the table. Roger stood and patted her back, happy to be able to help her with something so urgent, so simple: milk up her nose.

Things improved, Juliet began to relax. By August it seemed she'd reverted to the easy, sunny child she'd once been. She'd seemed to like her parents again. She liked the ramshackle house. She'd spent that summer as she'd spent earlier ones: hiking, swimming in the pond, helping with the garden and the dishes, walking dreamily through the fields. Late at night, she talked on the telephone. He and Ann heard the low murmur through the thin old walls of the farmhouse, felt the vibration of the invisible connection that stretched from their docile meadow to the crackle of distant cities. None of your old friends, the therapist at rehab had said. No one from that life. But Juliet was alone there in the house, with them. She saw no one else. There were no drugs there, in the sun-bleached field, the wooded hills.

Though it seemed drugs were everywhere now, seeping into kids' lives like groundwater. They were so available, so common, you couldn't ask your older, most obedient child not to take them, let alone your younger, wilder, more rebellious and more difficult daughter.

Vanessa, three years older, had been relatively saintly, they'd learned. Now through college, she was living in Somerville and working for a landscape designer in Cambridge. This summer, Vanessa had been their lifeline at times, coming up often for weekends, acting as intermediary between her parents and her sister. She told them her own story. Smoking pot, mushrooms: it would have horrified them at the time. Now it seemed innocent, adolescent.

What was it they'd missed? That exchange in the kitchen, between Juliet and Ann—the plates, the hose—that was completely normal, wasn't it? Or not? What was it that he should have foreseen? He felt again the sliding terror of what approached.

The last week, they'd gone swimming, the four of them, in the pond at the foot of their hill. At the near end of the pond stood the splintery wooden dock. At the far end was a stand of willows, overhanging the water, trailing long green strands into its depths. Beneath the willows the water was dark and murky. No one swam there, for fear of monsters: snapping turtles, eels, leeches. Logic suggested that all those things might be anywhere in the pond, but instinct warned that the dark shadows, the overhanging branches, were a haven for sinister forces.

That afternoon, Vanessa and Juliet stood side by side at the edge of the dock, wrangling languidly. Feet braced, they shoved hips at each other.

"Go in, then. Why don't you go in? You're such a *wuss*," Vanessa told Juliet, pushing her shoulder.

"*As if,*" Juliet said, shoving back. "I'm so much braver than you."

"Okay then, swim the pond. Go under the willows," Vanessa challenged.

Without a second's pause, Juliet threw herself full-length onto the cool green skin of the water in a long racing dive, hitting the top of the water flat, then sliding under it to disappear. There was a lengthy, expectant pause. The waves from her entry subsided, the pond turned silent. The surface was now smooth and unbroken, though somewhere beneath it was a living body, moving swiftly, its heart pumping, oxygen coursing through its blood. Waiting in the sunlight for Juliet to reappear, the others became mindful of held breath, aching lungs, throbbing heart, the weight of the silver-green water. The pond was still. Dragonflies glinted and shimmered above it.

Juliet suddenly exploded upward, surfacing in a swirling rush of air and bubbles, unexpectedly far away. Without glancing back she began to swim, turning her head to breathe with each stroke. Her hair, now black and glistening, clung flatly along her back and arms. They stood on the dock, watching her move along the edge of the water, toward the cave of willows. Juliet never stopped, never looked to see where she was. The long movement of her arms, the thrashing kick, disturbed the whole pond. Ripples rocked across its wide stretch.

At the far end Juliet disappeared behind the curtain of overhanging branches. The water there was shadowed and opaque. They could hear her steady strokes, but her progress was hidden. For a moment her disappearance seemed perilous, the silence fraught, as though they were waiting for a scream. Roger found himself holding his breath.

When Juliet reappeared, her arms beating long arcs through the still air, dark hair plastered over her polished shoulders, her flashing progress seemed triumphant. Risk now seemed absurd. There had been no danger after all, no monsters.

Juliet swam steadily back. Reaching the shallows, she stood, walking in slowly, against the weight of the water. Her face and body were streaming, brilliant.

Juliet looked at Vanessa. "So," she said. *"Wuss."*

What was it they should have noticed, foreseen?

The traffic hurtled past; the red car trembled. He should move, he was too close to the thundering stream. Though now he realized it would be hard to get out of here: the shoulder ahead narrowed to a point, then vanished. It would be difficult to get up enough speed, in the space remaining, to reenter the current. The red car, though willing, did not have much acceleration.

At the end of that week, Juliet had announced her plan to go back to Boston with Vanessa. It was late afternoon, and they were all out on the lawn. The girls were lounging on the grass; Ann sat in a decrepit aluminum chair, its woven webbing frayed.

She was shelling peas and dropping the empty pods onto a newspaper spread on the grass. Roger had just come up, carrying a hammer and a jar of nails. His summers here were spent in continual battle with loosening shingles, hidden leaks, rotting wood, and creeping damp, as the house struggled purposefully to return to the earth, and he struggled determinedly to prevent it.

Ann frowned. "Where will you stay?" she asked Juliet. "You can't stay at home." Their house in Cambridge was empty, and this was exactly the sort of thing that could get Juliet in trouble.

"She'll stay with me," Vanessa said.

"I just want to see Alicia before she leaves for college," Juliet explained.

None of your old friends. No one from that life.

Roger and Ann looked at her, worried.

"Juliet," Ann began. She was sitting very straight, her feet crossed at the ankles, dropping the peas into the colander in her lap.

But Juliet smiled at them. "Don't worry," she said. "Alicia's not in that crowd. I'm not going to run off and do drugs."

She'd said the words out loud.

Should they not have trusted her? Do you never trust your child again? When do you start to trust her? She'd been there with them for nearly three months. Her eyes were candid, her gaze open. They couldn't keep her alone with them in the mountains forever. It was the end of the summer, and they were all about to return to the world.

On Sunday afternoon, the two girls left in Vanessa's small dusty car, trundling slowly down the rutted driveway through the field. At the bottom of the hill Vanessa gave a honk; both girls stuck their bare arms from the windows and waved loosely. Roger and Ann stood on the lawn in front of the house, waving back. Then the car turned out onto the road and was lost at once among the trees.

He would have to make an effort to get out of here, to get back into the rushing line of cars. He would be late for his lecture.

He looked in the rearview mirror. The traffic streamed at him seamlessly. Maybe he should back up, to give himself more room. He set the car in reverse and turned to watch over his shoulder. He pressed cautiously on the accelerator. The car began to creep backward, zigzagging disconcertingly toward the cars flowing dizzyingly toward him.

When Vanessa called, the next night, they'd been asleep. At the first ring they were both awake, sitting up, hearts racing. Ann picked up the phone, Roger fumbled with the lamp.

"What is it?" Ann asked into the phone.

He looked at the clock: one-forty.

"Where is she? Where are you?"

"What is it?" Roger asked.

Ann shook her head, frowning. "Are you with her right now?"

There was silence while Vanessa talked.

"What is it?" Roger asked again.

"Hold on." Ann turned to him. "It's Juliet. She came home late and Vanessa's worried about her. She thinks she took some drugs."

Roger took the phone.

"Vanessa," he said. "What happened?"

"We met some friends for dinner, and then we went on to hear some music, and then I wanted to go home. Jules said she just wanted to see Alicia, by herself, and she'd be home really soon." Vanessa sounded frightened. "I know I told you I'd stay with her. I know I did. But she got really mad at me, and yelled at me, and told me to stop following her around. She promised she'd be right back. She came back a while ago, and now she's asleep, only I can't tell if she's asleep or out cold. Unconscious," she added, touchingly careful, as though verbal precision might help.

"How did she act?"

"Okay, I guess."

There was a silence. Roger closed his eyes to listen, trying to hear what was going on.

"Really okay?"

"I guess so. She said she had a headache." Vanessa sounded miserable.

He spoke to Ann. "She had a headache."

Ann frowned and shook her head. What did it mean? What did a headache mean? Anything?

"That's all?" he asked Vanessa.

"Yeah. She said she was going to bed."

It was quarter of two in the morning. Whom could they call? Was it an emergency? Juliet was already asleep, and they were two hours away.

Ann took the phone back. "Nessa, did she seem okay?"

Their bedroom was in shadow, except for the glow from the lamp. The darkened ceiling slanted down toward the eaves; on it, above the lamp, was a pale blurry oval. Around them the house was still.

They decided finally to let Juliet sleep. Whatever she'd done was already done. They'd get up early and drive to Somerville. They'd call the therapist at rehab. They'd find a local program, they'd call their own doctor, marshal their forces, find out what to do. Right then, seventy miles away, in the middle of the dark mountain pasture, the middle of the night, they could do little. They'd do everything the next day. They'd start in the morning.

Of course, for Juliet there was no morning.

She'd taken no more than her old dosage, but during those innocent country months her body had lost its resistance. The cocaine vapor thundered into her system, accelerating her heart, contracting the vessels in her brain. Within the hard bone cup of her skull, a narrowed artery gave way. The tissue ruptured, and blood spilled deep into the smooth inner surfaces of the brain. These were places sacrosanct, inviolate. The intrusion was intolerable: an irreversible distress signal was given. The violated brain closed down the central nervous system.

Closed down the central nervous system.

He had an image of offices darkening for the night, covers placed over machines, doors shutting, lights going off. *Closing down. Closing down.* He could not hold the two thoughts in his mind at once, the physiological and the personal. The rupturing artery and Juliet.

He was backing now directly toward the oncoming cars. The afternoon was waning, and some headlights were on. The approaching lights were hypnotically attractive, and he had to resist veering slowly into their path. He backed carefully, swerving slightly back and forth, correcting himself with small swings, until he'd created enough room to make a run. Then he waited for a gap in the oncoming stream. All you could do was go on. Was there anything else you could do? Back directly out into the stream?

When he saw the gap, he tried to measure it mentally, looking backward through the growing dusk. How big was it? Big enough? But he could feel something gather within him, some kind of excitement, and he understood that this was the moment, he was going. He had already gunned the little car; at once it lost traction on the gravel. But he was committed, the tiny motor roaring, the accelerator flat against the floor. He felt the engine laboring, gathering speed slowly, the breakdown lane narrowing rapidly ahead. He was racing it. At the very end of the lane, his turn signal sounding its repetitive bell, hoping the driver behind him would understand his need, see his danger, Roger pulled out into the traffic, his heart racing, rising to meet the moment. It was like a plane roaring down the runway toward liftoff.

The moment the wheels hit the pavement he knew his pace was too slow. He could feel the speed all around him: he was too slow. He felt the thunder of trucks alongside, felt himself borne down upon from behind. All around him was the assault of sound, the hurtling crush of speed; he waited for the impact.

It did not come. The car behind him must have seen him and understood; he felt its dangerous looming presence diminish, fall away. The little red car droned loudly, its engine straining upward. Finally it reached its capacity, and then miraculously, within moments, he was again a part of the flow. He was in it. *All you could do was go on.* But still, he stayed in the slow lane. The far lane, the fast one, seemed now unimaginably distant, suicidally fast.

Somewhere soon, he thought—though he had lost all sense of this trip—he was meant to get off the highway, onto a secondary road. This would lead him to the quiet streets of the university, and somewhere there he would find Allen Douglas Hall. The small band of waiting historians, the silent students—respectful? bored? derisive?—lounging in their seats. This community of dazing speed would be behind him.

When he reached the exit sign, he slowed gratefully and turned off. Curving sedately down the ramp, he felt himself returning once again to the actual world. This new road was two-lane, winding through wooded countryside, but the traffic still seemed fast. It was late afternoon now, not dark, but nearly dusk. You could still see without headlights, though their presence reminded you that light was fading, vision provisional.

After the stoplight at the Dairy Queen, the road curved down a small hill toward the town. On the left was a string of bright seedy places: muffler repair, Mexican fast food, a gas station. On the right was nothing: a strip of trees, some kind of construction. A metal fence, a single grooved and massive band, hugged the roadside.

When he saw the man, Roger thought he must be seeing it wrong—the man must actually be on the outside of the metal fence, not inside it. There was no sidewalk, and the shoulder was narrow, not for pedestrians. There was barely room for the man's body between the fence and the speeding traffic.

The man wore a trench coat, and beside him was a dog on a leash. Or not on a leash—a harness? Was it possible? Roger felt his scalp tighten. That this was a blind man, making his way along this shallow gulley, inches from the lethal stream of traffic?

Roger couldn't stop as he drove past; the traffic pressed him too hard, too fast. He watched the harnessed dog trying to lead the man away from the road, toward the fence. He saw the man stumble against the fence, then jerk the dog, heading it back toward the traffic. Roger passed by, inches from the man's trench-coated shoulder. The man held his head high, his chin raised, as though his face, pointed toward the sky, would help his body see. Ahead, unknown to him, the narrow walkway was about to end, slanting diagonally toward the road, funneling the man's steps toward the pavement, the hurtling cars.

There was nowhere on the right to stop; the metal fence was unrelenting. Roger put on his blinker and turned abruptly left, cutting across the traffic, into the muffler repair parking lot. Jumping from the car, he ran back up the hill. Across the road, he could see the blind man yank his dog from the fence again. At the top of the hill a truck rounded the curve. Roger ran heavily across the road in front of it, his heart answering the thundering approach of the truck. He ran clumsily up the culvert, pebbles loose beneath his feet, toward the blind man.

"Hello," Roger said loudly. "Can I help you?" Roger was breathing hard. The truck was nearly on top of them.

The blind man swiveled to face him. "I'm fine, thanks," he declared.

"You're in a dangerous place," Roger said. "Let me give you a lift." The truck pounded past, rocking them both, blasting them with its hot smoky stink. "Where are you going?"

"Middletown," the blind man said, smiling at the air. He was in his forties, his hair graying. He looked not prosperous but respectable. He acted as though there were no traffic drowning out his voice, buffeting his body.

"That's where I'm going," Roger said. "I'll take you."

"No, thanks, I'm all right," the man said. "My dog is pretty well-trained. She knows what she's doing. We're fine." The dog, a small golden retriever, stood unhappily, her head low. The cars rushed past them, loud and rhythmic.

What were the rules of courtesy, with the blind? You were meant to act as though they were perfectly competent: which they were, weren't they? Leading their own lives. It was rude, patronizing, to act as though they could not cope with things, as though you knew better.

Roger stood facing the traffic. Because of the curve at the top of the hill, drivers could not see them until they were on top of them. The cars hurtled past, the wind from each one rocking the two men. The murderous roar mocked their fragile armor of skin, flesh, bones.

He thought of the blurred oval of light on the slanting bedroom ceiling, the silence of the dark house. *What if you did know better?*

Roger took the man's elbow, gently—he didn't want him now to pull away, stumbling into the road.

"You're not safe here," Roger told him.

He was ready for the man to resist, to pull back from his grip, but the man did not. Instead he stood with his arm in Roger's grasp, saying nothing, his head slightly cocked, as though he were listening for something. The lack of resistance came as a shock, somehow painful: maybe this was what people wanted.

"I'm going to hold up my hand to stop the traffic," Roger told him, "and we'll walk across the road together. Then I'll drive you wherever you want."

The blind man did not move, and Roger watched the approaching cars for another gap. He was calm, as he'd been earlier, waiting on the highway. He was waiting for another hiatus in the lethal flow, the moment in which he would save their lives. When it came he would seize it, step out boldly, his hand held high to stop the deadly current.

He would save the three of them: the blind stranger, gazing aimlessly at the sky; himself, playing the endless loop inside his brain. The dog too, silky, dark-eyed, plumy-tailed, waiting sweetly to see what would be done with her life.

The Treatment

Here is what I do each morning. As soon as I wake up, barefoot and still in my nightgown, as though I'm on the way to my lover, I go downstairs to the darkened kitchen. I'm alone in the house: my husband leaves early, my daughter is away in college. I don't bother to turn on the lights, I go straight to the refrigerator and open the door to its icy glare. From it I take out a chilled golden globe, the size of a small orange. It's made of firm and springy plastic—solid, with some heft. The pearly outer sheathing is translucent, obscuring the glowing interior and giving it a muffled shimmer. I set the globe, with its neat coil of attached tubing, on the kitchen counter. For the next three hours it will lie there, slowly warming, so that when the fluid inside enters my vein it will not be cold and torpid but swift and potent. What's inside the radiant globe is Rocephin, a powerful antibiotic, which will cure me.

When you are not ill, when you are well, you think about yourself in a particular way. You take being well for granted: that is

who you are. You are a person like that, someone who does not
have to think about her body. It is a luxury, not having to think
about your body, but since you have always possessed it, you
aren't aware that it's a luxury. When you think about sick people, you think of them as different from you, set apart in some
unspecified way: they are Other. They are in that other place, beyond a mysterious divide. They have become different from you,
branded somehow, in a way you don't consider much. Even if
you do consider it you can't get very far. Why are other people
sick? Why are you not? There are no reasons, there is no logic.
Things are the way they are. In some interior subliminal place
you believe that you deserve your health. The person you are, it
seems, deserves to be healthy, just as the person you are seems
to deserve two legs, a nose. I had two legs, a nose, my health.

Ten days ago the line was first introduced into my vein. I lay on
a narrow examining table at the doctor's office, waiting while
the nurse laid out her instruments. She was pleasant and perky,
rather glamorous, with long blond hair and gleaming red finger-
nails. I lay perfectly still. I was prepared for everything, anything: nothing she did would distress me. This was the initiation
ceremony, the start of the healing. It was frightening, but I wel-
comed it, whatever terror it held. I was embracing the source of
my fear. The treatment would be my salvation.

The nurse pulled up my sleeve and exposed the white skin
on the inside of my elbow, the sacrificial site. She cleaned it and
laid it down, bare, before the row of instruments. She took up
a length of tubing, like a long transparent snake. Casually she
measured this against me—from elbow to shoulder, across the
top of my chest, and then down to just above my heart. Here
the mouth of the snake will dangle for six weeks.

When the nurse was ready to begin, she paused and looked
up at my face. "You're going to feel a pinch," she warned.

I nodded. I knew that *pinch* was code for "pain." The nurse looked back down, and I turned my head away. I watched the square white tiles in the ceiling while she worked, piercing my skin, violating my body. I could feel her movements. I didn't look.

"I hate when it spurts," I heard her say crossly. "Now it's all over the rug."

I said nothing, I didn't turn to look. No part of the treatment would trouble me: this was what would save me. I watched the grid of cross-hatching on the tiles while she slid the snake into the vein and sent it up the length of my upper arm, through the widening veins across the top of my chest, and down to the great thunderous vessel directly above my poor heart, deep in its hidden fastness, now invaded and violated. I said nothing. This would save me.

Taking pills three times a day means nothing. Anyone can do it, people do it all the time. There are no implications. It means only that you are correcting something, an aberration. Having a plastic tube inserted into your bloodstream, dangling over your heart, is different. This is a violation of your deepest recesses. This moves you into a darker place, more dangerous. This means you are ill, and helpless.

After three months, the oral antibiotics stopped working, and I went back to my doctor. We sat in his office, which is pleasantly cluttered in a domestic way. There's a bright hooked rug on the floor, a tall standing bookshelf, and a big ficus tree with glossy leaves in front of the window. There is no desk; Doctor Kennicott sits in a brown plaid wing chair. When he wants to write a prescription, he sets a polished wooden board across his lap.

Doctor Kennicott is a quiet man with a kindly manner, slightly bohemian. He has mournful brown eyes and shaggy graying hair and sideburns. He wears a white lab coat, khaki pants, and black leather running shoes. That day he sat in the wing chair, and I sat in a smaller chair across from him.

"My neck is stiff again," I said. "I can't turn my head any further than this." And there was more. As I talked, Dr. Kennicott frowned sympathetically, his mournful eyes attentive. His elbows were set on the arms of the chair, his fingers steepled just under his chin. When I finished, Doctor Kennicott nodded slowly.

"That often happens," he announced.

This puzzled and disappointed me: then why had we used that treatment? I'd never been to a doctor who had prescribed something which often, he knew, didn't work. I'd never been to a doctor who didn't just fix what was wrong.

"Then what do we do now?" I asked.

Dr. Kennicott pushed out his lips thoughtfully. "I'd suggest moving on to intravenous antibiotics."

"No," I said at once.

I knew about the intravenous treatment, he'd mentioned it before. I didn't want it. It was too serious, too alarming. I told him it wasn't justified: I wasn't that ill. I was basically healthy, I told him. Other people have this disease and are treated for it and recover completely. That happened to my daughter, and she was treated for it at once, and now she seems fine. I am basically fine, I told him.

The doctor said nothing while I explained this. He said nothing when I stopped. He sat in the wing chair, his hands steepled under his chin. He watched me quietly, waiting for me to understand. Finally I stopped and looked at him, alarm dawning.

To understand that you are seriously ill is to cross over into a different country. You are apart from other people now. Something separates you from them, something you cannot change. The realization is like a fall from a great height. You are silenced: there is no recourse. You cannot help yourself. Your body has failed you, and you are helpless. You must change your expectations of all things. You must put yourself in the hands of the healers. They may fail.

When I understood this I fell silent. I was in a new place. Things were not as I had thought; arguing with the doctor was of little use.

There's reason to think the spirochetes have been in my bloodstream for ten years, for who knows how long. They have set up their malign outposts throughout my body. They're in the nervous system, the muscles, the connective tissue inside my joints, my spinal cord. They have stiffened my neck and my shoulders. They have turned my muscles leaden and my limbs resistant, so that when I move it feels as though I am struggling against an invisible network of tightening bonds. The spirochetes may, too, have infiltrated my deepest and most interior spaces, the tender private whorls inside my cranial basin. This idea, though, is so frightening that I don't allow myself to think about it. I don't permit myself to slide into that well of terror, I can't afford to.

The treatment also frightens me, but I can't afford that fear either. I've given myself up to this, like a postulant giving up her soul to God. I'm allying myself with this larger power. The treatment will be my salvation. I can't afford to believe otherwise.

This morning, when the moment for the infusion arrives, I go back to the kitchen from my study. I'm dressed now, in jeans and a sweater: I work at home, getting my doctorate in early childhood development. I've finished the coursework and am writing my dissertation, which means that I don't have to explain to anyone why I'm now spending every morning at home, unavailable to the world, engaged in a private and fearsome activity.

At the sink I wash my hands with a liquid antimicrobial soap, a surgical scrub. It has a thin acrid smell, and afterward my skin feels raw and scraped. This is proper, this is part of the ritual: I am preparing myself for the ceremonial chamber. My gestures now are careful and precise. From my big box of medical supplies, from my ziplock plastic bags, I take out three

blunt-nosed syringes. The two white-capped ones hold saline solution, which will be injected first and last, to clean the tubing.
The yellow-capped syringe holds heparin, a mild anticoagulant.
This goes in after the Rocephin, so that the blood idling in the
tubing between treatments will not form clots. I lay all these
things out beside the globe. The instruments are ready.

I pull up the sweater on my left arm. Clasped along my elbow
is a white elastic fishnet sleeve, open-ended, that holds the appa-
ratus tight against my skin. I slide this off, letting a translucent
line of tubing uncoil downward into the air. One end of this is
taped flat to my skin in a serpentine loop before it disappears
into my flesh. The other end, interrupted by a small transparent
junction box, ends in a blue valve. This is called a clave, and it
is shaped like the head of a lizard, narrowing and blunt-nosed.
I open a foil-wrapped packet holding an antiseptic swab, and its
sharp alcohol odor blooms in the air, powerful and sobering.
With a little bad luck, any germ I encounter at this moment will
be transported directly to my heart.

Carefully I swab off the flat metal surface of the clave. Holding it aloft, sterile, in one hand, with the other I unscrew a
white-capped syringe. I push its threaded nose into the clave,
forcing the surface downward. Inside the clave are matching
grooves, and the threaded syringe screws neatly, perfectly, into
the protected tunnel within the clave. On the line of tubing is a
triangular cock, and I slide the line from the narrow vise end,
where it has been clamped shut, to the wide end. The line to my
vein is now open.

I press down on the plunger. The loaded syringe holds two
and a half milliliters of saline solution. I watch the transparent
presence creep down the coil until the tube vanishes within the
surface of my skin, and the liquid enters my body. I can feel its
cold arrival in my vein. Slowly I depress the plunger until I reach
the flattened air bubble at the bottom of the shaft. I unscrew the
syringe and set it down. Still holding the clave in the air, I un-

screw the small angel-winged cap on the Rocephin line and set its transparent nose into the opening of the clave. Like the syringe, it fits neatly into its tunneled grooves. This connection feels smooth and satisfying, and I am gratified by this, as though technical perfection means the treatment will work like this, in just this beautifully engineered way.

I sit down and lean back. Now I'm connected. The valves are open, the liquid has begun its journey into my body. The golden globe is pressurized, and for the next forty minutes, it will slowly contract, forcing the Rocephin steadily into my bloodstream.

I close my eyes. My part in this is like prayer: I concentrate on what is taking place inside me, I visualize it. I see the golden tide beginning its silent warrior's surge, past the heart and through the wide channels of the great arteries, the smaller ones of the arterioles, moving deep into the interior, into the narrow waterways of the capillaries. I see the golden tide moving into a still lagoon, deep in the interior. Calm water on pale sand. The movement is visible, a low relentless surge. Along the irregular shore a long ripple breaks in a narrow line of foam. There is a sighing hiss, a small seething commotion: the spirochetes, the tiny corkscrews of the disease, are sizzling in a frenzy of death. I hear them thrashing tinily, I see the surface of the water along the shore boil and churn as they jitter. They twist and sputter as it hits them, they are dying, dying in droves, dying by the millions, at the touch of the smooth golden surge.

During my first week of the treatment I had the predicted reactions: high fever, chills and headaches, brief wild stabbing pains in all my joints. I'm told that all of this is the result of the spirochetes dying off. I believe this is true. The infusions are the Asian hordes sweeping across the wide plains, overwhelming our enemy. I lay in bed, sick with fever, feebly triumphant.

Now the fever has stopped, and I'm better, but not well. I know I am ill. I feel as though I'm walking carefully, on some unreliable surface, not knowing what movement might cause a sudden terrifying crack and plunge. Yesterday I took the dogs out for a walk through the woods, down to the winter-dark pond and past it, up the hillside beyond. The woods are brown and mysterious now; the trees creak ponderously in the wind, and their gray filigree tops sway silently. The narrow path was soft underfoot. Walking along it, climbing the steep slope of the hill, I felt suddenly the delicate tangling grope of the snake inside my chest, a faint dry grappling sensation, just above my heart. When it happened my heart began to pound, panicky, shrinking from this dangerous alien presence. There was nowhere for me to go for help. It was I who gave permission for this. My brain believes it's good; it's my body that fears it. I tried to calm my heart: I refuse panic. Above me, the tops of the trees moved slowly, swaying against the gray sky.

This morning, Saturday, my husband, Mark, comes into the kitchen when I'm getting ready to infuse. He's been out in the village doing errands, and now he stands just inside the door, setting down packages. I know he sees my equipment laid out on the kitchen counter, but he keeps his eyes away from it, as though it were a naked body.

"I couldn't find the coffee you like," he says, unzipping his parka. His voice seems loud and artificial.

"That's all right," I say. "They have it at Sgaglio's. I'll get it tomorrow."

"I got everything else," he says. His eyes now fix on mine, faintly accusatory, as though I've contaminated the kitchen.

"Thanks," I say, conciliatory.

He ducks out into the mudroom, to hang up his coat. When he comes back in he shuts the heavy kitchen door hard.

"You're welcome," he says. Still without looking at my syringes, his dark gaze fixed on mine until it shifts to the door, he heads for his study. Mark is a philosophy professor, and his mind moves either in great wheeling arcs or in little tiny circles, depending on your point of view. I hear him sit down in his study. Alone in the kitchen, I turn back to my instruments, but now the sight of them fills me with dread. They look diabolical, like something from a horror movie.

When I'm ready, I tell myself that Mark was just uncomfortable, not horrified. Or abstracted, as he often is. I call in to him in his study, my voice playful.

"I'm about to shoot up. Want to watch?" I ask hopefully. If he'll be part of this, it will be less frightening, it will seem more normal—but he doesn't want to watch.

"No thanks," he calls in from his study. His voice is not playful, and after a moment I hear his door close quietly. I know he finds all this repugnant, and why should he not? Why should he have to share it with me?

He's not the only one. My friend Sarah came over one morning, and when she saw my syringes in their bags on the counter she jumped nervously behind my back. "I don't want to look at them," she explained.

I begin to wonder if I should wear a bell, to warn normal people of my approach. I feel frightened and isolated. I can see I am alone here.

Last night in bed, when Mark was ready to go to sleep, he closed his Kierkegaard and set it on his bedside table beside the clock.

"That's it for me," he said. He took off his glasses and rubbed fiercely at the bridge of his nose. He put his glasses on top of his book and turned off his light.

When he turned over on his side, toward me, I was waiting for him.

"Put your arms around me," I said, and my husband did this at once, gathering me wholly against him. My face pressed close into his chest, surrounded by his comfort, his healthy body. I said, "Tell me I'm going to get well."

I needed to hear the words.

I felt Mark's hand on the back of my head, stroking my hair. "You're going to get well," he said.

"Say it again," I said, pressing my face against his chest.

Tonight I'm alone. Mark's away at a conference, but a visiting nurse, Ginger, is coming. It's her second visit, she came once before, early on, to change the bandages. Now she's going to change the tubes. I'm uneasy about this, as I don't know what it means. Will she pull out the whole long snake that has burrowed its way so deep into my interior? Drag it from its secret nest above my heart? It's frightening to have it in there, but it would be frightening, too, to have it moved.

Still, I'm looking forward to seeing Ginger: I know I've done well, and I'm proud of myself. I'm looking forward to her praise: I'm a good patient. The pains are mostly gone, and both their arrival and their departure are proof of my prowess. The opening where the line enters my skin is pale and healthy, not inflamed. Each morning I have performed the infusion successfully, sending the golden tide deep into my interior. Each day, connecting the tiny spiral chambers, screwing them into the closed valves, unlocking the entrance to my veins, plugging myself into the heavy golden globe, I feel the elixir rush silently into my bloodstream and I feel charged with victory. I feel the spirochetes failing against this magnificent onslaught: they are overwhelmed, undone. I know we'll be victorious, and my nurse knows it too. She is the agent of my healing. Her presence plays a part, it will make this real. She'll infuse me with hope and conviction.

Around eight o'clock, Ginger arrives. She opens the back door and bustles cheerfully into the kitchen. "Hi there," she says, boisterously good-natured. The dogs sniff her, wagging their tails politely. "Good *dog*," she says crooningly, leaning unctuously over them and patting their heads too hard, "good *dog."* Ginger is in her early thirties, thickset, with bushy brown hair in a wild shoulder-length aura. She's wearing a knitted wool dress, a heavy sweater, and dark clunky shoes. She's somehow powerful and clumsy, like a shaggy little bull.

Ginger sets down her bag and takes off her padded jacket, already talking. "I just came from an auction in Poughkeepsie," she says chattily. "It was so fun."

"Great," I say. "Did you get anything?"

"A rocker," she says emphatically, pausing to look up at me, delighted I've asked. "A porch rocker. It's real old and funky. I really love it."

"Great," I say again.

I don't care what she bought, I'm so pleased to see her that she could read aloud from the telephone book. I listen happily as she gabs, watching her take out a big plastic packet, sealed and sterile. She spreads it open on the kitchen table—it is full of small intricate objects. I sit down. Outside it is turning dark, and we lean together under the hanging lamp. I lay my arm out on the table and roll up my sleeve. Ginger now takes off her big sweater and tosses back her heavy mass of hair. There is a lot of her at that table, breathy, fleshy, bulky. I wish her hair were in a bun. I wish she were lean and smooth, clipped and sterile, in a white uniform.

"So, how have you been?" she asks bumptiously.

"Fine," I say with pride. "Some aches and pains in my joints, but that doesn't bother me."

Ginger shakes her head fondly. "My patients who have this love feeling achy," she says, as though this were an endearingly foolish trait. "They think it means they're getting better."

I smile with her: I know they're right.

Ginger opens her sterile packets, ripping back adhesive strips, putting on thin gloves. I am nervous about this procedure, anxious about the hidden snake, fearful of what she is about to do.

Ginger yanks off the bandage over the plastic shunt where it enters my skin. As her hands near the opening, I turn rigid. She stops.

"Where does it hurt?" she asks.

"It doesn't," I say. "I'm just wary." In fact I am terrified.

"You think I'm going to pull the adhesive back against the tube," she says indulgently. "We're taught as rookies always to pull *with* the tube. You pull against it"—she makes a sudden ripping gesture, as though she is about to jerk the unprotected tube from where it snakes into my skin—"and you'd pull the shunt right out of your arm. Like, that is *not* therapeutic."

I say nothing, trying to calm my heartbeat. My whole system is running on alarm, my heart is pounding. That dangerous gesture, the perilous mimicking of violence, has shocked me. She now begins to do delicate things to the tube. I don't want to watch, and to distract myself I look at her face.

"Do you do this a lot?" I ask.

She told me before how grateful her patients are, and I want to hear stories of her successes. I want to hear how this disease is vanquished, how good she is at her task, how powerful and inexorable this treatment is. I am greedy for these stories, I want to count myself among this healing crowd.

Ginger looks up. "Oh, yes," she says. "I do chemotherapy all day long."

I frown: this isn't a word I want to hear. This is not a group I want to belong to.

"No," I say. "I mean do you do this, treatment for my disease, often?"

"Oh, yes," Ginger says again. She bends over the tube again. Her heavy hair falls over her shoulder, hanging in a bristly thicket over the instruments. I can smell it. "In fact I have one patient who lives right near you. He's been on intravenous treatment for two years."

"Two years?" I say. I've been told my treatment will last six weeks.

"Yes," she says, shaking her head. "He's in terrible shape. He's had your disease for years and it wasn't treated right away. He's nearly paralyzed. He's trying oxygen chamber treatments now. Nothing really seems to help him."

I say nothing. I wish she weren't bending so closely over my arm, which lies bare and vulnerable beneath her fleshy face. The transparent tube doubles down beneath my skin and disappears. The whole region of my arm twitches with alarm, with the extremity of its exposure. If she were to do anything now, just jostle the tube accidentally, the possibilities of pain are horrifying. The possibilities are ones I cannot permit myself to think of: infection, the lethal transmission of things directly to my heart, my poor vulnerable heart, with the snake dangling its toxic head directly over its chambers. I feel as though everything now is dangerous, that our passage together through this process has become perilous. Each step is crucial.

Ginger shakes her head again. "No, this is really a terrible disease," she says.

I cannot bear to hear what she is saying, it is dangerous for me to hear this. I say rudely, "Don't you have any better stories?" My arm, in her hands, feels exposed and frightened.

She looks up. "About this disease? No. If it isn't treated right away it's really terrible. You see, it mutates in your system."

I stare at her, appalled, willing her to stop telling me these things.

She looks earnestly at me, her huge bristling hair surrounding her face. "What happens is that the spirochetes, if they aren't treated right away, change form, so that the treatment can never catch up with the disease. Each time the doctor tries something new, the form is different. The disease goes deeper and deeper into your system. This man has it in his spinal cord, and it's gone into his brain, he has neurological symptoms. Now he's going to doctors who have it themselves, to see how they're treating their own diseases."

I stare down at my arm, mesmerized with horror.

As she talks, against my will, I am picturing the spirochetes in my own body, spiraling deeper and deeper into my defenseless system, burrowing their way into my spinal fluid, sliding unstoppably into the crevices of my brain. Each word she speaks makes this real, inevitable, incontrovertible.

All my feelings of triumph, of power and victory, are sliding downward, cascading toward ruin. She is destroying everything I have accomplished. I hate the words she is saying, I hate what she is doing to me. I want to rip the tubing out of my arm, I want to take everything she has touched and throw it from me and order her from my house. She is casting a spell, she is cursing my body, she is destroying the health and vigor of my flesh, she is shattering my hope. She is declaring the futility of everything I am struggling to achieve, she is showing me a future of misery and despair. She is deriding my belief in the golden tide. I hate her more than I could have imagined possible.

Looking down at my arm, I say in a strained voice, "I don't think you should talk this way to your patients."

Alarmed, she looks up. "What does your doctor tell you?"

"He doesn't talk to me like this," I say, my voice choking. "And you should never talk like this to a patient."

"I'm sorry," Ginger says. She is clearly upset. "I'm a very sensitive person. I wouldn't have upset you if I had known."

"I've had this disease for ten years and it hasn't been treated," I say. I am struggling, I am desperate to keep from crying. "I don't want to hear about this."

Shaken, Ginger bends again over the tubing. She is not touching the long snake, as it turns out. She's replacing only the outer section of it, the bit that goes from the clave to the junction, but I now hate having her touch me. She is contaminating me, her touch is dangerous, poison to my body. Her touch is a curse on me. I imagine tearing everything out of my arm, flinging the transparent coils away from me onto the floor.

She works for a few seconds in silence, then starts up again. "Last time I came," she says carefully, "we talked about your daughter, remember? Who has this too, right? And was treated for it?"

How can she not have understood me? Does she imagine I want to hear this about my daughter?

"I said I don't want to talk about this," I say again.

I am now swollen, huge with wrath and despair and grief. I am outraged that she should choose to use her power over me in this way, that she should have come to me disguised as a healer and have revealed herself instead as a black curse, an agent of doom and anguish. I want her to get out of my kitchen, out of my house, off my property. I want to sic the dogs on her. I sit in raging silence while she finishes. She pads heavily back and forth, finishing up, throwing things away. Her head is down, her face averted, she is clearly upset. I think she's crying. I don't care.

I want only to control my tears, to keep from breaking down in her presence, to achieve merely that, and in that one small thing I am victorious.

Assez

That summer we rented a house in France, with friends.

It was Steven who found the real estate agent. She sent us photographs, and Steven and I spent an evening in Westchester, looking at bright glimmering images of Provence. We sat at the kitchen table, shuffling the pictures back and forth, and finally Steven slid one over to me.

"This looks nice," he said.

I held the photograph up to study: it was a long farmhouse of golden stone, with a faded orange tile roof. In front of it was a flat stretch of pale gravel, shaded by wide trees. The swimming pool was shimmering turquoise, surrounded by high green hedges; along the garden paths were cypress trees—cool dark sentinels against a light-filled landscape.

I nodded: it looked like paradise. Also, I would have agreed with anything Steven said then.

We were the first to arrive. We took the overnight flight to Nice, and then rented a car at the airport. Dizzy with sleep lack and jet lag, we set out across the bottom of Provence to the village of Saint-Emilion, between Aix and Avignon. It was a three-hour trip on the crowded highway at eighty miles an hour, German cars surging terrifyingly past us, the hot glare of the Midi sun in our eyes. Along the highway were enigmatic messages in lowercase letters. BASTIDE ANCIENNE, one sign announced austerely, and we searched among the hillsides until we made out, for a moment, a distant stone silhouette. At Salon, we turned off the highway, and drove more slowly across a strange flat landscape: dusty fields, slightly ragged, empty in the sun. In the distance was a range of steep miniature mountains with bare jagged peaks: the Alpilles.

When we finally drove into the little stone courtyard of our house, it was early afternoon, and we were dazed with speed and heat and fatigue. Steven turned off the car and we sat still for a moment. Everything was silent in the afternoon heat, and the air shimmered. On two sides of the courtyard were the rough stone walls of the rambling house; beyond the other walls we could see the narrow silvery leaves of olive trees. All around us we heard a weird high insect shrill.

The front door was unlocked, and we stepped into the cool stone darkness of the hall. The shutters were closed against the sun, and the whitewashed walls were muted and mysterious after the bright light outside. The house was quiet, the air dry and sweet and aromatic. Steven was beside me, and he leaned over to set down a suitcase. As he straightened, his face moved into a soft shaft of light from a crack in the shutters.

Steven is tall and rangy, with dark hair and eyes, and thick beetling eyebrows. He is an intense man, with a dark and forceful manner, and there are times when his darkness and forcefulness are frightening. But just then, the beam illuminated a small intimate portion of his face: the tender hollow of darkened skin around his eye, damp with the heat. Below the clustered lashes was the liquid brown gleam of the eye itself, innocent and steady. I could smell his skin, the dense delicious musk my husband gave off when he was tired and sweaty. The sense of his presence, so vivid and so deeply known, gave me a surge of happiness, and I nearly reached out to touch him.

"*Bonjour!*" A woman called from inside the house, and we heard light clopping footsteps. Madame Garcin, the real estate agent, was in her fifties, with dark narrow eyes and a thick waist. She wore gold-rimmed glasses, a wrinkled linen dress, and high-heeled mules.

"*Bonjour, madame,*" Steven said carefully, in his terrible French. He gave a courteous nod. "*Nous sommes les Winstons.*"

I can't speak French. I can read it and understand it, but I can't speak it, and I don't. Steven can't really speak it either, but he does. He'll say anything, he has no fear. Right then he was rumpled and travel-stained: a dark beard was starting to thicken on his cheeks, and his sweaty shirtsleeves were rolled up. But still he looked easy and confident, and I was proud of him for speaking so freely, with that terrible accent, without embarrassment or hesitation. I was proud of him for being so steady and American, for being so sure of himself, and of who we were: *Nous sommes les Winstons.*

Madame Garcin showed us through the house. The downstairs rooms were cool and dim, with dark Provençal furniture set against rough whitewashed stone walls. The bedrooms upstairs were airy and pleasant, with high ceilings and faded toile curtains. The place felt clean and polished, and the red tile floors gave off a muted sheen.

Downstairs, Steven gave Madame Garcin the rental money, and she stood at the hall table to count it. She shifted the bills rapidly through her fingers and whispered French numbers under her breath. When she finished she straightened.

"*Merci, monsieur,*" she said. She held out her hand, standing very straight. "*Au revoir, monsieur, madame. Que vous soyez contents ici.*"

May you be happy here: I liked the way the French word joins the loose exuberance of happiness with the meeker and more domestic notion of contentment. And I felt graced by her wish. There is something charged and magical about a stranger wishing you well, like a traveler on the road in a fairy tale. It was a good omen, I thought, to have the first person we met wishing us happiness. We thanked Madame Garcin, and she clopped briskly to the front door, and then Steven and I were alone.

We had chosen the bedroom overlooking the garden, the pale blurred rows of santolina, the purple masses of lavender, the enigmatic cypresses. I hoped we'd chosen not just the view but the bed: it was the only double in the house.

It had been months since Steven and I had actually needed a double bed, months since we had actually "slept together." What we did was sleep apart, in the same bed. We did not touch. Even if Steven were asleep, if my leg brushed against his he flinched away from it, instantly. It was a muscular reflex. His flesh couldn't bear the touch of my flesh. It was like an electric shock to him.

We began unpacking. I opened the big shadowy armoire, smelling of lavender. There was lavender in the wide stiff-drawered bureau too; there were sachets of it everywhere, made of bright Provençal fabrics, tucked into corners. The smell was sharp and heavy, almost medicinal.

When I was finished, Steven was still unpacking, and his back was to me. I moved quickly, because I didn't want him to see me undressed. It's painful to show your body to someone who doesn't want it. I stripped to my underpants and slid into bed. There was no headboard, and the wide mattress was low and hammocky. The sheets felt rough and clean, and I leaned back and closed my eyes, and thought about the Chambertins, who owned the house.

I thought of their comfortably solid French bodies (as I imagined them), packed and firm from years of wine and cheese and pâté and olive oil and children and the pleasures of life. I felt safe and peaceful there, as if the comfort and steadiness of their lives (as I imagined them) would seep into mine as I lay in their bed.

As soon as I closed my eyes I began to drift. It's a moment that I love, the one before sleep when you feel yourself starting to give way, surrendering to that heavy irresistible sensation of exhaustion. It had become unusual for me, because sleep had become a rarity for me over the last few months. But now, being so sleep-deprived, so deliciously worn-out and now, this moment, feeling so deliciously safe in this low comforting bed, with my husband about to join me, I began to fall drowningly into miles and miles of deep sleep, as though I'd been drugged, and I gave myself up without a struggle.

When I woke up the light coming in through the shutters was deep gold, and the air crepuscular. Steven was lying on his back, his face toward me. His mouth was very slightly open, and his eyes deeply shut. I could hear the faint slow sigh of his breath.

When Steven and I were first together, when we first began sleeping together, in both senses of that phrase, we used to fall into unconsciousness lying face-to-face. We couldn't bear to turn away from each other. We lay with our legs tangled, our arms wrapped around each other, our faces touching. Steven's breath was sweet, like that of a horse, fresh as field grass, and smelling it was like breathing in a meadow. And in those days, as we lay together, close, touching everywhere, I used to listen to Steven breathing and then I'd hold my breath for a moment, timing the rise of my chest against the fall of his, so that I would breathe in as Steven was breathing out, and I could fill my lungs with that sweet sweet air. I couldn't get enough of him.

I would never dare do that now, set my face close against his, breathe in his breath without permission.

When you learn that the sight of you is no longer what your

husband wants, you find that the world has gone dark without warning. It's like an eclipse: a vast racing shadow has suddenly overcome the sky, the landscape is drained of color and the light has gone. You don't understand how it happened, or if it will come back. You don't know how to find out. You are blind and clumsy, fearful. Since the sight of you is not what he looks for, you hesitate to stand before him. Since the sound of your voice is not what he listens for, you hesitate to speak.

When I first found out about Alison, I shouted at Steven. I thought I had a right to shout.

"How can you do this?" I demanded. My voice was loud and angry. "A research associate? Some twenty-eight-year-old kid?"

Steven said nothing, his eyes black, his brows knitted. He leaned back in the kitchen chair, his arms crossed on his chest. He was still in his suit and tie, sweaty and wrinkled from his day in the office. He looked at me, silent and obdurate.

"You can't do this," I told him, outraged. "You have a sixteen-year-old son. You have a nineteen-year-old marriage. *You have a wife.*" I slammed my spoon down so hard on the table that I broke my glass. I was glad I'd broken the glass.

Steven said nothing, his gaze deep and hostile.

That night we spent arguing, and finally I went to sleep in Jeffrey's room. I shut the door and pushed a chair under the handle. I was crying. Later I got angry again, and shouted things out to Steven through the door. Then I cried again. I waited for him to come to the door in the dark, and planned what I would do when he did. Sometimes I thought I would let him in, sometimes I thought I would not. I slept a little, I woke and dozed and cried and dozed again. When I finally heard Steven getting up, moving around in our room, I lay in bed, clenched and angry again, waiting for him. I thought of what I'd say to him, the accusations I'd hurl. I was thinking of whether or not I'd forgive him, the conditions I would set. Now at least he understood what he was risking, after this night spent alone and in disgrace. I heard him going downstairs: he'd be making coffee, and he'd bring it up as a peace offering, before we began to talk.

When I heard the car I sat up in bed, rigid. I heard it back into the driveway, and I threw myself out of bed and across the room. I had to wrestle the chair away from the doorknob and drag the door open before I could run down the stairs in my nightgown. By the time I got outside, the car was already at the bottom of the driveway, turning out onto the road, and then it was gone. Steven had slipped into the great stream of movement surging back into the city, headed toward a world that did not hold me. I stood on the driveway, barefoot. The gravel was hard and sharp against my feet, and my arms were cold. The sky was just turning light over the roof of the garage, behind the mulberry trees. The windows in our house were dark. I was alone. That was when I understood that I had no right to shout. I had no right to do anything. He could leave.

If your husband doesn't want you, there is nothing you can do. You can't argue. You can't persuade him that he is wrong. Reminding him that he once promised to love you, and that he once did, is useless. Showing your feelings, revealing your vulnerabilities, once so useful and necessary in marital exchanges, is now forbidden. Weeping, your most frequent and involuntary response, is also the worst, and least useful. It makes your husband angry at you; it turns him into your enemy.

I tried not to weep in front of Steven after that, though sometimes I couldn't help it. When it threatened, I tried to think of something else to distract myself, to keep it from happening, the way Steven used to do during sex, to keep from coming too soon. Once he told me that he thought of baseball for this, and for years, whenever someone mentioned baseball, we'd catch each other's eyes. Now, of course, if I'd heard someone mention baseball, I'd have avoided his eye. It would have made him angry to see me looking at him then, just as it made him angry when I cried.

The friends who were sharing the house with us were John and Nina Stanton. John and Steven had been roommates in college, and they were each other's closest friends. I didn't know if Steven had told John about Alison; I hoped he hadn't. It was horrible enough for me to know; knowing that other people knew would make me feel flayed, as though the skin had been stripped from me, as though I was walking naked and skinless through the streets: the woman whose husband no longer wanted the sight of her.

I had seen Alison once, before I knew who she was. I went to Steven's office to pick something up, and a young woman came out of it as I was going in. She was wearing a tight short-skirted black suit, black tights, and high black heels. She had a glossy cap of thick dark hair, and that red red mouth. She didn't look to me like a research associate, but then I didn't know what one would look like. We passed each other in the doorway, and I could feel her gaze, powerful and alarming, like a dangerous ray. It was so powerful that I turned and looked back at her after I passed. She was still looking at me. She held my eye boldly for a moment, then turned and went on, composed and somehow triumphant. Crisp white collar and cuffs, like a French schoolgirl.

It was over now, Steven had told me.

"I'm not seeing her anymore." He said that at the end of a long night. It was five o'clock in the morning, and we were lying in bed, not touching. We'd been up all night, arguing, and the sheets felt gray and heavy, rumpled, twisted like ropes. There was no air left in the room.

"It's over," he said, his voice flat and cold.

There was a long pause. I couldn't really believe it.

I said, "Are you sure, Steven?" He didn't answer, and I said, "Please don't say this unless you mean it."

Steven was looking straight ahead. "I'm sure," he said. He sounded dead. He didn't look at me.

I didn't ask any more. I didn't ask when it had been decided, or why, if it were true, he hadn't told me until five o'clock in the morning. I didn't ask whose idea it had been; I didn't want to know that. What he said should have made me happy; it should have made both of us happy. It should have been the moment for him to take me in his arms and look at me, but instead we lay side by side, on our backs, without speaking. He didn't touch me, and I didn't dare touch him. I listened to his breathing.

I didn't know what to say: should I thank him, as though he'd done me a favor? Should I say I was sorry, since he was so clearly unhappy? Should I say I was glad, though he was not?

He said nothing more, and it seemed safer for me to say nothing, his silence was so dense and so unfriendly.

It was after this that Steven started talking about France. I could see that it would be a way for us to start out again. We'd be in a place where we could be kind to each other, a place we'd never argued, in rooms where we'd never run out of oxygen. It would be a place where I'd never been alone while he was with Alison, a place where he had never come back to me after being with her. It would be a place where we'd only have been together.

The morning after we arrived we drove into the village to buy groceries. Saint-Emilion was very small, really only two intersecting streets of shops, and then a few quiet blocks behind of houses. The two main streets were wide, lined by great sycamore trees with mottled trunks. The trees made a high green canopy of shade, and filtered sunlight fell in shifting patterns onto the pavement. It was hot, and the women had bare shoulders. They wore dresses in bright Provençal prints, deep reds, bold blues, bright ochers. They carried wide straw shopping baskets and wore flat slippers, which slapped against the sidewalks as they walked.

Steven and I went up and down the two blocks, in and out of the shops, finding bread and olive oil and cheese. When we were done, we each had a heavy bag, and when we reached the car Steven came around to my side and opened my door. He set his bag on the back seat and took mine from my arms. He set it inside, then opened the front door for me.

"Thank you," I said.

"You're very welcome," he said, punctilious.

A year ago, would he have taken the trouble to do that? Would I have thanked him so formally? Would we have been so aware of our obligations to each other? I couldn't remember. I couldn't be sure, now, how we had acted toward each other before, when love was common, everywhere, the element we breathed. When had we stopped? When had Steven stopped breathing me in, needing me to fill his lungs? I didn't want to know.

Of course I did want to know. I wanted to know what day he first looked up at Alison, as she leaned over his desk and as he smiled up into her face. I wanted to know what he first said to her, intimately, that changed everything—*How do you know things like that?*—and what she answered—*I know lots of things.* I wanted to know what midtown hotel he first took her to at lunchtime, and what room they were in, the room where they left the sheets hot and rank, torn off the bed, blankets and pillows thrown onto the floor, and then afterward, for the rest of the day he smelled her on his hands, his stupendous delicious secret, borne in on him every time he raised the phone to his face. I was dying to know all that, dying to know it, but I didn't ask any of those questions. I knew it was too dangerous. I could feel the black swelling urge beneath those questions, that knowledge. It was bad enough just imagining these things to myself: it would have killed me to hear the answers, to know how those things actually happened.

I wanted to kill him just knowing they had happened, and I knew I had to quell those thoughts if we were going to go on together. I had to quell that rage when it rose up in me, because we were trying to love each other. I had to stop these long swings into hatred and vituperation, I had to work my way back into loving him. Because I did love Steven, that was why I wanted to kill him. And I wanted him to love me, and I knew he was trying to quell certain thoughts and feelings of his own, he was trying to return himself to me, and to our marriage.

We were attached to each other, we were like climbers on a mountain, out of sight of each other, but with the long rope between us. We were struggling, each of us alone, chipping with hammers at the implacable stone, setting our feet into narrow crevices, but held together, each one knowing the other was at the end of the cord. That knowledge was holding us onto the face of the mountain, keeping us moving upward.

Of course, if your partner really falls off the mountain—a dead weight plummeting toward the earth—you cannot save him. In fact, the reverse: his velocity, the absolute plumb-line insistence of gravity, will pull you down too. But you can save each other from minor things, an ill-considered handhold, a crumbling rock, a loosened piton. Slips, not plummeting falls. If you're both careful, the major fall won't happen. You might make it to the top, still linked, and there you'll be, the sky spreading out around you in transparent splendor, the whole earth stretching out at your feet.

The Stantons arrived two days after we did, on the same flight. We heard them arrive, and came down to see them appear in the front hall with their bags and suitcases.

Nina was wearing a wrinkled tan suit and gold earrings, and sunglasses on top of her head. Her eyes were bright blue—turquoise, really—and her straight hair was streaky blond and thick, with straight chopped-off bangs. Her tanned limbs were smooth and rounded, slightly heavy, voluptuous; her breasts were generous. She had long narrow fingers and polished nails, and an air of splendor, sumptuousness. Her teeth were straight and white, but there was a narrow gap between the front two. The gap distracted you from her beauty, and made her look slightly hoydenish. And in fact Nina was slightly hoydenish, opinionated and unpredictable. She would say anything.

"Sweetheart!" Nina said, her voice rich and joyful. She threw her arms around me as though we had been separated for decades. "This is so exciting!"

Steven and John gave each other manly shoulder grabs.

"Hey there," Steven said, grinning, and John said, "Yo." Then John and I hugged, rather gingerly, as we do, and Nina called Steven "Sweetheart," and she embraced him, lavishly and full-frontedly, as she does.

"How was the flight?" I asked Nina.

At once Nina looked dark. "Oh, the *flight* was fine," she began. "It was the woman from Texas I thought I'd have to strangle. She was sitting across the aisle from John, and she kept *flirting* with him. It was all right when she was sober, but then she got drunk and began to sing. Frank Sinatra," said Nina and rolled her eyes.

John watched her, with a small smile at the corners of his mouth. John was quiet, a bit reserved. He was a handsome man, barely taller than Nina, trim and muscular, with small hands and feet. His eyes were amused and heavy-lidded, and his voice was wonderfully deep. He was an art dealer, specializing in seventeenth- and eighteenth-century European paintings, and he had a hushed and solemn gallery on East Seventy-eighth Street.

"I kept trying to sleep," Nina went on, "but every time I'd start to doze I'd hear *Dooby dooby doo,* in this terrible off-key whiskey voice. *Dooby dooby doo,*" Nina hummed, in her own voice, which was husky and delicious. "Waving her glass at

John. Finally I leaned across him and I said to her, 'Look, I don't care if you *run off* with my husband when we get to Nice, but would you stop serenading him while we're still on the plane? It's one o'clock in the morning and I'd like to get some sleep, especially if I'm going to have to talk to a divorce lawyer later.' "

John's small smile deepened. He took great pleasure in Nina, and she in him, which made them a pleasure to be around. They produced their own current of tenderness and affection, and I hoped it would catch us up in it. I hoped that Steven would be drawn back into the place he'd once occupied. I hoped he'd remember what good friends we all were, and how it was to love your wife.

Then Nina put her hands on her hips and looked around, shaking her head. "This is so great," she said throatily. She walked to the end of the hall and looked outside to the terrace, and to the garden beyond, still and silent in the sun. "This is *fabulous.*" When Nina liked something, you felt she was going to lean forward and take a big bite out of it. She looked around at John. "Let's just not go back. Let's just stay. Why should we ever go back?"

"Why should we?" John repeated, smiling at her.

That night in bed Steven and I talked about Nina and John as though we were allies, companions. Their arrival had changed things, altered the balance. We were no longer two people struggling perilously to become a couple; we were now part of a foursome, old friends. And Steven and I had given up the stage. We were no longer the center of everything, no longer the raging and weeping characters in our own wild drama. Now we had become the audience; a relief.

"Nina has so much fun with everything," I said. We were lying on our backs under the sheets, looking up into the dark.

"Zest for life," Steven agreed.

"But I always wonder about her stories," I went on. "Do you

think there really was a woman on the plane? Or if there was, did Nina actually say anything to her?"

"Who knows? It doesn't matter," Steven said cheerfully, and he yawned suddenly. "Nina's wonderful."

I wondered for a moment if he were jealous of John, for having such a wonderful wife. It was something I could not ask him; I couldn't raise those horrible issues—twisting and writhing—up from the depths. We had put those things away, and I turned myself from the thought.

And I could hear from Steven's voice that he was becoming happy, *content*. He put his hands behind his head and spread his legs out, under the sheets; the side of his leg moved against mine and stayed there, unflinching, solid, and I was so grateful, and so happy, to feel him back, next to me.

All that month it was hot and clear. The sky was the deep intense blue of Provence, the air was dry and sweet-smelling, and the cigales sang their strange high song in the trees. Each morning Steven went early to the village and came back with food, the paper, local news. We had breakfast outside, at the stone table under the chestnut tree. Some days we all went on excursions, driving across the flat countryside to Nîmes, to Arles and Avignon. We felt the Roman presence from two thousand years earlier in the great monolithic geometry of the Pont du Gard, the vast stone amphitheaters at Arles and Orange, which still hold operas and bullfights. We drove up into the low sunbaked hillsides, covered with wild rosemary and thyme and rustling grasses, past olive orchards and wide cultivated fields. The long rows of pale crumbly earth were edged with narrow ditches; these were filled with cool dark water, seeping invisibly into the dry fields. Some days we went nowhere, and had lunch at home under high green shade; we swam, we lay beside the pool, we read, we took siestas and ate dinner late.

One day Steven came home from the marketing humming and cheerful. I went into the kitchen to help put things away,

and Nina and John appeared in bathing suits, on their way to
the pool.

"What's the news?" John asked. Steven often brought us village gossip: the two feuding bakeries, the funeral procession
down the main street, the drunk who lay on the sidewalk and
refused to get up even when the big-bellied mayor himself stood
over him and ordered him to move.

"I have a report," Steven said. He took from his basket a
baguette and a small plastic container of olives.

"Tell us," said Nina, picking up the olives. "*Love* these," she
added parenthetically.

"I want you all to know," Steven said and paused solemnly
for effect, "that I am now a man known to the locals." His chin
was lifted with pride.

"Oh, well, now," Nina said, sounding impressed. She fished
out an olive and put it in her mouth. "Tell us about it."

"Today, as I was leaving the vegetable shop, I said, '*Merci,
madame,*' as I do every day, and the woman at the counter said,
'*Merci, monsieur,*' as she always does, and then she added, '*à de-
main.*'" Steven looked at us all. "'Until tomorrow'! She expects
me!"

"Now *that* is a real accomplishment," Nina said generously.
She held out the olives that he'd just brought, like an award.
"Have one of these. They're delicious."

"Thank you," Steven said. He gave a little bow and took
one.

"We're *clearly* in the right place," Nina said, turning to John,
"with the right people." She shook her head. "We'll just have to
stay."

It was a small thing, but it made Steven happy, and it was a
measure of his content that such a small thing would make a difference. Happiness was seeping into him like the cool water into
the dry fields. That afternoon when we went upstairs for our

siesta I could feel him watching me while I undressed. I didn't meet his eyes, I didn't dare, but I could feel him watching, and when I got into bed, lying with my back to him, he slid at once over to me, stretching his whole body against mine from behind, and I felt his hands slide smoothly, and so slowly and deliberately up, along my ribs and onto my breasts, and I closed my eyes, with gratitude and delight.

It was a lovely month, and it seemed that everything I'd hoped for had come true. On the last night we went out for a fancy farewell dinner at our favorite restaurant, in Fontvieille, a few miles away. The village was even smaller than ours, just one main street lined with old stone houses. We parked and walked to the restaurant: it was entirely silent around us. In those small Provençal villages there is no sound after dark, and there all the houses were shuttered against the night. No one was on the sidewalk, there were no passing cars. The sound of each footstep rang against the stone walls. The evening air was sweet and soft, and we walked through it full of anticipation. We were dressed up, the men in white pants and crisp shirts, Nina and I in dresses and heels.

The owner-chef came out to greet us. He was tall, with blue eyes and smooth pink cheeks, in a very clean white chef's uniform and toque. He nodded at everything we said; he seemed to approve of all our decisions.

Would we like a table in the garden?

"*S'il vous plaît,*" Steven said enthusiastically, and the chef bowed his head politely and led us out. The garden was walled, and there were low fruit trees in it, and flowers everywhere: tumbling from big urns, on climbing vines, in vases on the tables. Around us were the old stone walls of the village houses; their shuttered windows overlooked us. There were flickering candles on the tables, though there was then still enough twilight in which to see. The sky above us was a deepening blue; the first faint points of stars were beginning to appear. We ordered a bottle of the local rosé wine, which is light and sweet and makes you happy.

The pink-cheeked chef took our orders, bowed with courtesy, like a friend, and left us.

"You know, the French are really so polite," Steven said. "They have a reputation for being rude, but they're really incredibly polite. Much more polite than Americans."

"Well, to be fair, they can be incredibly rude," John said.

"They aren't really, it's just that they don't smile. That's why Americans think they're rude. We think smiling is being polite, but for them, it's what you say, not how you look. They say good morning and good-bye to everyone. They always say please and thank you when we don't bother. All they don't do is smile."

"And the incredibly supercilious manner?" John said.

"You just don't speak French well enough to know when they're being polite," Steven said, waving his hand, grinning.

"That must be it," John said, nodding.

"But you are getting really good in French," Nina said to Steven, swirling her drink. She was wearing glittery earrings, the color of her eyes, and a low-cut dress; her sumptuous tanned breasts were on display. "Aren't you?"

"Better, anyway," Steven said modestly. "I'm still actually terrible."

"No, you're not," I said. "Steven can say anything."

"Oh, really very little," Steven said, but he was pleased.

"The big challenges in a foreign language," said John, "are telling jokes, a dinner party, and calling from a pay phone."

"Phone calls are easy," Steven said, waving his hand.

"They are?" Nina asked.

"*Pièce de gâteau,*" Steven said.

"You know how to use the French pay phones?" I said, surprised, impressed. "How do you know things like that?"

"I know lots of things," Steven said and smiled at me.

The evening drew out. The candles grew brighter, illuminating our faces as the nighttime darkened around us. It grew later and later. The German couple at the next table paid their bill and went home, and so did the American family behind us. The silent Parisian couple sat over their coffee without talking, but we grew merrier and merrier. Everything seemed funny, that night. Steven was across from me, and I could see his happiness, his good humor, glowing from him.

When John leaned back in his chair and lifted his hand for the waiter, Steven lifted his hand too.

"I'll do this, Stanton," Steven said, pretending to be surly.

"I can take care of it," John said, pretending to bristle.

"I told you I'll do it," Steven said, and the two of them leaned back in their chairs, their arms raised high, jostling, easy.

"You two look like kids up in the bleachers," Nina said, "trying to catch the baseball. What is it, a pop fly? What *is* a pop fly?"

When she said the word *baseball,* I glanced at Steven. I hadn't meant to, but I did, and he was looking at me, and he smiled. I thought, We've done it.

The waiter came with the bill, but when we'd paid we didn't stand up to leave. We sat there, still talking and laughing, unwilling to let go of what we had.

The village around us was completely quiet by then, so we could easily hear the first scrape of metal against wood. It was a small sound, somewhere above us. I looked up, and Steven did too, and we watched each other, listening. Up on one of the houses overlooking our garden, shutters were being swung open. Then we heard the swift turning of metal, as the long windows were parted. There was a brief pause, and then we heard a man's deep voice, someone leaning out into the air above us. He spoke one word: *"Assez!"*

Enough: that was all.

Silence. We looked at each other, laughing and sheepish. The man was so precise, so perfectly assured, so courteous, and so inarguably right. It was really late. We looked around: the other tables all were empty. Everyone else had gone home. The waiter stood respectfully near the door, his hands crossed. He was waiting for us to leave, the whole village was waiting for us to leave. We'd had enough: the beautiful meal, the wine, the garden, the warm scented air, the black star-filled sky. And so we went out, and down the black silent street to our cars, walking slowly, arm in arm, giddy with the pleasure of that night.

When I look back at that evening, it still makes me happy. I like the memory of that invisible Frenchman, declaring his single word into the dark air like a charm. We all heard it, and caught each other's gazes, and we knew that he was right, that our night was over, that we had had enough.

You can't keep things as they are, but you can hold things fixed in your memory, and so I still have that evening, although everything was lost, after that.

Steven had never stopped seeing Alison. That month in France he called her every morning when he went to the market. It would have been the middle of the night in New York; she would have answered when she was still asleep, dozy and warm. Steven must have stood in the phone booth in our little village, next to the *tabac*, his head held down in order to hear her voice, pressing the phone against his ear, imagining the sight of her on the other end of the line. I suppose he was happier as the month went on because each day he was closer to seeing her again.

I would have given anything to have made that not happen, to have kept him from ebbing away from me, but I could not. I did what I could, and it wasn't enough. I couldn't make a current strong enough to draw him to me; he left. He married Alison, with that red red mouth, and I don't think about them now any more than I can help it.

And Nina's sumptuous breasts contained her death. First she had surgery, then toxic treatments, poison, deadly rays—oh, everything anyone could think of—and then finally, her immune system ravaged and gone, she died of a fever. She got a headache, and then the fever. Her temperature was one hundred and five when we got the last report from the hospital, and we were told by then that her brain had been destroyed, so we couldn't even hope they could save her. And John—it's so hard to believe it—died too. The last evening I had dinner with them, when Nina was wearing a brilliant scarf wrapped around her head to conceal the loss of her thick blond hair, John complained of dizziness. Oh, that's nothing, I said, inner ear infection, they give you antibiotics. I was so glad to be able to identify it and dismiss it. But it wasn't nothing, it was the other thing, the thing no one mentions until there is no other thing to say: brain tumor. Nina was sick for three years, but John was only sick for three months. He went into a coma and died two weeks before Nina's headache, the one that turned into the rising unstoppable fever. She died in twenty-four hours, before most of us even knew she was in trouble.

It's so strange to think that all that is past, gone, that it's over and can't be reclaimed. But that night in the warm garden, with the dark aromatic countryside all around us, the black starry sky overhead, we were happy. What we had, without realizing it, was enough. It was all we were to have, whether we wanted more or not.

Intersection

I live on a narrow dirt road, about a hundred and fifty years old. Great standing sugar maples line this road, and in the summer it is a cool shadowy tunnel, though the high arching boughs allow a dappling of light to sift through. On one side of the road the Audubon preserve plunges down a steep ravine into dim woods. The interior is crowded with wild grape and maple saplings that struggle under the high dense canopy of the forest. On the other side of the road a wooded hill rises gently, its few houses hidden on its open upper slopes.

At night, deer tap tentatively across the cool hard surface of the road. Possums and woodchucks and raccoons wind secretively along the stone walls that line it, and skunks parade down the middle of it, reeking fearlessly. And there is traffic in broad daylight as well: there are the harried squirrels who insist on living on one side of the road and working on the other. In the early mornings, joggers are rife, with dogs, black Labs and golden retrievers, that drift alongside the runners in erratic patterns. There are walkers, too, on the road. Every afternoon a woman strides by my house holding a tall stick in one hand and the leash to a saluki hound in the other: equal measures of order and chaos. And on weekends there are the young girls who trot past on horseback, their horses' ears pricked forward at a critical angle of curiosity—intense, polite, limitless.

One day last month I saw a woman walking along the road pushing a big baby carriage, the padded box joggling comfortably along on high springy wheels. It was an incongruous sight on the packed dirt road, under the hanging swags of grapevine and bittersweet, the high dim canopy of the woods in the background. The baby carriage looked so elegant and urban, the navy canvas sides were so darkly clean, the wide chrome wheels so bright. It was so obviously designed for smooth paved sidewalks, not the uneven surfaces of our dirt road. The young mother pushing it was looking straight ahead, and singing. I was driving past, but I could see from the tempo and the rhythm of her mouth that she was singing, not talking. She was half-smiling, her eyebrows lifted, looking ahead, up the road, thinking about the words she was singing, or about nothing in particular, in that dreamy, meditative, slightly exalted state brought on by song. She was wearing blue jeans and a sweater, and thick-soled running shoes, and she was pushing the carriage along with purpose and confidence, as though she were on a wide esplanade, or on her way to the Serpentine, in Kensington Gardens. I thought of the baby, lying in that swaying cot, watching overhead the slow unwinding of the reel of interwoven branches, the mysterious green canopy above. He was listening to his mother's voice as he watched the forest ceiling move past him, hearing her liquid presence in this airy green world. Perhaps he couldn't even see her face, perhaps he was so carefully lapped in fine pale blankets and coverlets that he could only see the trees and hear her voice, as he was carried along in that smoothly rocking cushioned ride.

In spite of all this fragile and slow-paced traffic, cars still rocket along the road as though they were its only travelers. It's dangerous to drive fast on a dirt surface. It's hard to stop quickly; wheels find little purchase on the smooth clay, and what produces an easy, obedient lessening on the highway will cause a wild, sickening skid on dirt. Two days ago I saw a small red car nestled confidingly into the base of one of the maples, its nose tidily concave around the convex trunk.

The cars hit our road fast. There's no preparation for it, and people don't slow down, turning onto it from the fast paved road at the bottom of the hill. This road has become busier and busier as big companies set up offices in the countryside, creating around them the suburbs they pretend to shun. People who drive that fast east-west road are rapid-transit types. They are in a hurry, on the way to the railroad station, or the mall, or the office complex. They hurtle, unseeing, past the scenery, which is spectacular. This road runs past one of the New York City reservoirs, a great shimmering untouched stretch of light and water, rimmed with silent woods. Deer swim out to the small wild islands in the middle of it, swans float nobly across it, and Canada geese come and stand on the spillway, dabbing at any small creature about to be swept over, in a bogus rescue attempt.

The cars on that east-west road are heading for an intersection three miles away, with a big six-lane interstate. The flat calm of the reservoir states simply that you are there; the interstate reminds you of all the other places you might be instead. Great distances are suggested here, and the interstate leads toward anywhere else on the continent. The road widens as it approaches the intersection, and official green metal signs appear, bold and bossy. Big cities are announced, and the points of the compass. There are lots of other places you could be, and speed will get you to any one of them.

Last summer a woman I knew was picked up out there, for speeding, by a state policeman. She wasn't yet on the highway, she was still on the smaller road, and might have been heading right through the intersection, though that was never clear. It was very early in the morning, five or five-thirty, and the policeman had pulled his car into a graveled space at the side of the road. There would be nothing going on at that hour; it was too early even for the most fanatical commuters to the city, too late for the most determined drunks. The sun would have been coming up from the wooded hills above the reservoir, sliding across the cold wet grass on the shoulder, which would be still soaked and white with dew. It was an in-between time for the policeman, the ragtag end of a shift that finished at six; nothing to do but wait for the numbers on his digital watch to change.

When the woman appeared she was heading west toward the intersection, on a straight wide and empty road. The policeman said later that she was doing eighty, eighty-five when he first saw her. He turned on his circling blue light and went after her. She pulled over, with him behind her, just before the entrance to the highway going north, and I wonder if she hadn't planned to turn up it. Canada? The wide blue of Hudson Bay? She could have had anything in mind, anywhere. At home she had left her husband asleep. Lunches for the children—sandwiches wrapped in aluminum foil, filled thermoses—were set out on the kitchen counter, ready for day camp.

When she pulled over, the policeman did too. Usually, when people are stopped, they stay in their cars, meek and chastened, awaiting the appearance of the policeman in the car window. But the policeman was still in his cruiser, checking her license plate number in the computer, when the woman climbed urgently out of her car and ran across to him, barefoot in the wet grass. By now the sun would have started altering the landscape. Her face would have been lit up by that clean early light, though maybe not her bare legs, her feet, cold and soaked by dew. She was wearing only a bathrobe, an old blue terry-cloth one that fastened with a cord at the waist. She ran across the grass toward the policeman and halfway there collapsed. He opened his door, startled, and of course not knowing what she was doing. By the time he reached her she was unconscious, or at least past speech: she had put the blade of the big kitchen knife so precisely between her fifth and sixth ribs that she didn't live to reach the hospital, though it was only twelve miles away on the interstate, and the policeman was going a hundred, maybe a hundred and ten, his siren on, the blue light flashing in circles, as though speed might save her now.

The way I want to see myself is like that woman with the baby carriage, striding steadily along the road, singing to myself and to the child, beneath the arch of dappled green light. Anchored to the earth by that small body, heavy and radiant as a star. Certain of the right thing and doing it. Pushing my life steadily along before me, unseduced by speed, unruffled by events. That's how I'd like to move through my days. I look at my life, and I see the bones of it, the structure of it, as solid and deep-rooted as the line of maples along our road. I tell myself it can't be turned to nothing by one minute of desperation along the interstate, by one long sickening skid, the embrace of a tree, a knife. Where I live is along those double lines of trees, whose roots go down a hundred feet. A place is just a place, and the grass beside the ramp at an intersection is less of a place than most. There are a hundred reasons for me to ignore that patch of grass, reasons for me not to draw myself into a moment's tense suspension each time I pass it.

It's not, of course, one moment of desperation that would deliver you to that place. The approach to it is gradual, there are miles of acceleration before you reach it. By the time you arrived, speed would seem the most important thing there was, it would seem the only thing. Speed, like a kitchen knife, is something anyone can get. It's like discovering that you have a secret weapon. You do, of course: yourself.

It's people that hold you to the earth—no job, no principles, no ethics could clamp you to it if you'd a mind to spin off. There are times when that connection falls away. There are times when the weight inside you is heavier than the weight of the whole world outside. There are times when dread falls over you like a great silence, and you are entirely alone. At those times, waking is the worst moment of the day: your eyes open, you know what lies ahead. There's no way out. Here you are again, conscious.

Her husband was questioned by the police: he'd had no idea. All those wrapped lunches, lined up on the counter, ready for day camp. Afterward he told a friend that if it hadn't happened as it did—if she'd done it at home, if he'd been there—he'd have begun to believe that he'd done it himself. It was the shock, you see: he was no longer sure of anything. It was the realization that what he'd thought he'd known about her was not the truth. She'd had a secret life, running right next to his, fast, black, lethal.

Last night my husband stood in the kitchen, putting plates into the dishwasher. The metal rack clanged noisily with each dish. Outside it was dark, the kitchen windows were black. I could feel the night around us.

My husband spoke with his back to me.

"Is that all?" he asked.

Those words hung perfectly still in the air, like the sound of a slow bell, and at that moment things seemed to give way. I understood that the words meant something, but it seemed I was unable to answer. It seemed I was unable to speak. I had been barely holding on somewhere, and at that moment I'd lost my grip. I'd come loose.

My husband didn't know any of this. All evening, while I watched the room darkening around me, we had talked. I had listened to his questions and answered them. I had listened to us talk while I listened to the gathering darkness. It was like hearing simultaneous translation, a double track running inside my head. I had been following both languages at once, trying to listen to each, holding them separate. I knew that only one language was legitimate, I knew the other was forbidden, and must be kept secret. But I had come to the end of something. I could no longer speak the public language. That track had stopped. What was inside me had taken over, I could not answer the question.

My husband turned to look at me. He stood for a moment, waiting, in front of the sink. The water was running. He held the dishwashing brush in his hand. His face was puzzled, his eyebrows lifted.

"Ellen?" he said.

I looked at him. It was as though I'd been filling up with darkness. Desperation had been running into me in a lightless stream, and just at that moment I was filled. It had taken me over and I was frozen, silenced. The water kept rushing into the sink behind my husband, busy, endless. It was the only sound. I could say nothing. My husband looked at me. He and I were in the same room, but there was no way for me to reach him.

I wonder what time she woke up that morning, I wonder how long she had been awake before she set out. I don't wonder how she felt; I know how she felt. It would be escape, relief, a place you'd longed for all your life. Putting that blade in at last, sending it finally home, would be ecstasy, clear and exhilarating as sex. Leaving yourself finally behind, setting yourself free, would be a moment pure and blissful, like the silver hiss of cold air in your lungs at the top of a snowy mountain.

The pull of that place is like the current that draws you over the falls, and there are times when that route seems the only one left to take. There are times when you start out on that widening, quickening, emptying road, and you know that once you reach the intersection, all those reasons, those hundred-foot deep roots that are so solid where they stand, will be left behind.

The turn onto that road is smooth, and once you're on it, you find yourself accelerating, no matter what scenery you're passing. You're hypnotized by the promise of relief, you're desperate for it. And as the speed increases the landscape empties.

Once you're out there on that road, whoever is at home, whoever sleeps trustingly there, relying on you for lunches, is behind you, gone, vanished altogether. And by the time you reach the intersection there is nothing left to hold you on here. Out there are only smooth ramps curving onto wide lanes, blank concrete strips, signs telling strangers about other places. The great silence, and the cold light.

Shame

They came in from the road, down the long rutted driveway. The ranch didn't look like much: a couple of big scraggly flat fields with horses grazing in them, and at the far end a huddle of low flat-roofed buildings, scattered among the live oaks. The horses—Arabians, with slim legs and elegant sculpted heads— looked as though they were always turned out to pasture. There was caked mud on their flanks and mud in their long arched tails, which swept the ground like bedraggled boas trailed behind a dirty beauty.

The house faced the long field. It was an old adobe, with a wide porch running the length of it. A ragged piece of lawn stood before it. Guinea fowl scratched noisily in a corner, and a small band of yearling horses grazed loose near a clump of lilacs.

Caro and Eloise pulled their car up behind the old yellow Mercedes that had just stopped. Jeremy and Teresa climbed out of this, Teresa's white hair and white jeans vivid in the sunlight.

She turned stiffly to shut the door, then looked over at Caro and Eloise. She made a wry face about something—her own stiffness, perhaps. Her small features puckered briefly, then her expression relapsed into interested amusement. Teresa was in her late seventies, and had always liked what she'd found before her. She was rich, though that didn't account for the pleasure she took in life. Even now, as forgetfulness took a firmer and firmer hold on her mind, she retained this pleasure; it was hers daily.

Jeremy came over and squatted by their car, setting his mournful face in the driver's window. He was Australian and in his mid-forties, slight and narrow-shouldered. He had pale green eyes, a pointed chin, and a disappointed mouth. His mouse-colored hair was in a short ponytail, which lay limply against his back like a small exhausted animal.

Jeremy spoke across Eloise, to Caro, in the passenger seat. "I *told* you it was a long way." He sounded triumphant.

"She believes you," Eloise answered for Caro. "She'll never doubt your word again."

"Good," Jeremy said. He smiled archly. "I like that."

Caro had only been in Santa Fe a month; she was doing research for her dissertation. Her topic was the Spanish colonial period, the relationship between the Catholic Church and the indigenous population. Each day, in the dim and silent document room in the state archives, she handled stiff parchment pages the color of dried grass, reading close slanting script in seventeenth-century Spanish. The hand of the Church had been brutal here and ruthless. The records were full of orders for imprisonment, torture, executions—hangings and public burnings. The Church had seen the New World as a wide wild landscape, rich but unclean, polluted with heresy. They'd used the tools of the Inquisition, trying to burn a whole continent clean.

What interested Caro, among other things, was the philosophical inversion—the process by which the Church had transformed itself from an inclusionary institution, one based on compassion and brotherly love, into an exclusionary one, one driven by hatred and discrimination. Zealotry interested Caro.

She'd gone back to being a student after her husband had left her. She'd applied to graduate school, driven not by love of scholarship but, really, by shame. It was that she couldn't bear to face the people she knew. She wanted a new community, people who knew nothing about her. Then, when she'd gotten in, she'd been surprised by how much she liked it all—classes, texts, discussions, research. Especially research: she loved the deep industrious silence of the reading room. There, surrounded by other silent readers, she was entirely alone, entirely engaged, taking soundings in the mysterious currents of history.

Now that the children had gone—Eliza already a freshman at LSU, Dawson at Tulane—Caro could leave, too, the neat brick house outside Baton Rouge, the dense glossy leaves of their famous magnolia tree (second largest in the county), the rich green of the lawn, mowed weekly by men in earmuffs.

Santa Fe was a new world, with its clear bright skies and low endless hills, the flat-roofed adobe houses, its strange dust-colored landscape, and the pellucid light. It seemed deeply exotic, an eccentric mixture of bohemia and frontier. There was a sense of fiercely guarded privacy, ancient secrets. It was a rich, layered culture, full of color and mystery. It seemed like another country, where Caro was leading a new life.

Jeremy, leaning in the window, spoke earnestly to Caro. This was her first visit to the ranch.

"Now, remember," he warned, "Edward is very difficult. He's ordered people off his property for disagreeing with him. Once when I spent the night here he got mad at something I said and locked me into my bedroom. I couldn't even get out to pee until he got up for breakfast. The correct attitude is *abject*."

"You know us, Jeremy," Eloise said, grinning. "Abject is our middle name."

Caro leaned toward him, across Eloise. "Honey, y'all forget I'm a Southern belle?" she said, deepening her accent. "In Baton Rouge, we're *known* for our charm."

She and Eloise had become lovers the night before. For Caro, Eloise was now haloed with a brilliant light. Caro hardly dared to look at her; she could not bear to look away. Leaning across her now to speak to Jeremy, Caro felt breathless, giddy, at the nearness of the golden body. Everything, the whole day, was illuminated by the glow of secret delight.

In the doorway of the house the old man appeared, stiff, upright, angular. He was wearing an ancient Canadian Mounties hat and faded khaki pants. A black patch covered one eye.

"What are you all doing?" he shouted at them, already angry.

"Oh, hello, Edward," Jeremy called out at once, his voice high and placatory. "We just got here. We're bringing the food in. We'll be right there."

"You see? A great host," said Eloise to Caro. "The way he makes you feel right at home."

Teresa stood still in the driveway, hand on her hip. She looked calmly at Edward, without moving or speaking, as though she hadn't yet decided to participate. The expedition had been her idea.

Teresa had moved out here in the fifties, when her husband was still alive. They had bought their own old adobe, outside Santa Fe, in Nambe, which was then an isolated village. The Anglo community had been small and eccentric, and Teresa had known everyone: Mabel Dodge Luhan and Tony Lujan, Frieda Lawrence, Dorothy Brett, O'Keeffe. Edward was part of the circle—he'd arrived in the thirties. Artists, writers, visionaries, cranks—they'd all had been drawn here by the light, the beauty, the mystery. It had always been a place apart, outside the borders of convention.

Now Teresa decided, and stepped carefully across the rutted

mud toward the house. "Hello, Edward," she called out, announcing herself.

"Look at the sneakers," Caro said to Eloise, delighted.

Teresa's black high-tops were striped with glittering lines of neon green.

"Teresa," said Eloise meditatively, "is a top fave. That's who I want to be, when I'm her age. Except I'd like my memory, too."

As Eloise reached for the car keys, her sleeve slid back, and Caro could see the edge of that delicate inner skin that stretched the length of Eloise's arm, the tender, secret part of her that she, Caro, now knew. At that moment, with the sun glittering on the hood of the car, the others calling out to each other, carrying picnic baskets, Caro felt a flicker of superstitious fear. She wanted to keep Eloise here, in their shared, sheltered space, their private air. What risk, letting the rest of the world see these beautiful round arms, the smooth planes of this face, the curving shock of short sleek hair? Caro wanted to preserve this moment of seclusion, the two of them cloistered, protected from the world. Who knew what it held?

"Hurry up," Edward shouted irritably. "What's taking you all so long?"

Caro swung open her door and stepped out into the clear mountain air. The ranch was a thousand feet up, maybe more. The landscape was brilliantly exposed, vividly present. Since she had come to New Mexico, it seemed some filter had been removed between her eye and the world. Everything was revealed to have finer textures, more intricate construction, richer colors. Everything was more real, more vital.

When Caro thought now of her marriage, it seemed like an old movie, jerky and confused. Those big twilight picnics at the lake, everyone drinking margaritas and eating pulled pork; Tom roaming from group to group with his roving, unfocused eye, disappearing as darkness fell. Caro had always assumed that

Tom would go on like this, smiling his bleary smile at someone else's wife but still being her—Caro's—husband. As a child, she used to hear her father come in late at night, slipping quietly up the back stairs past her bedroom. He was in his stockinged feet, his shoes in his hands. She'd assumed it would be like that with Tom—that he'd have dirty secrets she didn't want to know about, wouldn't have to learn. Instead, Tom had walked out on her for his secretary. It was such an insult; other husbands didn't do this, though lots of them had affairs. But Caro had been left. And the girl was so awful, that mean little mouth and those awful plucked eyebrows. Caro had always thought she and Tom were partners, if not lovers. She'd been flattened when he'd left, by the shame of it. For six months she'd worn dark glasses every time she left the house.

Now, all those awful tipsy picnics beneath the darkening trees seemed remote and inexplicable, black-and-white pictures from someone else's life. Here, under this pure bright sky, Caro was living in color, living for real, next to this fluent, golden body.

The two women walked across the bumpy lawn. Edward stood, imperiously waiting, on the porch. His face was broad and wrinkled, sun-ravaged, the visible eye fierce and blue. The dull black patch turned the corner of his colorless glasses, concealing his damaged eye along the side as well.

"Edward, this is my friend Caro," Eloise said.

"Hello," he said crossly, not meeting Caro's eye. "Always someone new." He looked at Teresa, holding her accountable. "I don't know how I'm supposed to keep track of everyone in the world."

Teresa, unruffled, folded her arms across the broad black and white stripes of her sweater. "I didn't think you *were* expected to keep track of everyone in the world, Edward," she said calmly.

Edward ignored her and turned to go back inside. One of his

shoes was built up higher than the other, and he walked unevenly.

"You have a *fabulous* ranch," Caro said. She heard her accent and realized she'd set out to charm him. "I'd just like to
move right in."

Edward snorted, not bothering to turn.

"Everyone says that," he said scornfully. "No one knows
how much work it is to run this place. It's impossible to find
people. The last boy I hired stayed two days."

Behind Edward's back, Eloise rolled her eyes, at the idea of
working for him. He wheeled suddenly around to face them.

"Is it too cold to eat outside, do you think? Should we eat in
the house?" he demanded.

"No," everyone said loudly and at once, like a comic chorus.

This was how they dealt with Edward, Caro saw—
energetically, and in unison. It gave her an odd feeling of
protection and belonging. She was a member of their troupe.

Jeremy had warned Caro about this part. "We bring *everything,* when we go to Edward's. If we were going to use his
kitchen we'd have to send a team of people up a week beforehand to sterilize it. It hasn't been cleaned since the last flash
flood."

"I think we should eat outside in the sun," Teresa said. She
was swaying gently, standing on tiptoe in her neon-striped
sneakers. "It's nice out here." Teresa's statements were mild but
absolute. She'd grown up on the King Ranch, and was used to
choosing what pleased her most. Sometimes she remembered
everything, sometimes nearly nothing.

It was Jeremy who looked after her, living in her small adobe
guesthouse. It was he who took charge of her days, reminding
her of things and people, appointments, plans; it was he who
kept track of her life. It was he who drove her around in the ancient Mercedes, and now, when Teresa was invited to lunch or

dinner, Jeremy was included. He knew all her friends; his life was now entwined with hers, as though they were lovers. Their arrangement was a mystery: no one knew whether or not money changed hands, whether Teresa paid him for his efforts, or if she simply let him stay rent-free, sharing her place, her meals, her charming life. What everyone did know was that Jeremy had stopped painting. He had stopped even talking about painting, though when he met Caro he told her he was an artist. It was the way he saw himself still, or at least the way he wanted the world to see him.

Eloise was a real artist, a practicing one, who showed regularly at a local gallery. Her work sold very well—people who bought art in Santa Fe were rich—but it didn't support her. Eloise had moved here from New York eight years ago, and to Caro it seemed that she found her way through the landscape like a bright stream, shifting course lightly and easily, unstoppable. Whenever Eloise needed money she took a job; just now she was heading a fund-raising drive for the opera.

Eloise's paintings—rich glowing watercolors, small lush oils—were stacked neatly in the tiny studio at the back of her house. Right now she was making hanging boxes, small perfect painted chambers full of evocative objects: beads, old coins, tiny wheels. One was a dark-mirrored niche flecked with glittering stars like deep space, with a taut cat's cradle of copper wire stretched across it. Caro thought the works very beautiful, but she was, she knew, biased.

She'd thought Eloise very beautiful, too, when they'd met, at a museum opening. Eloise wore a pale doeskin shirt that dripped soft fringe down her front; her fluted throat rose up from it, straight and strong. Caro had never had a woman lover before, never even thought of it. She was not sure, now, what it meant.

Though it seemed surprisingly natural, in a way. Women

were used to admiring each other's beauty, taking pleasure in it. They were all used to seeing each other as objects of desire: the images were everywhere, from Botticelli to the latest *Vogue*. Acting on it seemed less extreme, less scary, really, than sleeping with men.

In any case it had been easy for Caro to close her eyes and give herself up to Eloise's silken hands; it was like slipping down a waterslide in a river. It seemed at once exotic and secret, thrilling and safe: this was a foreign country, and Caro a visitor. She could do what she liked here.

"We can move this table out into the sun," Jeremy now said, setting his hands beneath it, ready to heft. The table, a long unfinished board, stood on the porch, in deep shadow, where it was dank and cold. On the wall hung a large Chinese ancestor portrait, its paper wrinkled from weather, its colors pallid and remote. Below this stood a heavily carved gilt table, cracked and peeling. Under the table were stacks of newspaper and a rusty bucket of pinecones; on it was a cracked leather halter the color of mud.

They pulled chairs out onto the lawn. Jeremy, Caro, and Eloise carried the heavy table across the bumpy grass. The yearlings looked at them boldly from among the lilacs, their dark eyes and pricked ears peering through the heart-shaped leaves.

Caro and Eloise took the picnic hamper inside, to heat up the casserole. Eloise had told her about the house. "You'll keep noticing things that are hidden in the mess. A T'ang horse on a windowsill, something gilt under a table. Last time I was here Edward told me to bring over a chair, but there was a pair of his underpants on it. I picked them up, and underneath was a piece of fabulous Chinese brocade."

The door opened onto the side of one long room. Sofas, tables, and chairs were in a huge claustrophobic clutter to the right. There was an empty expanse of floor, then a normal grouping of chairs before a fireplace. At the end, to the left, was a great mahogany four-poster, neatly made, with a scarlet bedspread. A scratched metal file cabinet stood beside it.

The rooms were dark and chilly. Winding their way back to the kitchen, they passed a stone-tiled corner filled with plants. Eloise pointed out two large gilt carp on the floor, faded and peeling.

"See what I mean? It's like one of those children's puzzle pictures, where you try to find the hidden animals."

The kitchen was large and gloomy. Counters and tables filled the space, all loaded with objects: old tools, half-empty bottles, a rusted chrome coffeemaker, jars of nails, an electric fan, decades of *The New York Times*. The stacks of newspapers loomed horribly over the room.

Margarita, Edward's housekeeper, appeared. She was Hispanic, small and thin, with graying black hair in a bun. She wore glasses, black pants, and a troubled look. She came into the room rubbing her elbows. She did not look at the countertops.

"You know how to work the stove?" she asked Eloise doubtfully.

"Yes, thank you, Margarita, we do," said Eloise, giving her a brilliant smile. "Don't worry about us. We're fine." Margarita turned to leave, frowning, still rubbing her elbows. A big black chow came in past her, his eye alert and suspicious, his tail furled tightly over his back in a thick spray of fur.

"That's Mr. Mao," Eloise said. "Edward raises chows."

"Oh, come here, darlin'," Caro said, leaning over and patting her knees at him. But Mr. Mao was circumspect and retreated under the table, where he stared out at her, unblinking. Eloise bent over the stove, trying to light it.

"Where would we have sat if we *were* eating inside?" Caro asked: there was nowhere to sit in the kitchen, and no table in the other room. All of this—the surreal chaos, Edward's misanthropy—seemed wonderful, hilarious, to Caro.

"God knows," Eloise said. The oven lit with a soft explosive *voom,* and she slid the casserole inside.

Eloise's last lover had been an artist too, very different from Caro: small, sleek, and French. Caro had seen photographs of Nathalie. She was gleaming and self-contained, like a highly polished stone. Caro found it hard to believe that Eloise would choose her—rawboned and awkward, as she saw herself, pure American, with short wide feet, freckles everywhere on her body (which had, after all, been publicly rejected)—after that smooth silken creature, dark-skinned, European, sophisticated. She was amazed by this.

Caro watched Eloise at the stove. She was dazzled by the sight of her: the springy shock of her short golden hair, the gestures of her hands, so sure and delicious. Caro didn't dare move toward her; she wasn't sure who might walk through the door. She couldn't quite believe that last night had happened. All that urgency, the liquid, glistening delight.

"Why does he have all these Chinese things?" Caro asked. "Why did he collect such spectacular stuff just to let it all rot?"

"He didn't collect it," Eloise said. She edged the picnic basket gently onto the counter, pushing it into the solid phalanx of clutter. "Edward used to go to Hawaii a lot. Years ago he met a Chinese man there, and they became friends. Just before their revolution, the man wrote and asked Edward to come and get his things and keep them for him until everything was over. So Edward went to China and brought everything back here, but he never heard from the man again."

"So it's here for *safekeeping*?" Caro asked. She looked at the stained walls, the sagging tables, the stacks of forlorn and mildewed objects.

Eloise grinned. Her pale eyebrows slanted up diagonally, giving her a devilish look. "That's it," she said. "Safekeeping." She looked around. "Amazing, isn't it."

"Amazing," answered Caro, looking at Eloise's burnished face, her wide-set turquoise eyes.

Years ago, Eloise had told her, just after college, she'd been engaged. Her fiancé was young and sweet; she'd thought she loved him. Six weeks before the wedding Eloise called it off. She'd told him what had happened—what she'd learned about herself, who she really was.

They were in a coffee shop, in a booth, facing each other. While Eloise talked, explaining, she felt herself being slowly consumed by shame. She felt it physically, heat rising up through her body, like fire. She felt as though she were confessing a crime. She couldn't bring herself to look at him. She kept her eyes down, and kept stirring the spoon in her coffee, over and over. When she finished, and finally dared look up at him, he reached over and took her hand. He wanted to get married anyway. He couldn't see why not: he still loved her. And besides, he said earnestly, he didn't mind her being with women too. In fact, he said, he kind of liked the idea. He said this last in nearly a whisper, smiling at her. The worst of it, said Eloise, was that he thought he was being kind and understanding. She had begun to cry then. She felt invisible, as though people on the street would walk past without seeing her, as though she no longer had a place in the world.

Now Caro and Eloise carried out trays loaded with plates and silverware. Waiting for the casserole to heat, they all sat at the splintery table, squinting in the brilliant sunlight. Crows argued loudly overhead, and a gigantic cottonwood lifted its complicated arms above them to the sky.

"How many horses do you have here?" Caro asked Edward.

"About seventy-five," Edward answered.

"And how many do you sell each year?"

One field was full of peaceful mares shadowed by long-legged foals; the herd obviously was increasing.

Edward made a dismissive gesture. "People don't know what they're buying," he said. "These horses are worth thirty, forty thousand dollars each. They're the purest Arabians in the world, now that the Egyptians have started messing around with their own bloodlines."

Teresa looked at Caro. "Edward was given a small herd, as a present from the Shah, before the war," she explained. "He's kept them pure ever since."

The Shah? Who in the world *was* Edward, wondered Caro, with his rich, shadowy, international connections? Was he CIA? Gay? But it was hard to imagine him working for an organization. Or being with anyone—man or woman. Caro was intrigued by his mysterious past, and amused by his preposterous bluster. Radiant with her new secret, Caro felt charged and potent. She would win Edward over, charm and comfort him, befriend him.

"Most of the people who come here don't know what they're looking at," Edward said. "They just want some backyard horse to fool around with. Show jumping." He looked disgusted.

"We saw another horse farm, coming in here." Jeremy offered new information. "A big breeding farm. It's about ten miles from here, down near the highway."

"Near *here?*" Edward asked, stiffening, proprietary.

"Out near the highway. It's called Broadmoor, something like that." At Edward's hostility, Jeremy turned cautious. "The people are named Watson, I think?"

"Never heard of them," Edward said with satisfaction. "Most of the people around here are newcomers."

"The sign said Trakehners, whatever *that* means." Jeremy rolled his eyes, now siding with Edward against the hapless Watsons. "Jumping and *dressage,* it said."

Edward's disgust deepened. "Oh, yes, I know who you mean.

They don't give a damn about anything except what they're doing. They're only interested in their own operation."

"Not like you," Teresa said out of what Edward first thought was loyalty. After a moment he looked up at her; she smiled benignly.

"The market for Arabians is all gone to hell, same as the market for chows," Edward went on, ignoring Teresa. "No one knows what they're looking at. You show people an animal that's the result of a thousand years of breeding, the purest bloodlines in the world, and they say, 'Are they easy to housebreak? Will he jump up on my car?'" Edward's voice turned unexpectedly to a thin spoiled whine, and everyone laughed.

"But he *will* jump up on your car," Teresa pointed out. "You can't train chows. You tell them that, do you, Edward?"

Edward waved his hand again. "I don't tell them anything at all. I don't want to sell this kind of dog to that kind of person." The wind of his contempt blew across them all.

Eloise went inside to bring out the casserole. After a moment Caro, emboldened by Teresa, said to Edward, "I have a chow, actually. Black, like Mr. Mao." She heard her accent, strong again.

"You do." Edward snorted, not looking at her, as though this proved his point exactly.

"I do. I love chows. I'm just crazy about Tina. I'm *crazy* about her."

"Well, I just hope you don't let her run around loose on the road," Edward said repressively.

In fact, this worried Caro. Her rental, a tiny half house on the outskirts of Santa Fe, had no yard. There was only a dusty place behind the back door, opening toward the scrubby hillside beyond.

"She stays inside all day, while I'm gone, but at night she *is* loose sometimes," Caro admitted. "There's no fence, and I let her out alone for a while. Sometimes she does go toward the road.

I'd hate for anything . . ." She did not want to say out loud what might happen. "Even if there were a one in a million chance . . ."

But this enraged Edward. "'One in a million'! 'One in a million'! That doesn't mean *anything*," he said angrily. "Why do you say something like that? What sort of person *are* you?"

His malice was so naked, so exposed, that Caro felt the shock of it against her face like a slap.

"If you let her run around on the road she'll be killed," Edward announced.

She'll be killed. Black and malign, the words hung in the air like a curse. Caro wanted to order Edward to take it back. She saw Tina's rapt, attentive face when she came home, the slow adoring sway of the tightly furled tail. Now, against her will, she saw Tina, dark head down, sniffing busily, trotting out toward the road in the dark. She saw the sudden radiance of headlights, heard the scream of locked brakes.

She should never have spoken Tina's name here.

Not looking at Caro, Jeremy said virtuously, "It's not really fair to a dog to keep it inside all the time."

Teresa looked at Edward, then away. She said nothing.

So Caro was not part of their troupe. No one would defend her from Edward; he could attack her at will. She felt publicly chastised, felt the shame of it. Her cheeks burned. She fixed her eyes on the ancestor portraits, faded and rippling, hanging on the damp wall. The place no longer seemed touching or comic— the venomous old despot with his sinister connections, his squalid household, cowed servants, sycophantic friends. It now seemed vile.

Eloise appeared, holding the casserole with two filthy pot holders. She smiled at Caro, who did not smile back. Eloise began to serve steaming spoonfuls onto the plates.

Edward watched her silently, wrathful.

Teresa leaned forward and put her hand on Edward's arm.

"Edward," she began.

"Oh, skip it, can't you?" Edward said. He was nearly beside himself with irritation. "Can't you just skip it? You don't have any idea what it's like to run this place." His voice rose. "Seventy-five of the purest horses in the world, and nobody wants to work here. No one knows what work is anymore. I can't get anyone to help on this place at all."

Teresa put her elbows on the table and looked at him seriously. "We'll find someone for you, Edward," she announced, her voice full of purpose. "We'll find you someone." She nodded resourcefully at Jeremy. "We'll start calling tonight."

Jeremy nodded back, blinking in obsequious agreement, as though Teresa, like he, were in her forties, as though she were clear and purposeful, with a mind that did not flicker on and off like a faulty fluorescent light. Jeremy nodded solemnly, as though he believed Teresa would complete any project she took up; he nodded as though he himself would complete all his projects, or any.

But Edward was not reassured. He shook his head like a bull in a ring, distracted by rage and pain. Without answering he bent stiffly over his plate.

Teresa, too, began to eat. She raised her eyes once and smiled benevolently at Caro, her fine white hair glowing in the sunlight, but said nothing. Eloise, beside her, gave Caro a bright solicitous look. No one spoke. Caro lowered her own head to the food—chicken stew laced with chiles. She said nothing more. She no longer wanted to befriend Edward; she wanted only to avoid his hostility. She no longer understood this excursion—why had they wanted to come? What pleasure could anyone take in visiting this savage old man? There was nothing he did not despise. What were they all doing here?

And what was she doing, falling in love with a woman?

Something had shifted, and now Caro felt a thin ripple of revulsion at the thought, a fine dry tightening of the skin. She hadn't, really, fallen in love, she told herself: one night meant nothing. She wasn't a lesbian. She didn't even like the word. Caro had been married for seventeen years and she had two children. That was who she was. She felt a slow coil of resentment toward Eloise, who'd drawn her into all this.

Caro wished the day were over. She wished she were back in the archives, picking up a heavy parchment page, losing herself in the narrow slanted script of the old language. She wanted to be alone in that deep silence, analyzing events. She wanted to think in historical abstractions: the Inquisition as a tool of colonial expansion, the Church as an economic power. The puzzle of zealotry, its fierce hot unreasonable flame, its hysterical potency. These were the things she wanted to consider. The landscape of the mind: that was where she wanted to be, it was where she lived.

Caro felt the cool mountain wind on her bare arms, and shivered. She was now repelled by Edward's viciousness, disgusted by Jeremy's toadying, saddened by Teresa's promises. And she could not look at Eloise—something in Caro had curdled.

She said nothing more during lunch. She thought of Tina, lying patiently on the stone floor, awaiting her return. But first there was the drive back alone with Eloise to endure. She could not now imagine their touching.

Caro hoped they'd leave right after lunch, but when the table was cleared Teresa asked Edward if they could go out and see the horses. They walked in a straggly group into the big field of close-cropped grass which held the mares and foals, forty or fifty of them. Some of the babies gamboled, long-legged, loose-jointed, absurd, skittering around their grazing mothers. Some lay curled up like dogs, hind legs tucked close, one narrow front leg outstretched, like a ballerina practicing a bow. Some lay spread out like flags. The mares moved quietly, cropping the grass, casual but deliberate, keeping their bodies always between the people and the foals.

"You have to be careful out here," Jeremy told Caro officiously. "These horses can be dangerous." She could see this made him proud. "That's why Edward wears the eye patch: he got into the middle of a fight between two horses."

"It wasn't their fault," Edward declared at once, protective. "He was trying to kick another horse, not me. Two stallions had been put in the same pasture by mistake. It never should have happened. It wasn't their fault." Frowning, he walked unevenly across the dry turf, pulling his built-up shoe along with a tiny hitch in each step.

There seemed little risk of danger now. The horses barely moved, raising their heads calmly, still chewing, to look as the people approached, dropping them again peacefully to the grass.

"There's my favorite, Edward," Teresa said. She was on tiptoe again, teetering across the bumpy grass on her glittering sneakers. Holding her hand out, she stepped up to a small bay mare with deep brown eyes and a short dished face.

"Don't put your hand out to her head," Edward snapped. "That's what the vet does. Don't go to her. Let her come to you."

Teresa stopped at once, putting her neon feet together, her hands clasped behind her back. She leaned forward, daring the mare with her chin. The mare blew out a gentle, wary breath from her silky nostrils, flaring them widely. She stretched her curving neck toward Teresa. The two profiles faced each other, the woman with her flat white hair and raised chin, her steeply sloping bosom; the mare's short pricked ears, her dark, liquid eyes, the fluid arching line of her neck, her small, inquiring muzzle.

"That's the prettiest mare on the place," Edward said.

He spoke so low that Caro had to lean toward him to hear. She thought she'd misunderstood him.

As Edward watched the two bending intently toward each other, another mare came up, moving her body confidently against him from the side. He turned and put his arms around her neck. He spoke casually, as though what he said were not astonishing.

"You're my lovely one," he said to the horse, "aren't you. You're my lovely one."

The mare stood still and calm within the circle of his arms, blinking, peacefully swishing her muddy tail, listening to his murmuring. She was used to this, it was how she knew Edward.

Here, Caro saw, was the object of Edward's passion, here was the other side of his rancorous self. Here was where Edward allowed himself tenderness. All the horses in this wide valley, the peaceful foals, blinking in the spring sunlight, the slowly grazing mares, the yearlings loose among the lilacs, the wary chow beneath the table: all of them were held in the wide unlikely glow of Edward's love. It was animals he honored and cherished, people he despised.

The abrupt shift from rage to gentleness, the startling discrepancy, and the distance between the extremes reminded Caro of her research. Edward himself was like the early Church, with its two paradoxical, contradictory sides, one gentle and compassionate, one raging and malevolent.

For this moment, all was peaceful. Jeremy stood with his hands in his back pockets, gazing out at the horses, waiting for a cue. Teresa faced her muddy mare, each leaning closer, now nearly nose to nose. Edward stood with his arms looped around the quiet horse's neck.

Without warning, Caro felt Eloise's arm slide around her shoulders, drawing her close. The touch on her body was intimate and proprietary; Caro flinched. She felt as though she were being claimed, as though Eloise were making a public declaration.

Before she could move, Edward released his mare and turned. His good eye fell on the two women, their bodies linked. *"What are you doing?"* he asked them, furious at once. Rage rose up in him like a geyser, it came foaming out in spates. The mare jerked her head in alarm, and moved protectively toward her foal. Edward ignored the horse, he was his other self now. "What are you, *perverts?*" He spat the word at Eloise and Caro. "What are you doing here? Who are you? I don't even know who you are."

Teresa stood upright, pulling back from her mare.

"Edward," she said pacifically, "you know who they are. That's Eloise."

"Shut up," Edward said, without looking at her. Flecks of saliva flew from his mouth, glittering in the sunlight. "Get out of here," he said to Caro and Eloise. *"Get out.* Get off my ranch. You're disgusting."

Caro and Eloise stood motionless, as though turned to salt by his hatred. Eloise's arm was still across Caro's shoulders.

"Get out," Edward said again. He took an uneven step toward them, as though he would beat at them with his bare hands. His tottery figure vibrated with hatred.

Meekly, Eloise began to pull her arm off Caro's shoulders, but now, unexpectedly, Caro felt something rise in her, answering Edward. She reached up and grabbed Eloise's wrist, holding it hard in place, against her shoulder.

Facing Edward, she felt an odd exultation. Here it was: zealotry. Here was the black star bursting into dreadful radiance. Here was hatred, hysteria, choking rage: here was Torquemada himself. She felt his anger sweeping over her, it was like standing outside in a hurricane. Edward would have burned them at the stake.

Caro stood straight, holding Eloise's bare arm across her shoulders like a mantle. Teresa and Jeremy were quiet. Edward stared back at Caro with his one good eye narrowed with hatred, his pupil black and bottomless.

Then Caro reached out and slid her other arm around Eloise's waist. She pulled Eloise close, holding her hard, hip to hip. Shame: she'd had enough of it. She didn't care what she was doing now—declaring herself lesbian, witch, anathema, the Antichrist. She didn't care what happened next. She stood waiting, daring Edward to go on.

The Football Game

We slowed down as soon as we got off the highway in New Haven. Everyone, it seemed, was going to the game. Our car became part of a long crawling procession that was snaking its way toward the athletic fields where the parking was. Finally we turned in to a field and bumped across its wide green expanse. A man in jeans and a sweatshirt waved us briskly toward the end of an evolving lineup, and we pulled up next to another station wagon and stopped.

"Here we are," Mr. McArdle said. Mr. McArdle was my roommate Karen's father. He was in his late forties, cheerful, slightly stooped, and balding, with small merry blue eyes. This was the kind of thing he said: obvious and unimportant, but sociable and friendly. You didn't have to listen to him, but it was nice that he was talking.

"I wonder if the Braithwaites are here yet," said Mrs. McArdle, looking around at the other cars. Then she turned to look at us in the back seat, encouraging. "You girls all right? Are you looking great?"

I liked Mrs. McArdle. She was kind and energetic, and she said things my mother would never have said. But all the McArdles were different from the members of my family. For one thing, all the McArdles loved to sing. Before dinner they sang grace together, harmonizing, and taking parts. Karen sang second soprano; her older sister sang first. Mrs. McArdle closed her eyes, listening to the different voices, and once I heard her say afterward to Karen, "You know, kiddo, you had that second soprano line just exactly right. It was perfect." She shook her head in a brisk wag of appreciation.

I was amazed by all of this: by the idea that a family would do something in harmony, taking parts to create a line of transient beauty together, just for the pleasure of it, and then by the idea that praise might be handed out so freely, without cost or guilt. I had never been told that something I had done was just exactly right—*perfect*—in my whole life.

I watched their family with awed respect, taking notes for my life. Karen's older brother, Ned, was at Williams, and her older sister, Marian, was through college and already married, to a musician. Their family seemed to unwind, like a spool, into a perfectly woven fabric, the texture sound, the pattern beautiful. My own family was not comparable. For one thing it was too small: it consisted only of my parents, my much younger brother, and me. We had no pattern. I myself had no idea where I was unwinding, the world as I was discovering it seemed wild and erratic and unfathomable, and my younger brother was worse off than I was. We knew nothing, our family was stuck in a bizarre backwater that I longed to escape. When I stayed with the McArdles, I memorized the things they did, devouring their solutions, storing them up for my future.

Mr. McArdle worked for a bank in New York. He went off on the train every day from Bedford Hills, wearing a gray suit and carrying a briefcase. This seemed both proper and glamorous to me, as though he soared off daily into another galaxy, returning miraculously safe each night to the small protected planet he had created. When I was staying with them, visiting Karen, I saw him when he got home, his suit wrinkled, his face creased from the strain of his mysterious interactions with the larger world. I sat on the deck with them in the summer evenings, while the McArdles had martinis, and we listened to the katydids in the trees, and watched the night drawing closer over the sloping lawns, over the heavily laden trees and the misty meadows of Bedford Hills.

All this seemed infinitely preferable to my own parents' life, so unconventional, so awkward, so stubbornly outside the American norm. My own father arrived home from work at four o'clock in the afternoon, stamping out of his cold studio, with his white wave of hair and his deep interior frown, his paint-stained blue jeans and loose jacket, his battered work boots. My father was an artist, and we lived in a converted barn in Vermont. The barn was composed of big drafty spaces, with not enough heat and no privacy. A second, smaller barn nearby was my father's studio, and it was even colder.

My father was an abstract expressionist. He had studied with Adolph Gottlieb, and he made huge canvases full of slashing brushstrokes. His paintings now were all black and white, though the earlier ones, stacked in dusty rows in the horse stalls, were full of bold and anguished color. I could not bear to look at them, they were so freighted with my father's burdens.

I could hardly ever remember seeing my father dressed in a normal suit. When we visited my grandparents in Oyster Bay, my father wore a tweed jacket and a polka-dot bow tie. For a big formal family party he wore his black dinner jacket and a black bow tie. But I had never seen him wear a gray pin-striped suit and a regular long flat normal tie, with dark subdued stripes, the kind that Mr. McArdle wore always.

When my parents came to see me at boarding school, they looked odd and out of place. My mother wore fragile dangling earrings, and her long hair was piled loosely on top of her head in a swirl. She wore long full skirts and black stockings, and little low black heels. My father's hair was in a sort of pageboy, nearly chin length, but without bangs. His hair was long and coarse and turning white, and he often swept it back with his hand, combing it roughly with his outspread fingers.

Once I saw him do that at my school, during Parents' Weekend. He was standing on the Oriental rug in the formal front hall, in the middle of the other parents. All the other fathers were in gray flannel suits and raincoats; my father was in his baggy gray flannels and his old tweed jacket. My father has an imperious profile, and he is tall and thin, and his head rose high above the other fathers. I saw his arm go up to his hair, and the sight of his wild raking despairing gesture among those neat decorous heads twisted at me. I could not bear to see him there, so different and so strange. I wanted to run from the room and pretend I had never seen him before. But I could not, because I knew my father, I knew those moments of concentration and delight and confusion that made him make that gesture, and the knowledge that I knew him like that made my heart contract, as though it was unbearable to know someone so well, to see his life so intimately.

The McArdles evoked none of this pain, because it seemed that they did normal things without effort. Though normal things were exotic to me. Mrs. McArdle was breathlessly interesting: for example, she belonged to the Garden Club. I knew about the Garden Club from hearing my parents mention it. My mother would say scornfully, "She's the kind of person who would belong to the Garden Club," or irritated, she would ask my father, "What do you want me to do, join the Garden Club?" Once I understood that the Garden Club was part of this other, stable world, and that it was the focus of my parents' derision, I determined to join one as soon as I could, because I wanted to be as unlike my parents as possible. I believed that my parents had deprived me of the kind of life that their parents had had—a life of convention and stability, which were things I longed for.

My father's obsession with aesthetics, his unanswerable pronouncements at the dinner table about form and space and color, his gloomy hostility toward the world, his gigantic and powerful opinions about everything, and the silent intermittent presence of his despair—all of these things sucked the air from our family conversation and blackened the big drafty spaces of our house. Our singing in harmony before meals was unthinkable.

All of this I blamed on my father's decision to abandon his own father's life, his choice not to enter the army of commuters who stepped onto the train each morning from leafy parking lots, heading into the noisy, bustling metropolis, where they all did something useful together, something powerful and important that wound the clock of the country, kept its internal gears in continual interlocking mesh. Those men returned in the evenings to pleasant houses with air-conditioning, to children who lived near their friends, children who were allowed to have television sets and eat junk food and listen to trashy music. Because of my father's unfathomable decision, all that easy, graceful Elysium of American life was denied to my brother and me. Instead of doing what normal children did (whatever that was—we would never know), we made tree forts in the woods, we played Indian trackers in the meadows, we made up secret languages, we resented our parents' rules. We were silent at school when the other children talked about television programs. "Television is trash," my father declared with majestic disgust, when I once mustered the nerve to ask why we didn't have one. "Television is for idiots." My father's idea of recreation was to walk with us through the woods, carrying his binoculars and watching for birds—something which I liked when I was small but which seemed antisocial and strange as I grew older.

When I was sent, at the age of fourteen, to the girls' boarding school outside Philadelphia where my mother had gone, I felt I had escaped from prison. I was being allowed at last to enter the larger, normal world, where people like Karen and the McArdles lived, in regular houses, not barns. Moreover, I was tacitly being allowed to enter the world of sex, the existence of which was not admitted in our household. When I was in sixth grade, I had dressed up for Halloween as a sort of Superwoman Witch. While I was getting myself up, my mother saw me standing in front of the mirror.

I was interested by what I saw: I had dark cherry red lipstick on, and I had outlined my eyes in black. I was wearing black tights and leotard, and a black cape, and I had set my hand on my hip, and thrust my hip out to one side. I could see that the image in the mirror was no longer the one I was used to. What I was used to seeing was a child ready to play, in a T-shirt and blue jeans folded carefully up at the bottom, and sneakers. Or a child dressed up for some occasion, in a pale smocked Liberty print dress sent by my grandparents. But either way the image was sexless: I was a child, and my torso was smooth and straight. My proportions were mysteriously right, the way children's are, as though there is some classical equation that applies to all children's bodies the way there is for Greek temples: the length of the legs equal to one and one-fifth the length of the torso, something like that. It's not until adolescence that things begin to go awkward. Then the legs become too long or too short, the head suddenly out of scale, the rib cage inexplicably outsize, the hips too high on the frame. But all children are the right size.

Now in the mirror I could see something else: the cocky tilt of the hip, the sultry black rimming of the eyes were mimicking some other form of life. I was pretending to be something I was not, but I was using the same, regular body that I'd always had. I could do it, I could see that. It was a strange, dangerous feeling, and as I stood there, eyeing myself with curiosity and excitement, I saw my mother standing behind me.

"Don't stand like that," she said.

I pulled my hip in. "Like what?" I asked.

"It makes you look 'sexy,'" she said, and the word in her mouth was shaming, unthinkable.

"It does not," I said stoutly, denying everything, as I always did. But I knew guiltily that, in fact, I might have looked sexy, that my body could now do that, that it could move, unbidden, into an illicit realm, the large trashy popular world that my parents shunned, where anything might happen, where everyone else lived.

By the time I was fourteen I was interested in looking sexy, though at school this was not encouraged. We wore uniforms, decorous green pleated tunics, tied with sashes. These could not be too revealing; they were loose, and the hem had to be no more than four inches from the floor when you were kneeling. They were strange garments, but we didn't care. We didn't care how we looked in our tunics, since when we wore them we only saw each other. We only saw boys under special circumstances: at tea dances, glee club concerts, the junior prom. These events happened seldom, were brief, and took place under strict supervision. I wondered what boys were like.

What were they like? My brother was too young, really, to qualify, and none of my friends at elementary school had been boys. Those boys had their own weird lives, shooting each other with rubber bands, snorting gleefully over unintentionally obscene references made by anyone. The boys were, all of them, strange, clumsy, big-footed, restless, violent, unknowable. Who knew what boys were like? At boarding school, for the tea dances, we spent all day preparing. We washed and cream-rinsed our hair, and put it up in giant rollers. We shaved our legs perfectly, perfectly smooth—as though, while we were dancing primly under the eyes of the chaperone in the discreetly lit room at Lawrenceville, there would be an opportunity for a boy to discover the delectable truth about the skin on your panty-hosed calf. There would not. Still, the ritual of preparation was central.

At the football game the McArdles were taking us to, I knew there would be boys—college students, a different brand from the smooth-cheeked boys at Lawrenceville. These would be older, thicker, and more daring and advanced; they would know more, they would be more full of that coarse interesting life that had so far eluded me. And my body had begun to look sexy on its own, I knew that. I was now fifteen years old, and that's what fifteen-year-old bodies do.

We got out of the car and put down the tailgate. It was a clear sunny day, cool, the air with a brisk edge of excitement. Mrs. McArdle opened up the picnic hamper. There were egg salad sandwiches and pretzels and cookies, and big thermoses of martinis for the grown-ups. The Braithwaites came over to our station wagon, and some other people.

"This is Karen's roommate," Mrs. McArdle said, introducing me to Mr. Braithwaite. He was thickset and ginger-haired, with rough skin and corrugated seams down his cheeks. He smiled at me.

"Boarding school, eh?" he said and shook his head cheerfully. There was a friendly gleam in his eye. "Hated boarding school. Only thing I liked about it was playing ice hockey. Hated every minute of it besides that."

I smiled at him. I knew you were supposed to hate boarding school. At the beginning of each semester we made chains of paper clips, one for each day until the next vacation. We hung them in our rooms and took off a clip each night, as though we were all longing to go home, where our real lives were. The other girls talked about the parties they would go to, once they were home, and I would smile, listening, as though I knew what they meant. But I didn't look forward to going home, to my dark cold room in the corner of what had been the hayloft. I knew I would see no one there but my small ignorant family, in that wintry northern darkness. My father might or might not be speaking; either way there would be no parties of my friends, for my age. For me the holidays were blank and desperate spaces, blank holes cut out of my year in the real world.

"What do you think?" Mr. Braithwaite now asked me, conspiratorial. "You hate school?" He smiled at me. He was standing quite close; he held me in his gaze. He seemed interested in me, in my opinions, and I was grateful.

I smiled back. "I don't hate it," I said. "It's not so bad."

Mr. Braithwaite held my eyes a moment longer, smiling into them. I was aware of his friendly, tweedy bulk, the weight of his body near mine. I saw his wife look over at him from where she stood, a glance; he saw it too, and he raised the silver beaker he held. The sides of it were beaded with cold sweat from the martinis. "Well, good," he said, smiling. "Cheers." He moved away.

Karen and I were the only people our age there, and we talked mostly to each other. Karen knew more than I did, of course, about the world she lived in. She was much more sophisticated than I was, which irritated me. I felt I deserved to be more sophisticated, since I cared so much more about this world than she did, and it was frustrating that I was not.

"Let's get out of here," Karen said in a conversational way. Delicately she set the entire half of egg salad sandwich in her mouth and chewed solemnly.

"Where shall we go?" I asked.

"Anywhere but where Mr. Braithwaite is," she said. "One

more martini and he'll be shoving us up against the side of the car."

I was hurt by this: this was my friend she was talking about, the man who took such an interest in me. I was also hurt to learn that he was unfaithful to me.

"Let's go," I said.

We walked across the field; the ground was damp and springy, and the grass green and live underfoot. The autumn sun was warm on our faces. Around us people were smiling and calling to friends, carrying picnic hampers and plaid blankets. The women were in neat bright wool suits and low heels, the men in tweed jackets. It seemed busy and complicated, like one of the paintings we had been studying at school. It was like a medieval market scene where everyone was full of life and pur- pose and color, a scene that looked at first just like a pattern, a kind of mosaic, but then if you looked closely you could see that each of these little blotches of color was a real person, doing something important: the baker was carrying a tray of rounded loaves, the woman was leaning out the window, the dog was licking something up from the cobblestones. It was a place where everyone had their own little scene to act out, but everyone's scene was a harmonious part of the whole, blending into it, everyone's gesture was made in exactly the right place for the composition.

Karen and I made our way, from the milling group of grown- ups, toward the football stadium, which we could see looming above the low horizon of parked cars. We were surrounded by color and movement and expectation, moving along as part of a throng. Throng: I liked that word. It was completely separate from my own life up until now. My parents could never be a part of a throng. Now—my own doing—I was.

Karen and I, of course, were in our own bright wool suits and stockings and low heels. Our hair was bright and freshly washed; we felt ourselves glinting in the sun. Everyone in this crowd seemed to know each other; we had all practically been introduced. We all had connections to one of these schools or the other, we were all part of the same throng.

There were college boys all around us. We could feel their presence, we could feel them looking at us; we smiled at each other, at nothing in particular. Two boys who were walking near us started talking loudly, for our benefit.

"Jesus, Jackson," the taller one reprimanded his friend, "you're going to drop that. You'll disturb these young ladies." He looked at us, ostentatiously reassuring. I didn't look straight at him, but I saw him.

"You're going to drop it, Jack," he said, now more confident.

"You carry it then," said Jack, holding the bag out to his friend.

"Please," said the tall one theatrically, closing his eyes and declining, holding his hands up, palms out, in an absolutely-not gesture. The tall one had reddish brown hair, crumpled and wiry, bold dark eyes, and wide cheeks. He was handsome in a greedy rushing way. The shorter one—who was too short for me but not for Karen, who was much shorter than I was—was the better looking of them, with thick dark hair and heavy eyebrows.

"Okay, then, shut up," Jack said, taking the bag back against his chest. The taller one turned to me and smiled.

"Going to the game?" he asked, brilliantly.

I smiled back.

We talked to the boys until it was nearly time for the game to start. The taller one was Brad, and they were both at Yale. I didn't care about the game, I had no interest in watching people hurtling around rupturing ligaments. Still, the game was why we were here. I understood the ritual: the game was today's center. It was the excuse for everything else: the bright wool suits, the thermoses of martinis, the electrifying eye contact. I couldn't pretend I wasn't part of it, couldn't admit I didn't care. We said good-bye and made a plan to meet at halftime. We were in our seats with the McArdles by the kickoff.

"Where were you?" asked Mrs. McArdle, smiling at us.

"We met some friends," Karen said, frowning vaguely into the distance. And it was sort of true. Brad and Jack were now friends of ours, it was just that they hadn't yet been friends when we'd met them.

"Anyone I know?" asked Mrs. McArdle.

"No," Karen said, looking bored. "Some guys from Yale." The game started, and everyone began to yell. We were sitting on the Dartmouth side, and instead of watching the disorganized capering on the field I looked over at the Yale side, trying to distinguish Brad and Jack from the huge crowd. Of course I could not: I hardly knew what they looked like close up, let alone across a football field. But I was already thinking about Brad, the proprietary boldness of his dark glance, the attractive greediness of his presence, his burly shoulders.

"We don't have a chance," Mr. McArdle said philosophically. "We never do against Yale. It's always a rout at New Haven." He was a small man, with an easy, self-deprecating manner.

"Who *did* you use to win against?" Karen asked.

Mr. McArdle shook his head dolefully. "No one," he said. "We never won. That I can remember. They were all routs."

We all laughed. Mr. McArdle was always like this, yielding and pleasant. It seemed that he took nothing personally, or seriously, and this made me feel oddly safe. He would never fill the room with black gloom over the question of the picture plane.

We were all watching the field, and I wondered if Karen and her mother were thinking about the game. Mrs. McArdle had been coming to these games for years, making egg salad sandwiches and thermoses of martinis and carrying the plaid blanket and sitting in the cold for four hours. What had she thought about? It was a little like going to church, which I had done with my grandparents. You were part of a crowd, dressing up, sitting down, all taking part in a grand spectacle. But did you have to think about it the whole time? Because I could not keep my mind on the play for an instant. On the field the ball appeared suddenly in the air, arcing up over a disheveled group of figures. The crowd roared. The ball disappeared again, and the figures ran in circles. The crowd roared again.

"He's useless," Mr. McArdle said sadly. Then something else happened and Mr. McArdle was suddenly on his feet, cheering, along with everyone else on our side.

At halftime Karen and I stood slowly. Karen thrust her arms out stiffly and yawned.

"I think we'll go stretch our legs," she said.

"Have a good time," her mother said.

The boys were where they'd said they'd be, which was good: Brad was tall, he was strong, and now I knew he was reliable.

"Here they are," Brad said, his eyes taking possession of my face as we came up. "I told you they'd be back." He was talking to Jack but looking only at me.

"So what do you think of the game?" he asked.

I shrugged my shoulders. "It's like all football games," I said. "I don't know what's going on."

"You don't understand football?" Brad said, acting surprised. "All right, I'm going to explain it to you. Brad's going to teach you about football." He draped his arm around my shoulders, to give us privacy. "Now," he began. He dropped his head down, close, next to mine. I could smell his hair.

I didn't know what Jack and Karen were doing. I was watching Brad's black eyes, and he was watching me. I don't know what he said about football.

We were back a little late after halftime, sliding into our seats just after the kickoff.

"Sorry," Karen said, but her mother just smiled at her and turned back to the game. Mr. McArdle had the silver beaker in his hand, and it was freshly beaded with chilly drops. He had become more animated, and he had things to say to the players.

"You're a bum!" he called after the ball appeared again and vanished. He said to the crowd around him, "He's a bum! He can't catch!" The crowd seemed uninterested in him; everyone had their own points of view, and they all seemed more animated now. The afternoon was drawing down, the shadows were beginning to spread in long liquid pools across the field. The wind was picking up, a sharp chilly presence against our faces. Brad and Jack had offered us drinks from the bottles they carried; Karen and I had each taken a daring sip. It was bourbon, they said: I felt a quick burning shock in the back of my throat. In the stadium, Mr. McArdle kept the thermos at his feet. He took sips from the beaker, and periodically he refilled it from the thermos. When someone ran down the field, Mr. McArdle raised the beaker in the air, his arm stretched up straight in stiff salute.

Yale won hugely. It was a rout, just as Mr. McArdle had feared. As the game drew to an end, as the irrational clock on the big board went into its last mystifying revolution, the crowd grew more and more excited, in a loose, unfocused way. It no longer seemed as though anyone cared about the score or the play, only about the idea of the game, and its ending. That idea had taken over the whole stadium, and everyone seemed to be drawn into this swift rushing current. As the clock ticked backward toward zero, a hum of response mounted, voices chanted with it, and when the clock finally stood at 0:00, a big roar rose up from the stands. People began to swarm out onto the torn-up field, a loose swirling crowd, apparently in a hurry, for some reason, though there was nowhere for them to get to.

We did not hurry. We folded our blankets and gathered our things together, and finally we stood to leave. By then everyone was standing, but no one was moving, the exits were clogged. Karen and I stood, waiting, impatient though not showing it. Brad and Jack were going to meet us at the bottom of the stairs and walk us back to the car.

"God," Karen said, rubbing the side of her nose with distaste. "These people are *not moving.*"

I said nothing. I didn't want to draw dangerous attention to our impatience. It seemed to me that anyone would see it for what it was: an illicit longing for an unsanctified rendezvous. I wasn't sure exactly what the McArdle rules were, though I knew how my parents would have felt.

We were standing in single file. Mr. McArdle was behind Karen, and he answered her, though she was not talking to him, really, and was facing away from him.

"You in a hurry, Kar?" he asked.

She did not answer. She rubbed the side of her nose again, looking around the stadium with a neutral gaze.

Mr. McArdle turned to his wife, behind him.

"She in a hurry?" he asked. "She have an engagement?"

Mrs. McArdle shook her head vaguely, not looking at him, and after a moment Mr. McArdle turned back and stood facing Karen again. She still did not look at him. The line began to move, and we shuffled forward.

The boys were waiting for us at the bottom of the staircase. I saw Jack's face, looking up into the crowd. At first I didn't see Brad, and I felt a dip of anxiety. Then I realized that the dark spot next to Jack was the top of Brad's head. He was bending down over something, and I saw his face come tilting swiftly up, something in a paper bag held to his mouth. Then his face went down again. In another moment his face was turned up, like Jack's, to the crowd. They were looking for us. I felt Karen's hand give my ribs a swift pinch, and I nodded. I didn't know what to do, but she took the initiative.

When we grew closer, Karen said casually, "There are our friends."

Her parents said nothing, and I thought they hadn't heard. We moved forward slowly. Brad began to wave comically, his big hand flapping back and forth as though he needed to get our attention. Karen and I gave discreet flips of our hands.

"Who's that?" Mr. McArdle said.

"Those are our friends," Karen said. "I told you. They're from Yale."

"Yalies are bums," Mr. McArdle announced. It was impossible to tell if he were joking, as he had been before the game, or if he were serious. His voice had an edge of angry impatience to it. Karen didn't answer him, and he put his hand on her shoulder from behind. "Find someone from Dartmouth."

"Sam," Mrs. McArdle said, mildly reproving, "Karen doesn't have to find someone from Dartmouth." She sounded amused. "Look, there are the Townsends." She waved at someone further along.

Perhaps Jack thought she was waving at him. He waved now too, expansively. Then Brad waved, in slow motion, his whole body rocking with his gesture, reeling like a robot. And then Jack waved like a puppet, holding his hand up stiffly and flapping his fingers, a fixed grin on his face. I giggled nervously at this display. I didn't know if the McArdles were watching or what they thought of it. Was what we were doing permissible? I could not imagine my own parents allowing it, but then I could not imagine them here at all, inching along in this crowd, my father's white mane towering over everyone, his brow knotted in concentration, and my mother following behind him, her manner vague, and her long skirts catching on the edges of the bleachers. God knew what they'd have brought as a picnic: wheat bran and raisins.

When we were close enough, the boys called out to us by name. We smiled at them, descending the metal stairs in the press of people, but we didn't answer back. "Don't act cheap," my mother would have said. "Don't draw attention to yourself." What my father would have said, his eyes fixed on me, I did not allow myself to imagine.

When we reached the ground, Brad and Jack were there, grinning.

"*Hola,*" Jack said, raising his fisted hand in an exuberant salute.

"Hi, guys," Karen said. Delicately she swept a lock of hair back from her face. "These are my parents." She turned sideways, so that her father now stood face-to-face with the boys. I was surprised to see how short Mr. McArdle was, next to them. He stared hard at them, but his gaze seemed slightly unfocused.

"Mom and Dad," Karen said, "Jack Tompkins and Brad Farlow."

"Hello," Mrs. McArdle said at once, stepping smoothly forward and shaking both their hands. Mr. McArdle stood looking. The boys shook hands, smiling, with Mrs. McArdle. Then Karen, not waiting for her father to speak, stepped ahead, almost brushing Jack's shoulder with hers. I moved over next to Brad.

"We'll meet you at the car," Karen said to her mother, and I saw her mother nod. Her father was now looking at Karen in that same focused but unfocused way, and his mouth was set in a belligerent line. He looked as if he were about to speak, but we didn't wait to hear him.

We headed into the crush of the crowd. Brad put his hand under my elbow to steer me. I felt his fingers close tightly around my flesh, exquisitely warm, proprietary, cherishing, steady. He leaned close to me, from behind, and spoke into my ear.

"So what did you think of the game?" he asked, as he had earlier. His breath was tickling, invasive, and I ducked my head.

"Well, you won," I said.

Brad squeezed my elbow. "Of course *we won*," he said. "Of course we *won*. Dartmouth," he said, "couldn't come out on top in its own wet dream." His voice was loud and euphoric, and I felt a tiny jolt of shock and excitement, to hear that kind of talk out in the open. This was the world I'd been looking for—wild, unpredictable, dangerous in an unnamed way. Brad steered me through the crowd, his hand firm and manly. I felt taken care of, taken charge of, on my way to some unknown and adult destination. I didn't know where we were going; I hoped Karen knew where the parking lot was. The crowd was thick around us, everyone pressing mindlessly ahead. Once I hung suddenly back, to avoid running into the man ahead of me, and Brad's grip tightened on me deliciously.

The boys took us across another field, which they said was a shortcut. We stopped behind one of the athletic buildings and leaned against the brick wall, and the boys took their bottles out of the paper bags and offered us more swallows. I leaned my head boldly back, all the way. The bourbon tasted hot again.

"Woof!" Brad said, watching me. "Go, baby!"

Karen took only a small sip, as though she were merely being polite. We stood and talked, and I watched Brad's dark eyes, the way they fixed on mine. They seemed electric, brazen, filled with some kind of power. How did he dare do that, stare straight into me? It was wonderful. Emboldened, I stared straight back. He was leaning close to me, I could feel how close his whole body was. I could feel the rough grid of the bricks against my back.

Karen pinched me in the ribs again, through the thick wool of my suit jacket.

"We have to go," she said, "they'll get mad."

"Okay," I said, though I did not turn to her.

Brad was smiling at me and talking in a low voice. "I can't believe how shiny your hair is," he said. He sounded truly amazed, and I felt proud: all that preparation was paying off.

And he was right: my hair was, I knew, shiny. It was the cream rinse.

But Karen was pushing at me. "We have to go," she said again.

"Okay," I said again. Karen turned to Brad.

"We're leaving," she said. "We have to meet my parents."

"We'll walk you over," Jack offered.

The four of us moved again through the crowd, now thinning. Brad's hand was on my elbow again, and I hung back deliberately, to feel its presence. Karen and Jack, I saw, walked separately from each other; she was ahead, moving fast.

When we reached the parking field, the car was the last one left in the row. The field was mostly empty, green again, and from the long slanting of the light we could suddenly see that it was late. Mr. McArdle was leaning against the car, his arms crossed on his chest. Mrs. McArdle was inside, in the passenger seat. Mr. McArdle watched us as we approached.

"Hi," Karen said as we came up to them. Her father stared at her.

"Where have you been?" he asked.

Karen waved behind her. "We were walking around with our friends."

Her father stared at her stonily. "Why were you doing that?"

"Daddy, we were just *talking*," Karen said. The boys were still holding the bottles in the crumpled paper bags. I had slid my elbow out of Brad's grasp, and now I shifted my weight where I stood, so that there was a discernible distance between us. Mrs. McArdle got out of the car and started around to where we were.

"Why did you go off, knowing that your mother and I were here waiting for you?" Mr. McArdle asked. At the end of each sentence his mouth closed like a bulldog's, the lips turned down, the lower jaw thrust forward. He did not look once at the boys.

Karen rolled her eyes, but carefully, and one corner of her

mouth hitched up in exasperation. "Daddy, don't make such a big deal out of it," she said.

"I'LL DECIDE WHAT I MAKE A BIG DEAL OUT OF," her father suddenly shouted. A car in a nearby row started up and drove away, leaving us more alone in the field.

Mrs. McArdle had reached her husband. "Now, Sam," she said, coming next to him, "this isn't actually so terrible." She put her hand on his sleeve, but he pulled his arm away from her with a tearing motion.

"You think it's fine that Karen goes off for the whole afternoon with these clowns?" he demanded. His voice was still raised, his eyes were still on Karen. He had not once looked at the boys, and not once at me.

"Clowns?" Brad spoke up, and my heart sank. There was a hostile pause. "I don't think that's very correct nomenclature, sir," he said belligerently. "I would call that significantly rude, myself." He had trouble with some of the syllables in *significantly*, but he kept going.

Mr. McArdle stood up straight and took a step toward him. He moved almost eagerly. "I don't think I was talking to you, was I," he said to Brad. There was a pause. "Was I."

"*Daddy*," Karen said, and he swung around on her.

"I was talking to *you*," he said, his chin pushing out. "I was asking you where you have been, all afternoon, with these clowns."

Now Jack spoke up, allying himself with Brad. "I don't think you're anyone to call us clowns," he said insultingly.

Mr. McArdle now seemed to jump forward. His hands had turned into small pale fists that were held up in front of his chest. His chin thrust stiffly out, he said angrily, "What's that?" He was leaning strangely forward as though he were in a strong wind, and then he moved sickeningly toward Brad, whose heavy shoulders towered over him. It was terrible to see the two bodies so close. Brad stepped forward, too, and at the same time Mrs. McArdle moved toward her husband. But it was Karen who reached her father first.

"*Daddy,*" she said again, and from her voice you could hear that she was beginning to break. She rushed straight into him, pushing against his chest. He never looked at her, his little fists still raised at Brad. He twisted sideways, dodging away from her, and ran again at Brad. Brad was leaning forward, and his own hands were now raised, made into fists. Mrs. McArdle put herself in between the two men; Jack was to one side, outraged, uncertain.

"*Stop it,*" said Mrs. McArdle, her voice high, and Karen closed in again, pushing with both hands on her father's narrow chest. Her father seemed now unbearably small, his limbs shrunken with age, next to Brad, his ruddy, glowing body.

"Stop it, Daddy, stop it." Karen was crying and grappling with her father, who was pushing at her arms. She turned to the two boys. "*Get out of here,*" she cried, "*leave him alone.*"

But Mr. McArdle had somehow gotten too close to Brad, and had touched him or shoved him, and now Brad surged dangerously on the other side of Karen.

"Who are you calling clown, old man?" he said.

"*Get out of here,*" Karen cried again, her voice deep and breaking. "Daddy, stop it. Stop it, Daddy."

Mrs. McArdle, too, stepped in between the two men, and though Mr. McArdle bobbed between them, trying to shake them off like a bear with terriers, they would not let him pass. They kept pushing at him, blocking him, and Karen was now weeping loudly, the sobs coming up in her chest, as her father glared furiously past them at the two boys.

"Old man!" Brad jeered, again. Now he was leaning heavily forward too, his head lowered, his fists ready. His tie swung loose in the air.

I stood there motionless, in my bright wool suit.

I could not imagine what to do: all this was my fault. It had been my fault from the start. It was I who had first spoken to Brad, I who had let my elbow stay in the grasp of his hand, I who had taken the biggest swigs from the bottle, I who had ignored Karen's signal to leave. I could not bear to imagine my father when he heard how I had behaved: the way his face would fill with contempt, the way his eyebrows would lower and knit, the way his mouth would draw down at the corners with distaste, the way his eyes would rest on me with blame.

And I could see that I had not understood anything. About what the McArdles were like, about my reading of the simple message of their family, their voices lifted before the meal. I could see that I knew nothing about the larger, seductive world, or what boys and men were really like. I knew now that they held in them something frightening: unstoppable violence, rage and hostility, belligerence.

But I could also see that the same unnamed thing—what I felt when I saw my father sweep his hair despairingly away from his face, what I felt when I saw his anguished black brushstrokes— was there in the rest of the world, the world I had thought was so normal and so calm. It was right here, right now, I could feel it in the terrible sound of the boys calling Mr. McArdle *old man,* in the sight of his pale little fists held up against his chest. It was in the feeling that came over me as we stood there on the abandoned field, covered with long blue shadows and the chill of late afternoon.

I could see that Karen and Mrs. McArdle pushing and pulling, Mr. McArdle struggling fiercely against them, was another kind of harmonizing, that they were each taking parts in their own dark, sad, private melody, and I could see that Karen was caught up in the same net of intimacy and pain that held me to my father.

I saw that I had had no idea of what a family was, really, or what the normal world was like. I could see now that it was much larger than I had imagined, more complicated; that it was more dangerous and beautiful, that it was immanent with love and sorrow.

Pilgrimage

Who knows how these things start? An idea comes over you, it casts a spell. You find yourself in the grip of a passion, something private and secretive, one which you would not happily admit to, over which you have no control.

I don't remember when I first heard the name Madeleine Castaing. I think it was years ago, from a decorator friend. He told me that she was a legendary French antiques dealer, with an extraordinary eye. Her shop was on the Left Bank, and famously eccentric. So, apparently, was she: she wore a thick dead-brown wig, which was tied with a string under her chin. No one mentioned this, he said.

But she didn't interest me then. I didn't go often to Paris, and anyway, my decorator friend knew a lot of grand people who meant little to me. I saw an article, later, that showed her in the famous wig and in the legendary shop, but still I wasn't smitten. Still later, I read that she'd died, and that the eccentric shop was still there, on a narrow street near the Seine.

Then what happened? Somehow, Madeleine Castaing started

slowly to infiltrate my consciousness. I began to read about her whenever I saw her name. I began to pore over photographs. I tried to understand her aesthetic, I tried to catch a furtive glimpse of the string under her chin. She had a strong, handsome face, dark eyes, wide mouth, and a commanding manner. Her taste was, apparently, unlike anyone else's and was always described by the writers in worshipful but imprecise language. It seemed that her style was ineffable, it was somehow in a realm beyond the power of words: I was more and more intrigued. Castaing began to seem like a character out of Henry James, the mysterious Madame Merle, perhaps—elegant, imperious, and unknowable, the possessor of certain shadowy secrets that were never to be shared. I became entranced by Madeleine Castaing, by everything about her.

So, when my husband said he had to go to Paris on business and asked if I'd like to go, I did. I told him that there was an antiques shop I wanted to visit. I tried awkwardly to explain my fascination; I told him about the legend, the brown wig tied under the owner's chin. But what sort of things are in the shop? he asked. I tried to remember the photographs, though I could only summon up the atmosphere: somber, raffinée, and slightly decadent. But what had it *looked* like? I didn't know, I admitted, but I was certain it was fabulous: charming, outrageous, and incredibly sophisticated.

Before I left, I'd meant to get the shop's address. By then my own friend had died, too, but his business was being run by his daughter. I meant to ask her, but I forgot. Actually, I didn't think it would matter: Castaing was famous. Our hotel was in the same quartier, and I'd get the address from them. By now, my mind was so imbued with the idea of Madeleine Castaing's breathtaking, spellbinding presence that I assumed everyone else's was as well.

At our hotel, I asked the pleasant concierge for the address. "*Comment?*" she asked. "How do you spell it?"

I wrote it down. She frowned and pulled out the directory.
After a moment she looked up and shook her head.

"No Madeleine Castaing," she said.

I stared at her. "No Madeleine Castaing?" It was not possible.

"No. But there is a Madeleine SomebodyElse, and a Frédéric
Castaing. Would you like their addresses?"

"Would you give me the Frédéric?" Perhaps it was a relative,
running the shop.

The address was not too far off, in the Rue de Fürstemberg.
I took my *Indispensable* and set out on the cobbled streets. But
the Rue de Fürstemberg was elusive, and for nearly an hour I
toiled up and down the narrow cobbled streets of the Left Bank,
searching for it. When I finally found the street, I discovered
that the shop owners had discreetly declined to display their
numbers. Now footsore, I walked up and down, too shy to go
in and ask. Finally I deduced which was number three: a brand-
new and very modern fabric house. There was no Castaing. I
couldn't believe it. My search was at an end. My pilgrimage had
failed.

Back at the hotel I told my husband. "I should have gotten
the address before we left," I said ruefully.

"Well, it may be out of business by now," he said. "It may
have closed."

"It must have closed," I said. "I should have gone when I
first heard about her. I should have gone years ago. Now she's
dead and the shop's closed." Now the shop seemed to me like
the most important place in Paris, dense and fumy with the rich
ethers of Madeleine Castaing's existence. I couldn't believe my
foolishness. I'd missed it, I'd missed my visit to the shrine, out
of sheer carelessness.

The next afternoon, my husband and I set out for a lecture
at the Louvre. On a narrow street near the Seine we saw a small

shop with a slightly shabby white awning, bearing the discreet black initials "MC."

"Look," I said, grabbing his arm. "Do you think it might be? It's the right neighborhood. The right initials." We peered through the window into a dim room, full of furniture.

"Let's go in," my husband said.

We were greeted by a pleasant blond woman of a certain age, wearing a sleek sweater and skirt. She had a pointed nose and humorous eyes; she was elegant but not icy.

"*Bonjour,*" she said, smiling at us.

"*Bonjour,*" I said and asked, in my best French, the name of the shop.

"Madeleine Castaing," the woman said.

I could hardly speak. "It is?"

I explained my journey, my attempts to find it, my disappointment.

The woman shook her head, smiling. "No, it has never been in the telephone book. I don't know why, but that's the way it is."

Frédéric, she explained, was the son. He was on the Rue de Fürstemberg, but upstairs. And he sold autographs, not antiques. This explained the confusion, though none of it mattered now. I was here, at the shrine.

I stared at the room, trying to absorb it, to memorize it. The walls were faded green, pale apple green, with a black classical frieze beneath the ceiling. The paint was unapologetically peeling off in many places. Near the door was a small card table covered in bottle green baize. Its legs were made of antlers; on the baize were five or six cards, faces up, glued to the fabric. On the table was a lamp with a deep green glass shade, slightly askew. Small exquisite painted chairs stood about the black-patterned carpet.

"Would you like to see upstairs?" the woman asked.

"Yes," I breathed, "please."

With a smile and a tilt of the head, the woman led the way up a tiny curving staircase carpeted in black plaid, a bit tattered. At the top of the stairs were two tiny rooms, a salon and a bedroom.

"These were hers," said the woman. "This was where she lived."

Where she lived!

By now you would think that for my whole life I had thought only of Madeleine Castaing, that I had spent years and years studying her. There was nothing else in my head. It was like being on some powerful, dangerous, chemical rush: I was alone with my obsession. I was overwhelmed by the atmosphere, by the mesmerizing sense of her rich and complex presence. Standing in the inner sanctum, I was rapt, staring at the tiny spaces full of extraordinary objects, trying to memorize it all.

What did she have? What were the objects? It's hard to say. There was some Regency bamboo furniture, some lacquered things, some inlaid mother-of-pearl, some tortoiseshell. A small black shoemaker's last, very elegant. Many black things, all very elegant and many of them rather battered, which lent them great fascination. There was something about her eye. There was something about the juxtaposition of all these objects that made them, together, brilliant. I had never seen such sophisticated taste. It was beyond me. I was humbled, and even more adoring. I could never have seen these things, separately, and known to bring them together like this. I could not have done it.

The bedroom was tiny. There was a minuscule low bed, with white lace hangings and a white crocheted spread. A small silver dressing table stood against the wall, holding an odd assortment of things, some ivory, some silver. The curtains were tacked up, literally, with thumbtacks. Everything was falling to bits, everything was astonishingly chic, everything was part of a magically coherent whole. I stared, unable to stop my gaze anywhere, unable to take it all in, unable to make sense of it. I could not speak.

We came back downstairs. There was a photograph on the woman's desk. "That was her," she said, pointing to a beautiful dark-haired young woman, stylish but very natural, leaning against an outdoor wall.

"*Comme elle est jolie,*" I said rapturously.

"And here she is an hour before she died," the woman said, holding up another photograph. There was an elderly woman holding herself very straight, sitting on a bed. She had thick glossy black hair.

"One hour before she died," I repeated. It seemed unlikely, in fact it seemed, really, impossible, but like the wig, this was something that would not be discussed.

"She was so-and-so years old," the woman said.

My numbers are not so good in French, and I often get them wrong. I knew this was a large number, but I hadn't caught what had come after *quatre-vingt,* so I wasn't sure if she'd been in her eighties or her nineties. But I knew it was an impressive age, and I nodded respectfully.

"Not bad," said the blond woman, looking down at the photograph.

"Wonderful," I said, in my best French. "*Une merveille.*"

But my husband and I were late for the lecture.

"I'll come back tomorrow," I promised. "I'm so glad to have found you."

The woman gave me an enchanting smile and a little nod. "We will be waiting for you, madame."

The next afternoon I made my way back through the cobblestone streets to the intersection, wondering if the shop had been an illusion, a place you can find only when you are late and can't stop.

But no. There it was, and inside was the slim blond woman, elegantly erect, arms smoothly folded on her chest.

"*Bonjour, madame,*" she greeted me. She knew me. I was now a person known at Madeleine Castaing, and my posture improved with the responsibility. I began looking around again, trying to drink in the objects. My new friend stood politely near me, and we talked some more. I mentioned my friend the decorator. Had she known him? But of course.

"*Il avait du goût, le pauvre,*" she said.

I agreed, proud. I was now the friend of a man with taste. We were getting along very well.

"You know the shop has been sold," she said.

"This place? No," I breathed. My favorite shop in Paris, sold? It was sacrilege.

"Yes," she said. "We will only be here for two more months."

"This is terrible," I said.

"*C'est dommage,*" she agreed. "We are moving nearby. It is pleasant enough, but it is not the same."

"But the shop will not close," I said, partly mollified.

"No, no," she said. "We will be nearby. Would you like to see the new place? There are things there as well."

Of course I would. She went back to the tiny spiral staircase and spoke down into it. I hadn't noticed yesterday, but it curled downward as well as upward. From somewhere below us a tiny black man appeared, round-faced, graying, with a gap between his two front teeth.

"Auguste, would you show Madame the new shop?" my friend asked. He nodded solemnly, and we set out. The sidewalk was not wide enough for us to walk side by side, and he preceded me. He wore a long green loden coat, with a high back pleat that opened at each step. At the far end of the block he unlocked the door, and we stepped inside. Here again the walls were pale green, with painted friezes, but the ceilings were higher, and the feeling grander and colder. Again I tried to memorize the furniture; again I could not. There was a pair of painted bookcases, with much of the decoration rubbed off. A metal clip-on lamp was clipped carelessly onto one of them, rubbing off more paint. I found everything enchanting. I looked around and around, turning in distracted circles. The tiny black man in his loden coat politely did not watch me.

"*Merci,*" I said finally. He nodded, and we paraded back down the sidewalk to the first shop, the true source of Madeleine Castaing, which would be irrevocably lost in two months. By now I was determined to buy something from it, a single object, no matter how small.

In the shop again I began hunting.

What I was actually, vaguely, looking for was a pair of big carved wooden candlesticks. I had never seen these in reality, and had no clear picture of them, but I was confident that I would one day find them. Or something like them: anyway I wanted a pair of objects for the mantelpiece. There was nothing like them here; heavy carved objects were not Madeleine Castaing's style, and looking at these arcane and deeply sophisticated things, I became embarrassed at even having considered something so gauche as heavy carved wooden candlesticks. How could I have? I would have to educate my eye. I looked from object to object. My new blond friend stood quietly nearby, smiling.

In the window was a pair of small black vases.

"Could I see those?" I asked.

But of course. My friend took them out and held them up for me. They were black ceramic, neoclassical. The handles were swans, sleek and supple, the long slim beaks just touching the rims. I held one. It was smooth, a bit battered; small chips showed a reddish glaze under the black.

"Could you tell me the price?" I asked.

She could.

I did the conversion from francs: somewhere between three and four hundred dollars, a bit closer to four.

"What can you tell me about them?" I asked Madame, turning one upside down.

"Absolutely nothing," she said with amused pride, shaking her head. "We know nothing about them at all."

Here was a challenge. There were no words to surround and bolster up the idea of the vases. There was no connection to a period, a studio, an artist, even a country. There was no date, no provenance, nothing to support the price but the look, the infallible eye of Madame Castaing. I turned the vase over and over, trying to come up with a logical base for a decision. They weren't what I was looking for; I wasn't even sure that they were big enough for the space. But they were objects from The Shop, the real one, before it moved. And then they were elegant in a deeply sophisticated way, they were chic, subtle, charming. These would be the Madeleine Castaing vases, triumphant evidence of the pilgrimage. "Oh, I bought those from the old shop," I would say, "before it moved. It's all different now."

There is no logic to this kind of decision. I could feel myself reeling closer and closer to the edge of the cliff, I could feel the siren call of the abyss. I ran my hand over the urn, as though this would somehow help me. The abyss sang to me; I understood that I could not resist; I felt myself stagger, beginning to fall.

"I'll take them," I said to my friend, and as she heard the words she gave me a smile I had never before seen on a French face.

"I will miss them," she said in a dégagé way, "but I am glad you will be giving them a good home." We were friends, now, for life: I was adopting her children.

"I will," I promised happily. I looked at the vases now with the fond tenderness of ownership.

I began to wonder, belatedly, about customs, about brokers and shipping. "Would it be possible," I asked timidly, "to have them wrapped up so that I could carry them home myself?"

"*Oui, oui, ma chérie, il sera possible,*" my blond friend

said, teasing and comforting. She ticked her way back to the tiny snail-shell staircase, where she thumped on the floor with a walking stick. "Auguste!" she called, and my tiny guide appeared again, rising up from the depths like Erda. "Could you wrap these vases up for Madame?"

He disappeared again and reemerged with a translucent load of Bubble Wrap. I stood glowing, the vases on the desk before me, now mine. Auguste took out a sheet of wrap and began painstakingly to shroud the first vase. It disappeared into the opaque blanket, and he turned the bundle this way and that, sealing it carefully with tape.

I watched him with anxious satisfaction, pleased, with the golden proprietary rush that ownership brings, but already worrying that I had made some profound mistake. A nervous buyer, I began to wonder now if my husband would like these. I wondered if I would have to pay duty on them. Suddenly I felt a cold grip in my insides: *the numbers.* I swallowed. The thought I had was too terrifying to consider, but too terrifying to ignore.

"Attendez un instant, s'il vous plaît, monsieur," I said to Auguste, who stopped moving like a clockwork toy, one hand raised in the air, holding up the sheet of bubble.

"Madame," I said, "I am worried about the arithmetic, if I perhaps have made an error. I wonder if you could find out the exact number of the conversion to dollars. Could you give me the exact figure? Do you have a machine?"

Madame had a machine, but it did not work. A friend of hers, glossy-haired and bored, had come in. She sat next to the desk, leafing through a densely illustrated magazine, paying no attention to us. Madame sat down at her desk, stabbing with her long nails at her tiny computer.

"Ça ne marche pas," she said with irritation to her friend. Her friend looked at the machine, pursed her lips, raised her eyebrows, and turned once more to the magazine.

Madame said to me, "I'll call the bank for the right rate." She dialed a number. I waited nervously.

I knew I had done the conversion right, multiplied by the right number; what worried me was the zeros. I was afraid I had left one off. It was a thought so terrifying that I could hardly admit it. My heart was thudding as I waited for Madame to reach the bank. My error was one of such profound stupidity that I could not reveal it to this new friend, who was so fond of me and who had, up to now, such a high opinion of my taste and intelligence.

"*Bonjour, monsieur,*" Madame rattled pleasantly into the telephone. She delivered the price and explained her request. She waited; she listened. She thanked him at machine gun speed and hung up. She turned to me. "Oui, madame, it's just what I told you before." In French she repeated the number she had given me earlier. We had gotten nowhere.

"But could you write down the number in dollars?" I asked pathetically.

She stared at me for a moment and then gave a disgusted click. "But I forgot to write it down," she said and sat down to call the bank back. I looked at Auguste. His eyes were on Madame, his hand still raised, holding the sheet of frozen air.

"*Bonjour, monsieur,*" my friend rattled off again. She listened again and this time carefully set down the numbers on a scrap of paper. "*Merci, monsieur,*" she said crisply. "*Au revoir.*"

Smiling, she handed me the scrap of paper. My heart now thundering, I read the number. There it was: thirty-four hundred dollars for a pair of terra-cotta vases of unknown origin and unknown date, probably twentieth-century, chipped and scraped and battered. In fact, it wouldn't have mattered if they'd been handmade by Marie Antoinette, I couldn't afford them. I swallowed hard. My heart was by now making nearly too much noise for me to talk over it.

"Madame," I announced, "I have made a mistake. I made

the conversion wrong." I couldn't admit to the missing zero. "I will have to discuss this with my husband." While I spoke I kept my chin lifted and my back very straight, hoping that she would still see me as a person of substance, someone who might very well go off and discuss a pair of thirty-four-hundred-dollar vases with her husband and come back later and buy them.

But my new friend was smarter than that, and besides, she was no longer my friend. As she heard me speak, her face froze. Warmth drained from the landscape as in a nature film. Winter appeared, spreading suddenly and completely across the countryside; the air chilled, and ice settled in for the season. Auguste silently lowered his hand. He began methodically unwrapping the vase.

"*Merci beaucoup, madame,*" I said determinedly, my chin high. "*Au revoir.*"

"*Au revoir, madame,*" the blond woman said, her back to me, already on her way to her desk where her friend waited, flipping through the pages of her magazine.

Passing Auguste, who was pulling the long roll of wrapping off the vase, and who did not look up, I made my way in disgrace to the door. I looked at nothing in passing. I pushed open the door and stepped out onto the street. I hurried down the narrow sidewalk toward the hotel and the pleasant concierge, my pulse racing, my heart hammering, as though I had just barely escaped the whistling rush of the guillotine.

Who knows how these things start? But when they're over, they're over.

A Perfect Stranger

Martha met Michael Kingsley at the station. She was standing on the platform and worrying about recognizing him as the train slid quietly alongside. She had met him only once, at a dinner in London a year ago, and now, when she tried to conjure up his face, she found nothing. A long nose, she thought. Tall, in his seventies, probably gray-haired. What else? Would there be more than one man like that on the train? Should she have told him she'd wear a red rose? Should she never have gotten herself into this in the first place—inviting a perfect stranger for the weekend? Jeffrey, who had opposed it from the start, would feel no sympathy for her now.

It was midafternoon, well before the commuter rush—Jeffrey would not be home for hours—and the train was not full. Martha saw her guest in the lighted car before the train came to a halt. He was standing in the aisle, very erect, and tall, a head and a half above the man in front of him. His huge eagle's beak was in profile. *Of course*, she thought, *the nose*. He was balding and graying, with a noble dome and regal posture. He wore a tan raincoat and was frowning deeply, his great bristly brows knitted. When he stepped off the train, Martha was before him.

"*Mister* Kingsley," she said, smiling, holding out her hand. She made the name sound like a joke; she wasn't quite ready to call him Michael. Though as she said it she suddenly worried: was he actually *Lord* Kingsley? Or Sir Michael? There was a title somewhere in his family. She should have asked someone on the committee what to call him—had she just insulted him?

His face cleared into a smile. "Oh, you're Martha, aren't you," he said cordially and seized her hand. "You *are* kind, to come all the way out onto the platform." A huge soft suitcase weighed him down on one side, and his tall thin body listed heavily to the left.

Martha wondered about suitcase-carrying protocol: she was strong, and thirty years younger than he, but a woman. He was elderly, and quite rickety-looking, but a man. Should she offer to carry his suitcase? Would it offend him if she did? Would he have a heart attack if she didn't?

"Can I help you with your bag?" she asked tentatively.

"Oh, no," he replied, giving a short high whinny of amusement. She could hear him puffing as they walked along.

On the way home she took the narrow dirt road that crossed the reservoir, instead of the paved road parallel to it. Martha always took guests this way, which was cheating, really. It made their neighborhood look like wilderness: the wide untouched water, the woods coming right down to the edge. Everyone exclaimed over it.

"Goodness, how pretty this is," Kingsley said, as the car pulled out onto the causeway. "I had no idea we'd be so far out in the country here. I'd have thought an hour from New York would mean the thick of the suburbs."

"It is nice, isn't it," said Martha, pleased. She added snobbishly, "We don't, actually, like that word."

"But why not? I think Americans do suburbs *remarkably*

well," said Kingsley. "I gave a talk on *Turandot* last year in
Chicago and stayed in a place called, I think, Forest Lake? It had
beautiful brick houses and enormous old trees. I thought it was
perfectly lovely."

"Oh, yes," murmured Martha, who thought those big,
dressed-up manor houses on small lots were pretentious.

"But I shouldn't call these suburbs," Kingsley went on, looking out the window. Near the dam was a pair of black-faced
swans, motionless on the water, pale and mysterious in the gray
light. "I should call this country," he said generously.

"We like to think of it that way," Martha said, pleased again.

Beyond the reservoir they had to cross the main road, a fast
east-west thoroughfare full of kamikaze vehicles tailgating each
other at high speed. Martha hoped Kingsley would not notice
the intersection; beyond it they were back on another dirt road.

She wanted the weekend to go well. She'd only recently
begun volunteering for the Music Festival, and this was her
maiden venture. She'd been put on the Lectures Committee but
somehow had fallen afoul of its head, Jean Singer. Jean disliked
her, and at meetings she frowned impatiently whenever Martha
spoke, resisting all her suggestions. When Martha had offered to
put Kingsley up for the weekend, Jean looked around the table.
"Any other offers?" she asked and waited. When no one else answered, Jean turned to Martha, her mouth pursed. "It looks as
though you're our hostess," she said and added rudely, smiling,
"Are you equipped?"

Martha was determined that the visit would be a success, de-
spite Jeffrey's reservations and Jean's misgivings. In fact these
spurred her on: she was determined that the weekend would be
flawless, a pleasure for everyone.

"What a nice house," Kingsley said, as they came up the
driveway. "This is what you call 'clap-board,' isn't it."

The guest room was on the third floor, and Martha wondered again about carrying his suitcase. Wouldn't it simply be polite? She was the hostess, after all.

"Let me take that for you," she said in a firmer voice as they got out of the car, but Kingsley refused to yield.

"I have it," he said.

Going up the second flight of stairs, she could hear his breathing. Perhaps the nose acted as an amplifier; they were very long breaths.

He had worried that he would not recognize her on the platform. It was one reason he had taken an early train, so there would be fewer strange women to choose among. Perhaps he should have asked her to wear a red rose, though he didn't really know her well enough. Sense of humor was the last thing you understood about foreigners, and Americans were especially tricky. He hardly knew this woman; he had met her only once, at that dinner at the Ward-Jacksons'. He thought he remembered her as pleasant-looking, though perhaps with too small a nose? Silky straight colorless hair, like a child's; he could not remember her face. He did remember they had talked about Nabokov. He had been pleased to discover she was a reader, though her ideas were peculiar. She smiled too much, as Americans do, but he didn't mind that. He liked Americans: their energy, their profound and rather childish earnestness. He liked the things about America that Americans themselves seemed to despise: the huge shopping malls, like Oriental treasure troves; the car washes, fast and steamy and meticulous; the wonderful roads, wide, smooth, perfectly maintained. He liked the self-confidence of Americans, their boundless belief in the possibilities of achievement, their intuitive grasp of technology, their generosity. He liked the glitter and swing of their cities, the brutal hardness of their sidewalks, the punishing speed of the walking pace in New York. The speed everywhere. And their easy openness: it was so kind of Martha and her husband—was it Geoffrey?—to invite him, a virtual stranger, to stay. He never knew, when he was invited to give an opera talk, whether he'd be put up in a hotel or in someone's house. He generally preferred the house, he liked meeting new people.

When Martha slowed the car to cross the reservoir, Kingsley understood that he was meant to admire the view. It was bleak. The woods were still winter brown and gray, the sky and water without hue. Two evil-tempered swans hung about the spillway.

"Ah," he said, after they scuttled perilously across a rocketing stream of traffic and onto another unpaved track, "another dirt lane."

"Yes," Martha said happily. "We're very proud of these. The town tried to pave them, years ago, but some local women came out and lay down in front of the bulldozers, and they had to stop."

Kingsley pictured the confrontation: courageous women in corduroy trousers and silver-buttoned loden jackets, neat curled hair, stretched bravely out in the mud. Had they closed their eyes, he wondered, as the bulldozers thundered above them? Sung hymns?

It was strange the way Americans felt about unpaved lanes. In his own Suffolk village everything was paved except the farm tracks. The narrowest country lanes, set deep between ancient, towering hedgerows, were paved. The point of paving was that it improved roads, made them traversable. This American notion of keeping them muddy and rutted was wholly eccentric.

He wondered about his lecture. He had several talks on *Tosca,* at various levels of sophistication. The Music Festival here was well-known, so the audience ought to be reasonably knowledgeable. Still, he must ask his hostess what she thought. It was terrible to put people visibly to sleep, which he had done.

He hoped she wouldn't try to seize his suitcase again; it was disheartening. Did he look so decrepit as not to be able to carry his own luggage? He couldn't remember how he looked, actually, his face now so familiar, so much a part of his surroundings that he could hardly see it. It was like looking at his own kitchen shelves, trying to assess them. There was the mottled, balding dome, rising higher each year from the graying thicket that surrounded it; there were the deep creases to the corners of the wide thin mouth, the flat swags of skin below his eyes, the wild luxuriant eyebrows. The vitality that used to pulse elsewhere through his body seemed to have been diverted into other channels; it now animated his hair. Not the hair on top of his head, which was lank and spiritless and mostly gone, but the odd patches of ancillary hair, once meek and inconspicuous. Now these sprouted fiercely: his eyebrows, the insides of his ears, his nostrils—all were coarse and bushy gray tangles. Did he look old? Presumably, but how old? Did he look feeble? He was still quite tall, surely that counted for something?

The house was pleasant, and old by American standards. Odd that so many American houses were made of wood, though of course, America was a vast young country. A hundred years ago, when this house had been built, the great forests here had still been standing. In England the great forests had been cut down five hundred years earlier, and the wooden houses from those days had long ago burned down. In his part of Suffolk, houses had been made from rose-colored brick for the last three centuries.

Two dogs came out of the house to greet them, tails swaying gently: Labradors, of course. All Americans seemed to have black Labradors or golden retrievers. Perhaps there was an embargo on other breeds; perhaps they had a longer quarantine. Or did Americans not have a dog quarantine? He could not remember. There were so many things the English shared with Americans, so many things here that felt familiar, and then these inexplicable lacunae appeared—the reckless allowance of rabid animals to drift in and out of the country, for example.

"Good dog, good dog," Martha crooned, shooing their noses away from his crotch. "That's Artemis, and that's Apollo." She pointed. "Say hello," she told the dogs. The dogs wagged indiscriminately.

Kingsley's father had kept pointers, for shooting; light-limbed, excitable dogs, with pale-rimmed eyes. Kingsley himself hadn't had a dog since his wife died, eight years ago; her ancient dog had only briefly survived her. It had been a Norfolk terrier called Jackal, a bright-eyed irritable creature who slept on the bed between them and bit Kingsley periodically on the leg. Kingsley used to call the dog a Norfolk terrorist, long after, his wife told him, it was amusing.

"Lovely," Kingsley murmured now at the aimless dogs. He wondered which floor he would be staying on; the house was tall.

"You're on the third floor," Martha said apologetically. They had come in through the kitchen, and she showed him up the back stairs. "Let me take your suitcase."

He shielded it from her determinedly and labored up the two flights behind her. He could hear his panting breaths in the narrow stairwell and coughed, to disguise them.

"Only one more flight," Martha said, anxious.

Martha heard him now not only panting but coughing, and she hoped he wouldn't fall right there on the stairs. What did you actually do in CPR? Besides leaning heavily on the chest of, and placing your open mouth on, that of a perfect stranger. She had once taken a course: there was an acronym about how to begin. FISH, perhaps, but what did it mean? Was it about airways? She did not want to think of what Jeffrey would say—not to mention the Lectures Committee at the Music Festival—if Kingsley were to have a heart attack right there in their house.

"Well, here we are," she said, looking around. The guest room, long and narrow, high up under the eaves, which she thought of as airy and charming, seemed suddenly dark and small. The white curtains had yellowed, she saw now, and hung limply. The space was nearly filled by Kingsley's craggy height.

"What a nice room," he said happily.

It was totally private, with its own bath. Americans were good about private baths, and their plumbing invariably worked. The room itself was pleasant and cottagey, simply furnished, slightly shabby, comfortable.

"Would you like some tea?" Martha asked. "Or a nap? What would you like?"

Alone, Kingsley unpacked. He took out his lecture suit, but there were no free coat hangers for it. The closet seemed to be full of Martha's clothes from the nineteen seventies, and possibly her wedding dress: something long and white and satin, in a plastic garment bag. Kingsley hung his jacket over a magenta-flowered silk blouse and jammed his trousers into a press with a lime green miniskirt. He wondered again about the audience, and if he had brought another pair of socks. Inevitably, when traveling, he forgot something crucial, though when he was laying things out beforehand it seemed as if his entire wardrobe were traveling with him.

His ankle still hurt, giving off a subtle interior throb with each step. It had been like this for some time; he could not remember exactly when it had begun. There were so many murmurs of distress from his body now, a quiet and continual susurration, that it was hard to remember when one voice rose slowly above the others, when it fell, or vanished altogether. He thought the ankle had been hurting for several days; he could remember no knock against it, no collision with chair or wall. Back at home he would go and see the new doctor, the woman. Women doctors were such a good idea, so much nicer than the men. The old doctor, Toland, had asked him suggestive questions which were always veiled rebukes. If Kingsley came in with a cough, Toland would inquire, "Been walking about without your coat?" Then his lips would rise slowly over his yel-

lowed teeth in an unfriendly grin. This new woman—calm and
plump, with short graying hair—was just as good as Toland,
and comforting. After seeing her Kingsley always felt better;
after seeing Toland he had felt guilty and doomed.

Kingsley limped to the bed and lay down. It was only his
ankle, far away from the important things. The brain knows
where it lives. An ankle was remote, negligible. The entire leg
could be jettisoned, if necessary, if the worst had happened, cancer. At his age everything suggested cancer; the droop of an eye-
lid, the first stirrings of nausea in the early dawn, discolored skin
along the back of a hand. Kingsley stretched out on his back and
gazed up at the ceiling. It was wallpapered with small blue
sprigs on white and reminded him of home.

Dinner that night was just the three of them. When Kingsley
came slowly down the narrow back stairs, careful of his ankle,
he found Martha's husband in the kitchen, standing by the stove,
near his wife. Geoffrey was a tall man, bulky, with a long jaw
and shaggy graying hair. He wore thick glasses that magnified his
eyes, making them alarmingly large and fluid. He stepped forward at once to greet Kingsley, his hand held out hospitably.

"I'm Jeffrey Truesdale," he said. "It's so nice to have you
here."

"Very kind of you to have me," Kingsley said, smiling, "a
perfect stranger."

"Not at all," Jeffrey assured him, shaking his head. "Our
pleasure."

They ate in the kitchen, which pleased Kingsley, at a small
square table by the window. The Labs lay sprawled beside them
on dusty green dog beds. Martha served the plates at the stove
and brought them over. It turned out that Geoffrey was a reader,
too, and deep in the middle of a Faulkner biography.

"How is it?" Kingsley asked.

"It's interesting," Jeffrey said, "because Faulkner is interesting. But the writing is dull and academic, and it's too long. *Much* too long."

Kingsley himself preferred long books. He liked something with heft and stamina, a place where he could establish himself, where he could linger and return.

"I've read your Faulkner," he said, nodding, remembering. "Rather wonderful, I thought. So intense. Your American novelists enter into the interior world, don't they, in a way that ours don't."

"Oh, but Virginia Woolf does," Martha said politely.

"Well, yes, she does, it's true," Kingsley said, politely back. He couldn't bear Virginia Woolf, her novels so prissy and tedious, the essays so full of feminist nonsense. But Americans, he knew, loved her.

"I think the trouble is computers," Jeffrey declared. "They've made writing too easy. If writers still had to write on typewriters, or better yet by hand, it would take more effort, and books would be shorter and better." He offered Kingsley the salad bowl.

"Thank you," said Kingsley. He poked discreetly through the salad, trying to find sweet broad leaves of lettuce among the bitter spiky greens Americans seemed to like. He thought of long great books. "What do you think of *Decline and Fall of the Roman Empire?*" he asked. "*Bleak House. War and Peace.* Written by hand, pretty long, and pretty good, wouldn't you say?"

"Exactly," Geoffrey said, pleased. "Those writers were geniuses. They're the ones who should write long books. Those writers were driven by passion, they wrote masterpieces. But nowadays any nitwit can write a long book, and some other nitwit will publish it." Geoffrey beamed at him, his eyes huge and glowing.

"Well, yes, I see what you mean," Kingsley said, not sure that he did. Why weren't unwieldy books the fault of writers and editors, not of computers? It seemed like muddled thinking to him, but tonight his own thinking seemed muddled. He could feel jet lag and exhaustion invading his mind, slowing him down.

Passing the bowl to Martha, Kingsley changed the subject. "Now, there are two things I should very much like to do while I'm here."

"Tell me what they are," Martha said, smiling.

She hoped that the two things would be possible to arrange. She also hoped that Jeffrey would not make any more literary denunciations. She had heard this theory before (actually more than once), and was afraid that Kingsley found it dull. Why else had he changed the subject?

"Number one," Kingsley said, "I'd like to take you both to lunch somewhere agreeable, on Sunday. And then I'd like to see a historic house near here. Is it called Lindmere? A friend from our National Trust told me about it."

"Lyndhurst," Martha said with enthusiasm. She tried to remember where it was: on the Hudson somewhere? "What a good idea. I've never actually been there. And how extremely kind of you, about lunch." "Extremely kind": was she slipping into Anglicisms? She saw Jeffrey give her a look. She was.

Later, in their bedroom, Jeffrey lay under the covers, reading, his long legs stretched out, the ponderous book resting on his chest.

Martha held on to the closet door for balance and kicked off her shoes. "Now, that wasn't so bad, was it?"

"It's only Friday night," Jeffrey said, not looking up from his book.

Martha pulled her sweater up over her head. "Come on," she said, her voice muffled. "He's very pleasant." She freed her head and looked at him. "Admit it."

"He's perfectly pleasant," Jeffrey said, still not looking up. "But he's *here*."

"Well, he had to stay with someone," Martha said. She slid her arms from the sleeves.

"But why with us?"

"I've told you why," Martha said, exasperated. "I thought Kay Bowditch knew him, and that he'd stay with her. I only volunteered as a gesture. Then it turned out Kay didn't know him, and no one else did either, and there I was, having made the offer, and Jean Singer staring at me over her glasses."

"He could have stayed in a hotel." Jeffrey raised his head.

"I told you this too," said Martha. "The committee always puts him up in someone's house, it saves money. But the point is that Michael Kingsley is not only a very nice man but a very distinguished scholar of Italian opera. You're acting as though he's some verminous undesirable who couldn't get through immigration."

"He's a complete stranger," Jeffrey complained. "I'm acting as though you've imposed a complete stranger on me for the weekend."

"Well, there's nothing I can do about it now," said Martha crossly. "Don't take it out on me."

"Who should I take it out on?" asked Jeffrey.

Martha did not answer, walking into the bathroom and firmly closing the door. She was pleased by *verminous* and turned the water on full blast. It was unfair of Jeffrey to complain now, when it was too late to change anything, but she was determined to rise above it. She met her eyes in the mirror, her gaze full of resolution.

Though she had to admit, in the steamy privacy of her bathroom, the mirror slightly flecked with toothpaste, that she was slightly intimidated by Kingsley: by his looming height, his alienating accent, his grand English manner. And she worried that what she was offering—the stuffy guest room with its limp curtains, the meek suburban countryside—was somehow wanting.

"I'm sure it's no fun for him either," Jeffrey said loudly to the closed door and lowered his eyes again to his book.

He opposed houseguests on principle, and he felt ill-used. Martha hadn't consulted him about this, she had simply announced it as a fait accompli. All week long, Jeffrey's days were spent in noise and motion; on the weekends he wanted silence and stillness. He wanted to sit undisturbed in the fat faded brown armchair next to the fireplace, turning the pages of a book without interruption. He wanted no conversation, no schedule, no scrutiny. He wanted no looming stranger's face, no unknown footsteps creaking about overhead, no third presence at the table, no questions throughout the meal. He felt ill-used, and also rather noble, for rising so well to the occasion. Feeling noble fed his sense of aggrievement. He had said all along it was a poor idea, and his wife had ignored him.

When Martha came out of the bathroom he did not look at her, and when he had finished reading he closed his book without speaking. He turned off his light, put on his black eye mask, and settled himself on his back. He lay like a Crusader on his tomb, his arms straight at his sides, his nose in the air, closing himself off to the world.

Upstairs, Kingsley turned out his light at once, ready to sink into sleep. At his age, jet lag was like a deliciously potent medication: sleep had become increasingly fugitive. At home, sometimes he lay awake until one or two o'clock; sometimes he slept at once, earlier, but then woke for the day at three. Sometimes he turned on the light to read, sometimes he simply lay still in the dim room, drifting in and out of the currents of the night, listening to the small sounds of the house as it moved through the long dark hours.

Kingsley wondered again about the audience. He must ask Martha. He thought of the intent look on her face as she had listened to Geoffrey talk: it was a pleasure to be with a couple so visibly happy with each other. He wondered where the dogs slept, and if they would remember him if he went downstairs early, or if they would view him as an intruder and let loose a pandemonium of barks. He could see them now, the two of them standing by the table in the kitchen, wagging their tails and barking; confusingly, they were barking out the Anvil Chorus from *Trovatore*. The room, high up among the tops of the willow trees, with its slanting ceilings and faded flower-sprigged wallpaper, was closing around him, the dogs became distant and silent, Kingsley floated gratefully into the dark current and was gone.

In the morning, Martha had already left their bedroom when Jeffrey awoke; he found her down in the kitchen with Kingsley.

"Good morning," Jeffrey said to Kingsley, bowing his head courteously. "Good morning," he said to Martha, bowing again, more courteously. Martha bowed in response, but she understood his courtesy toward her as ironic and did not answer.

After breakfast, Martha asked Kingsley if he would like to have some time to go over his notes, and he spent a peaceful time alone in the sunny sitting room. Martha worked at her desk; Jeffrey read upstairs.

In the late afternoon they all drove over to the Music Festival. This was held in a faux-Gothic castle built by a rich industrialist in the nineteen twenties. It was a meandering complex of half-timbered buildings, the rooms high-ceilinged and gloomily opulent, full of dim tapestries and elaborate chandeliers. Kingsley's talk was in the huge Music Room, which was Venetian, with gilt stars painted on the deep blue ceiling. It was nearly full.

Kingsley stood on the raised stage, flanked by two enormous black wrought-iron candlesticks, macabrely twisted. He set his hands firmly on either side of the podium, taking hold, and the audience quieted.

"We all love the character of Tosca," Kingsley began forcefully, looking down at them over his glasses. "How could we not? Tosca is beautiful, loyal, and high-spirited. She is moved by passionate love to heights of unimaginable bravery, and she triumphs over one of the greatest villains in the history of theater."

Martha settled into her seat, relieved: she liked it.

"But Tosca," Kingsley declared in his sonorous voice, now letting go of the podium and folding his arms with melancholy finality, "must die." He paused. "In Italian opera, the men are courageous, and the women must die: think of *Tosca, Lucia, Bohème, Butterfly, Otello, Norma, Traviata.*

"This happens not because these women are expendable," he went on, "not because we don't care about them, but the reverse: these women are beyond price. These women are the vessels of our profoundest emotions, they bear the burden of our feelings. We care more about their deaths than we would about the men's, which means that their deaths are more powerful, more dramatic, and more utterly heartbreaking."

Martha looked around surreptitiously. Jeffrey, beside her, and old Mrs. Cort, who was famously difficult, were both frowning deeply, but in an interested way. They looked intent and absorbed. Jean Singer sat two rows behind her; Martha couldn't see her without craning her neck.

Kingsley was going to be a success, and she hoped this would restore her to Jean Singer's good graces. Her guest was going to be a success, and the rest of the evening was out of Martha's hands. After the talk was dinner with the trustees, then the opera itself. Tomorrow would be easy: the Sunday paper, then lunch at the Auberge. Afterward she and Kingsley would drop Jeffrey off at home; she would take Kingsley to Lyndhurst—she'd called, and they were open until five—and then straight on to the train. It was practically over.

She settled in to listen. Kingsley's deep voice and elegant diction were somehow comforting—his Englishness, his accent, his beautiful manners. And she liked what he said about women—their fragility, their vulnerability, their importance. He was right, she thought. Just listening to him, she felt fragile and important. She hoped Jeffrey was paying attention.

After all the congratulations and good nights, late that night, Jeffrey and Martha went into the bedroom, closed the door, and were alone again.

Martha stood by the bureau, unsnapping her bracelet.

"I'm very pleased," she said. She shook her head, smiling. "Very pleased. It went really well. What a relief."

Jeffrey sat down on the chair to take off his shoes.

"Didn't you think?" she asked. She put her bracelet into a saucer on the bureau.

"Didn't I think what?"

Martha looked at him. "Don't you think the evening went well?"

Jeffrey shrugged his shoulders. "Well, opera at a small suburban music festival is not going to match up to the Met," he said. He set his shoes, exactly side by side, next to the chair.

"I didn't say, 'Did you think the performance was as good as one at the Met?'" Martha said, nettled. "Of course it wasn't. What I said was, 'Don't you think the evening went well?'"

Jeffrey stood and began unbuttoning his shirt, his eyes on the carpet. "Went well?" he said judiciously. "Well—ideally, would I have spent an evening watching mediocre opera and having dried-out chicken for dinner, sitting next to a tedious woman who can only talk about her son?" He looked up at her. "Ideally, no."

Martha turned away and stepped out of her heels. She picked them up and put them inside the closet.

"Thanks for your support," she said, taking off her skirt. She snapped it onto a hanger. "It's really great to know I have it."

"Any time," Jeffrey said. He took his shirt off and went into the bathroom. He flung the shirt into the hamper; she heard him slam the wicker lid. He came back into the bedroom and put his hands on his hips. He was wearing only his shorts and his reading glasses, and his eyes were bleary and enormous behind the lenses. "Any time you want to bring around complete strangers, and inflict them on me without asking," he said, "and don't bother to even tell me, beforehand, you'll get this kind of support."

"Jeffrey—" Martha began and then stopped. Kingsley's room was directly overhead, and the acoustics, she knew, were excellent.

"What?" Jeffrey asked, but his wife only pointed venomously at the ceiling and shook her head.

She put on her nightgown and got into bed without speaking, sliding into her side and curling up in a tight ball in her corner. She went to sleep quickly, but in the morning when she awoke she was stiff. She was still curled up tightly, exactly where she'd begun. Jeffrey had slept on the other side of the bed, his face turned toward the window.

Breakfast was quiet. The three of them sat in the kitchen with the paper until it was time to leave for lunch. They took Martha's car—newer and cleaner than Jeffrey's dusty station wagon—and headed north, to a restaurant a dozen miles deeper into the country. The narrow road skirted hillside pastures, where horses in trim plaid blankets stood dozing in the sun; the day had turned bright and cold. Martha drove, pleased by the smooth meadows, the blanketed horses, the wintry sunlight, by the fact that the weekend was all but over.

At the restaurant, she parked the car, took out the key, and dropped it on the floor mat. In the country she always did this, it saved searching later through pockets and bags. Jeffrey, in the back, got out of the car as Martha did. Kingsley, in front, took longer, slowly extricating his legs. Martha and Jeffrey shut their doors and waited as he unfolded himself. Kingsley, finally outside on the gravel, took careful hold of the door handle, pushed down the inside lock, and then, before Martha could speak, firmly closed the door. Martha heard the smooth electronic internal shifting, the sickening sound of all the locks sliding obediently and irretrievably down into their wells. The car was now impenetrable, shut fast, its key neatly inside on the floor. Martha looked at Jeffrey: he had seen it too.

"This looks lovely," Kingsley said cheerfully, gazing around at the bright sky, the big trees. It was hard to walk on the thick gravel without a limp; he moved slowly, to disguise it.

"It's one of our favorite restaurants," Martha said, wondering if the spare key was in her pocketbook. Or was it in the mug over the kitchen sink? "Do you have an extra?" she asked Jeffrey under her breath as they went inside. They were still at odds, but this was an emergency. It superseded their hostilities, or at least she hoped it did.

"To your car?" Jeffrey shook his head. Perhaps it did not.

"*Bonjour, madame, messieurs,*" said the headwaiter. He was bald and smiling, with black eyes. He wore a long white apron wrapped around his waist.

The new car had a special locking system. The salesman had told them with unctuous pride that, without a key, it could be unlocked only by a registered representative of the company. At the time that had seemed like a selling point, but now Martha wondered how they might find a registered representative of the company on Sunday, out in the country, sixty miles north of New York City. They sat down at the table.

"I liked your talk very much," Martha told Kingsley.

"Yes, so did I," said Jeffrey with enthusiasm, unfolding his heavy white napkin with an air of settling in. "It was such an interesting premise. I was completely fascinated."

Under the table Martha groped for her pocketbook and began rifling through it. Blindly her fingers encountered unknown objects, and she closed on them hopefully. A hairbrush bristle stabbed her deep under her fingernail, into the quick, and she winced.

"What about German opera?" Jeffrey asked. "How would you describe the differences between German and Italian opera?"

She wasn't sure if Jeffrey were declaring a truce, taking charge of the conversation so that she could devote herself to the search, or if he were simply being elaborately polite to Kingsley and ignoring her. In either case she was grateful for his participation.

Kingsley began to explain. Under the table he flexed his foot delicately, testing: the throb came at once.

Martha tried to keep her face bright. "Really," she said periodically. "That's interesting," she offered, during a pause. She gave Kingsley a disconnected smile.

"Have you always been interested in opera?" she asked.

What was that, she wondered, as he answered. But it was not the key, it was a fingernail clipper. Why on earth did she have a fingernail clipper in her purse?

"And did you study music at school?" Jeffrey asked.

This could be it, Martha thought, if it were encased in a little plastic sleeve. Hopefully she envisioned the key in a plastic sleeve. It might certainly be. But no: it was a tube of lip gloss. Jeffrey glanced at her as he lifted his glass; she couldn't read his look.

"Actually, at university I read classics," Kingsley said.

"Rather a long way from opera," Martha suggested. She heard herself lapsing again into Anglicisms, and Jeffrey looked at her. She had found a wad of fraying Kleenex, and four pens, the keys to the house and two quarters, or perhaps nickels. The bristle stabbed again under her nail. She was ready to bring the pocketbook up over her head and empty it out onto the tablecloth. The wine came, and the two men tasted it.

"Very nice," Jeffrey said, nodding at Kingsley, who had chosen it.

"Not bad, is it," said Kingsley, agreeing. He liked Geoffrey, who seemed pleasant and intelligent, but he wondered what was going on between him and his wife. Yesterday they had seemed so amicable, but today they hardly spoke. And he wondered what Martha had been grappling with under the tablecloth since they arrived.

When the check came Jeffrey reached for it, but Kingsley was firm. "Absolutely *not*," he said, with a short triumphant whinny. "You are *my* guests now."

"That's very handsome of you," Jeffrey said.

"How very kind," said Martha abstractedly.

The time had come for Martha to make an announcement, to say something that would explain how everything had changed, how the entire configuration of the afternoon was being altered, without revealing to Kingsley even a hint that his small conscientious gesture had locked them all from the car and shattered their plans.

As they waited for the waiter to return, Martha cleared her throat. It was just past two-thirty, and there was still time to do everything, if things worked properly. She'd thought of a friend who lived nearby: she'd call Linda and ask her to rescue them.

"Now," she announced, "we have a slight change of plan." Kingsley looked at her inquiringly. "We're going to Lyndhurst, but we might—we might have to go in Jeffrey's car."

Kingsley nodded courteously. "Whatever suits you."

Martha looked at Jeffrey. "Why don't you make the call to the company, and I'll call Linda. Maybe she can pick us up and take us back to get your car." She prayed for him to understand, and to agree.

There was a moment's silence, then Jeffrey nodded. "Right," he said.

Martha smiled brightly at Kingsley. "I'm just going to call a friend." In the phone booth she dialed Linda's number, praying for her to be home. She wished she'd thought of Linda earlier and called before lunch—though she'd been hoping the key would turn up in her purse. She listened to the distant burr. *Oh*, *answer, Linda,* she thought, *answer, answer, answer.* On the fourth ring someone picked up.

"Hello?"

It was a man's voice. Maybe Linda's son? What was his name?

"Hello—Jordan?"

"Yeah."

"Hi, this is Martha Truesdale. Your mom's friend." Jordan lived in Colorado, and Martha had met him only once.

"Oh, yeah, hi."

"Is your mother there?"

"Actually she's not. She won't be back until around five. Can I take a message?"

Martha took a deep breath. Well: things were not going to go smoothly, that was how it was going to be.

"Jordan, I have a huge favor to ask you." She explained.

"Sure," Jordan said. "I'd be happy to come and get you, except that right now I'm waiting for a friend to call, who's driving across the country and calling from his cell phone and I don't have his number. He said he'd call at two-thirty, and it's almost that now. So it should be just a few minutes. Then I'll come and pick you up."

Martha thought for a moment. There was no alternative. There were no cabs nearby; any car service would take an hour to arrive. She knew no one else up here well enough to ask.

"Great," she said to Jordan. "Thank you so much. We'll be in the parking lot." Before going back outside, she rifled through the bottom of her bag one more time. Jean Singer's disapproving face floated into her mind.

Jeffrey had called the car company, and while Kingsley was in the men's room Jeffrey reported to Martha that, although there was indeed a twenty-four-hour service, the man on duty today was off on a family outing, an hour away. He'd be there as soon as he could.

"So you'll stay here and wait for him?" Martha asked.

"What choice do I have?" Jeffrey asked.

"Thank you," Martha said, but Jeffrey was looking past her at the front door. She turned too and smiled radiantly at Kingsley as he reappeared, walking slowly across the gravel.

The three of them stood in the pale wintry sun, waiting for Jordan. The impenetrable car stood ten feet away, gleaming, on the gravel. They did not look at it; Kingsley politely did not ask why they were not getting back into it. Martha looked at her watch: nearly three. Lyndhurst was open until five. If they were home by three-thirty, and it took half an hour to get there, they would be fine. When she'd called Lyndhurst, the day before, she'd gotten only a recording with the hours on it. She would have to call again, and wait to get through, for directions. She wished she had already done that.

Jordan arrived at quarter past. He pulled up in an ancient Volvo station wagon, muddy, and low in the rear.

"Hi there," he said, smiling out his window. He had a plump jowly face, a buzz cut, and an offhand manner. "Sorry about that. My friend never called. I finally gave up and came over."

"You've missed your call for us? That's so nice of you," Martha said. She was already pulling the door shut behind her, already in the back seat, which had a grainy feel to it. Discarded objects swirled around her feet. "You sit in front, your legs are longer," she said to Kingsley. She still did not quite want to call him Michael. "See you later," she called out to Jeffrey; he lifted his hand stoically as they drove away. Kingsley sat in front like a statue.

Jordan drove very slowly along the winding roads. He had a standard shift, which sounded troubled each time the gears were changed.

"Got to be careful with this car," he said cheerfully. "She's lasted over a hundred thousand miles. We're trying for two."

"Tell me, where do you live?" Kingsley asked, polite, interested, and Jordan began to explain. Martha, in the back seat, sat with all her muscles tensed, urging the car onward. It took them twenty-five minutes to get home. Jordan drove them up to the back door, still talking.

"No, man, I really love the mountains," he told Kingsley. Martha opened the door and got out. "That's what draws me. The outdoors. I couldn't move back now. Ever been out west?"

Kingsley sat in the front seat, not moving. "Not to your part. I've been to San Francisco, and Seattle, but that's not what you mean, is it?"

Jordan shook his head, grinning. "Come to Colorado," he said. "I'll show you what the real West is like."

Get out of the car, Martha thought, get out, get out.

Kingsley turned to Jordan. "How very kind of you. Perhaps I shall."

"Be my pleasure," Jordan said, nodding happily.

"Thank you so much for driving us here," Kingsley said, beginning to lever himself slowly out of the front seat.

"Thank you so much, Jordan," Martha said, heartfelt, urgent, leaning into the window. "I'm going to run, but it was so nice of you to pick us up. I can't thank you enough. And give my love to your mom. Tell her I'll call her."

She headed for the back door. It was now twenty of four. She unlocked the door and left it open for Kingsley, who was making his majestic way in from the car. She pulled the big telephone book out from its disorderly stack and began flipping through it. Lyndhurst was not in the white pages, she found: it must be in the blue pages, but under what? Government listings in each town? She didn't know what town it was in. Historic houses? Kingsley came into the kitchen behind her.

"I'm just going to get directions," she explained, searching through the blue pages. Where had she found it yesterday? She ran her eye down the columns: Emergency hot lines. Poison center. Domestic violence.

It was under the "State" section, then Historic Houses. She dialed and waited while the recording listed the hours. At the end of the recording she pressed 0 for operator and waited until she was cut off. She dialed again and waited while the recording listed the hours. She pressed 0 again and heard another message, advising her to wait. She waited while the recording played American folk tunes. Kingsley stood politely by the sink, trying to be unintrusive.

He wondered what was going on. Somehow the day seemed to have gone off its tracks at lunch, with Martha struggling with her pocketbook under the table and then the silent argument with her husband—was that why Geoffrey had been abandoned in the parking lot? And the mysterious Jordan, whom Martha had evidently never seen before, with his ancient mud-stained car, full of socks and crumpled drinks containers, ferrying them slowly back to their house, his car straining and sighing at every shift.

Now, somehow, it had gotten very late—he saw Martha keep looking unhappily at the clock as she tried to get directions. He did not actually care about Lyndhurst. A friend in London had mentioned it to him and he'd thought it would be a pleasant outing, something to fill an empty afternoon. But now it seemed more sensible to pack and start out for the train station at once, if the trip there were to be as difficult as this one. Three miles might take hours.

Martha had finally reached a real voice, and he heard her asking for directions. She wrote down route numbers.

"And how long do you think that will take us? We're near Cross River," she said. She looked again at the clock. "Thirty-five minutes. That will be all right. You're open until five?"

The person on the other end said something Martha did not want to hear. Her voice rose.

"But the recording said you're open till five."

More unwelcome information.

"Thank you," Martha said and hung up. She stared for a moment at the telephone.

"Something wrong?" Kingsley asked.

"It's too late," Martha said. "I'm so sorry." She sounded desolate.

"Oh, that's perfectly all right," Kingsley said, unsure of how to remedy this. What had upset her so?

"It will take longer than I thought to get there, and they're open until five, but they don't let anyone in after four-thirty. We can't get there before then." She sat still for a moment. She was determined to pull the day out of its downward spiral toward failure.

"I know what we can do," she announced, looking up decisively. "We can go to the local historical society. It's right nearby. It's not as good as Lyndhurst, but it will give you some idea of American houses. We'll go over there."

The Historical Hall was two miles south, a rambling, gloomy old house with an odd assortment of furniture. Martha stood up, remembering, for some reason, the day the town had tried to pave the road. Lying on her back, on the smooth hard-packed dirt, looking straight up, into the green canopy of trees overhead. The suffocating stench of hot tar, the sense of exultation.

"Lovely," said Kingsley. He did not want to go to the historical society. He would have been happy to read in the sunny drawing room until his train, but it seemed that Martha was determined to go through with the project. She seemed caught in the grip of something.

Martha walked briskly to the garage and backed Jeffrey's car out. She would take Kingsley to the hall and then to the train, and then she would come home and face Jeffrey.

Kingsley waited for her in the driveway. He liked Martha, her small round face, her cheerful air. He liked her resoluteness, the way she made her way quietly around obstacles, like a deer moving through a wood. Whatever lay between her and Geoffrey was opaque to him, a mystery; he knew better than to try to puzzle out someone else's marriage. It would be impossible for him to know which was more characteristic—the first easy partnership or the later silent conflict. Kingsley suspected that they rubbed along all right, that they loved each other.

Fights meant nothing, really. He remembered his own rages toward Evvie, whom he had loved dearly. Once, years ago, at Christmas, he had locked her out of the house. She had walked, furious, from window to window in the dark, knocking loudly on the panes. He had feared they would shatter. It shamed him now to remember it; he hoped no one else had ever known. No outsider should look too closely into someone else's marriage, you could never know enough to understand those vivid glaring scenes, someone else's anguish.

Martha pushed open the car door for Kingsley, who climbed creakily in. She turned the car around and headed down the drive again. She thought of Jeffrey throwing his shirt into the hamper, slamming down the lid, and felt a brief surge of heat, exasperation.

Once, during a fight, she'd driven off in the middle of the night. She'd been in a fury when she left the house, boiling, her cheeks hot with rage. She drove across the county, speeding over the dark highways, tunneling through the night. Three A.M.: she'd decided to drive straight through to Chicago. Rage was uplifting, somehow: she'd been in a state of exaltation. On the wide empty curves, her car drifted easily to the outside. She felt she could go on forever.

Now Kingsley said diffidently, as they started off again, "Are we quite sure that this place will be open?"

"It doesn't matter if it's not," Martha said, confident. "I'm on the board. I know where the key is."

At the bottom of the driveway she turned onto the dirt road, moving slowly on the loose gravelly surface.

She remembered starting off down this road that night,

fueled by anger. Surging along the smooth deserted highways, swinging off one, sliding down the ramp onto another. The highway at night, empty and singing: you wanted to press your foot down on the accelerator until it met the floor below.

But forty minutes later, just before the Tappan Zee Bridge, she'd pulled over on the side of the highway and stopped. Her headlights bored into the mist over the Hudson. She turned off the engine and sat in silence, watching the light over the dark water. The river was wide there, the far shore invisible.

By then, for some reason, everything had changed. During the drive, the long curves, the silence, the silence, amid the black emptiness of the night, her rage had ebbed. It had evaporated somehow. Why would she want to drive to Chicago?

By the time she parked on the shoulder, what she was thinking about was something else: after the last miscarriage, when Jeffrey had wrapped himself around her and held her all night. Even in his sleep, his muscles tightened around her each time she moved. She was held in his close embrace until morning. And she remembered the time in Asolo, walking in the narrow street, the cobblestones damp and slippery after the rain, when he had said, so quietly, and without looking at her, "You make me very happy."

When she pulled out onto the highway again, it was too late to get off before the bridge, and she had had to drive all the way across the river and pay the toll before she could turn around. By then she was longing to get back; the toll seemed like a penance, something she owed for her rage.

Now, driving Kingsley toward the hall, Martha stopped at the bottom of their dirt road before turning out onto the faster paved one. She waited for a small parade of cars to pass and thought of that night parked on the edge of the bridge, and of the ebbing of one feeling, the rise of the other. How strange the shift had been that night, how complete.

These things came in waves, she thought. She pulled decorously out onto the paved road, following the line of cars. She thought of Jeffrey being charming to Kingsley, throwing himself into the conversations. And in fact, she thought suddenly, it was true that she never had consulted Jeffrey about having a guest. It was an imposition, he was right. In his own house.

These things came in waves, she thought again. Something set them off: a visitor, the suspension and suppression of normal life, rising tensions. When this happened, she and Jeffrey became foreign to each other, contentious strangers. Each of them willful and self-absorbed.

Later it would pass, and they would meet again, as themselves. They would recognize each other, with relief. That night when she had driven off, when she returned from the Tappan Zee, Jeffrey was standing in the driveway, waiting. He was in his blue striped bathrobe, barefoot.

In fact, this was the path that emotion carved between the two of them. This was the way their marriage worked: it was not opera, not so heroic or grand. It was simpler, more domestic: a ballad, a folk song. Something more evenhanded. They were in this, whatever it was, together, both of them struggling with the waves of emotion, both carrying burdens of anger and love. *You're everything I want,* he'd said afterward. What more could she ask?

Kingsley could see now, as they rattled once again down the dirt road, how things would go. He could picture the white-painted door of the historical society, locked solid and unyielding, dazzling in the late afternoon sun, and the key not, as it was meant to be, beneath the heavy iron bucket under the window. He could see Martha, silent and frustrated, looking beneath every object in the yard of the Historical Hall. Geoffrey standing stoically alone in the parking lot, ten miles away, waiting for some mysterious arrival. Jordan driving slowly home, his strange, nearly naked head bobbing up and down to unlistenable sounds.

He could see himself, Kingsley, back at the house after the failed attempt on the Historical Hall, standing in Martha's kitchen, dolefully reading the train schedule to discover that today, because of a seasonal change, the last train to New York was not running at all.

But Kingsley would be somehow gone from this, magically removed from the complicated tangle of these predicaments, the impenetrable mystery of the car—what had happened to it?— abandoned in the parking lot, by the next day. All these questions would be behind him, unimaginably resolved. By then he would be in another country, another world: he would be back in Suffolk by tomorrow evening.

He would set the key into the stiff lock at the back door, pushing the door open into the silent kitchen. He would step inside, onto the cold slate floor. He would see the long battered silvery sink, the row of old apothecary jars above it, the table piled untidily with mail. The air would be quiet, stale, familiar, his. He would move about those cool unused rooms at will, without thinking; he would feel himself expanding freely into the space, without the constraints of other people, their gazes, their awareness. He would walk about as he chose, no longer troubling to conceal his limp. There would be the wintry smell of dampness.

What had shamed him, that Christmas, was his cowardliness. His own act, so cruel and outrageous in its intent, had been physically so civil, so discreet. He had merely turned the key quietly in the lock—and with that gesture he had forced Evvie into the role of the crazed outsider, someone near hysteria, violence. Bearing the burden of his emotion. He'd never apologized for that, he hadn't been able to. He was too ashamed to mention it, though he'd said he was sorry for other, lesser, things. Regret was one of the things you faced, after death. That was his burden now, knowing, too late, the part love had played in his life.

Inside the room Kingsley would take off his raincoat and drape it over the back of a wooden chair, he would bend over the mail on the table, and he would be once again inside the deep intimate space of his own familiar, mysterious, darkening life.

ABOUT THE AUTHOR

ROXANA ROBINSON is the author of three novels, a biography of Georgia O'Keeffe, and two previous short-story collections. She has received fellowships from the Guggenheim Foundation, the National Endowment for the Arts, and the MacDowell Colony. Robinson's fiction has appeared in *Best American Short Stories, The Atlantic, The New Yorker, Harper's, Dædalus,* and *Vogue.* She lives in New York City and Westchester County, New York.

About the Type

This book was set in Sabon, a typeface designed by the well-known German typographer Jan Tschichold (1902–74). Sabon's design is based upon the original letter forms of Claude Garamond and was created specifically to be used for three sources: foundry type for hand composition, Linotype, and Monotype. Tschichold named his typeface for the famous Frankfurt typefounder Jacques Sabon, who died in 1580.